The Dark

Andrew Neiderman is the author of numerous novels of suspense and terror, including *The Devil's Advocate* which was a major film starring Al Pacino and Keanu Reeves. He lives in Palm Springs, California, with his wife, Diane.

THE DARK

Andrew Neiderman

severn House

This first hardcover edition published in Great Britain 2002 by
SEVERN HOUSE PUBLISHERS LTD of
9–15 High Street, Sutton, Surrey SM1 1DF,
by arrangement with HarperCollins*Publishers*.

Copyright © 1997 by Andrew Neiderman.

British Library Cataloguing in Publication Data

Neiderman, Andrew
   The dark
   1.   Psychotherapist and patient - Fiction
   2.   Suspense fiction
   I.   Title
   813.5'4 [F]

   ISBN 0-7278-5834-3

Printed and bound in Great Britain by
MPG Books Ltd., Bodmin, Cornwall.

Prologue

The elongated shadow of Doctor Henry Flemming's 520 Sel Mercedes sedan washed over the mauve tiles of his wide, circular driveway as he turned in to his Brentwood Park Tudor house. Above and behind the vehicle, the twilight sun resembled a wafer of blood in the western sky. There was barely an ocean breeze coming east from Santa Monica. It was as if the world were holding its breath.

Flemming triggered his garage door. It lifted like a curtain of metal to display a garage so neat and clean it could be a stage on which were displayed a vintage red 54 MG convertible and another Mercedes, the smaller, silver gray 300 E his wife used. Doctor Flemming, a man who looked to be in his late forties but was closer to sixty, gazed with curiosity at the front windows of his home. The filtered sunlight glittered on the panes, changing them into mirrors that reflected the sprawling red maple, some of the manicured hedges, and the grand weeping willow. But the house looked dim, deserted, strangely quiet.

He pulled into the garage and got out of his car, a rich, dark brown leather briefcase carrying his psychiatric evaluations in hand. On the flap were the gold-embossed initials H.F. He paused for a moment and looked back as the garage door, again like a metal curtain, came down to shut out the quiet but lush Brentwood Park world. The garage light, which automatically went on and off with the opening and closing of the door, provided only dim, yellowish illumination of the white walls, hanging garden tools, and cabinets.

Flemming didn't linger there. He opened the door to the house quickly and stepped in, pausing with puzzlement at the darkness he confronted.

Not only wasn't this corridor lit, but neither was the kitchen on the left, nor the hallway of the house ahead of him. The living room was just as dark.

'Lydia!' he called, and waited for a response, gazing up the winding staircase with its mahogany balustrade. The upstairs was just as dark as the downstairs. There was no response. 'Lydia!' He raised his voice and his heavy apricot-tinted eyebrows rose with the effort. He had clear hazel eyes, a strong, straight nose, and firm lips. His face, tense, looked carved in granite at the moment, the jawline taut. There was just a slight twitch in his right eyelid as he listened for his wife's response.

Impatient and annoyed, he straightened up. The shoulders of his Armani suit jacket hung snugly. He turned on the hallway lights and the chandelier above him exploded with dazzling brightness, raining down illumination over the rich oil paintings, the plush carpet, and the case of Oriental collectibles. He checked his Rolex and shook his head, glancing at the stairway one more time before heading down the long corridor to the door of his den-office. It, too, was dark, even darker than the other rooms, since it was on the southeast corner of the house and the blinds were drawn shut. He hated that and he knew he hadn't left them that way. Either Lydia's damn housekeeper did it or she had done it, Henry thought.

He reached around the doorjamb and slapped the light switch that turned on the standing lamps and the desk lamp. Without gazing right or left, he marched toward his desk, but something made him pause halfway and he stopped and turned. It was Lydia, sitting in the deep, red leather chair quietly, her hands in her lap covered with a dish towel.

'What are you doing, sitting in here in the dark, Lydia?' he asked.

His wife of nearly thirty years smiled softly. She was a petite woman with soft, nearly golden hair, blue eyes, and rich complexion. Her features were diminutive, especially her nose. Doll-like, she seemed more like Henry Flemming's little girl when she stood next to her six-foot-two-inch husband.

'I was waiting for you,' she said.

3

He grimaced.

'Not a light on,' he muttered, continuing toward his desk. 'The place looks dreary. I guess we're going out to eat or sending out for something, since you're not in the kitchen preparing anything,' he continued, opening his suitcase and pulling out folders. He paused and looked up.

Lydia had risen to her full five feet one inch. In her right hand she clutched the model ten .38 Henry had received as a gift from the California highway supervisor he had treated for depression almost ten years ago. The man had lost a partner in a shoot-out and blamed himself. His partner was a young officer with a two-year-old daughter. Henry had helped him successfully return to work.

'What . . . what are you doing?' he asked. The gun was pointed at him. The hammer was cocked.

Lydia stepped forward, still smiling softly. He widened his eyes just before she pulled the trigger. The impact of the .38 at such close range was terrific. Despite his size, Henry flew back against the desk chair, which turned over, him following.

Lydia came around the desk and looked down at him. He was still alive, stunned, his eyes bulging, the blood pouring freely from his chest cavity. In a few seconds, he'll go into shock, she thought.

He started to mouth the word 'Why?'

But he saw the answer in her eyes, and he knew it anyway. It was almost as if he wanted this to happen, because his last willful, voluntary bodily act was to smile.

Which, of course, would confuse the police, but not Lydia. It would convince her she had **done** the right thing.

1

Grant Blaine took the stairs two steps at a time instead of riding the elevator up to his seventh-floor office. He was thirty-five years old, six feet one, and trim because he always avoided the easier physical alternatives, and this after he had played racquetball for nearly an hour and a half this morning at the Club. Carl Thornton beat him five games to three, but Carl, a forty-one-year-old wunderkind with his own psychiatric group, had been at it longer and was always more competitive about winning than Grant. It was a criticism of Grant that his wife Maggie had as well, especially when he complained about her ambition and what he termed her 'overdrive'.

'You're jealous because you don't have the edge,' she would reply. 'You were born with the silver spoon in your mouth, not me.'

She had come from the Midwest, the eldest

daughter in a family with three children, all girls, a family euphemistically described as of modest income. Her father, a postal worker, and her mother, a paralegal, had always struggled to make ends meet. If Maggie hadn't won all those scholarships, law school would have been out of reach.

But now, at thirty-one, she was already a prominent Los Angeles criminal defense attorney. After only two years at her present firm, Simms, Krammer and Beadsly, she had been promoted to junior partner, and there was a solid rumor they were about to offer her a full partnership. She had handily won her last three high-profile cases. The firm believed they had a female trial attorney who was attractive as well as intelligent and the partners were well aware that lately the courtroom had become the new arena for theater.

As he rounded the corner of a landing and attacked another flight of steps, Grant thought about Maggie becoming a full law partner. His mother, who originally thought he had married beneath his station, had come full circle and was prouder of her daughter-in-law than she was of her psychiatrist son. He had been an only child, admittedly spoiled, pampered, but he had a halfway decent practice and had garnered respect in the psychiatric community.

He and Maggie had met while Grant was still in his residency at Bellevue in New York. Maggie was attending NYU Law School and they were both invited to a party after the opening of an

7

off-Broadway play. She realized he had been watching her and laughing to himself. Tall and svelte, Maggie was a five-foot-ten-inch redhead with a strikingly resonant speaking voice who always made an impressive appearance wherever she was and especially now in court. Boldly, which was her style, she approached him and demanded what was so funny.

'I just like the way you handle the artsy-fartsy crowd,' he replied. She thought a moment and then she burst out laughing, too.

After nearly six years of marriage, the only troubling concern between them seemed to be when they would begin to have children. The question loomed unanswered, periodically making itself more visible as the omnipresent biological clock ticked.

Grant paused at his office doorway, caught his breath, straightened his posture, and entered. Fay Moffit, his secretary, was already behind her desk, working.

'Oh, Doctor Blaine,' she said, standing, a mask of tragedy over her face. 'Your wife wants you to call her immediately.'

'My wife? What's up?'

Fay shook her head, but he understood, she knew. She just wasn't going to be the one to say. He hurried into his inner office and sat behind his desk. Maggie's personal number at her office was under 2 on his speed dial. She picked up the receiver after one ring.

'Grant, I have horrible news. I was just on my way to the police station.'

'Police station? What's up?'

'Lydia Flemming shot Henry.' After a short pause, she added, 'He's dead, Grant.'

'What?' He almost laughed. What a ridiculous idea. Lydia Flemming shot someone? Shot Henry?

Henry Flemming had been Grant's mentor. Henry had hired him to be part of his group when Grant finished his internship and decided to practice in Los Angeles. Henry had been Grant's father's shrink, right up to the day Grant's father died of cardiac arrest while walking to his import-export business office in Beverly Hills. That walk had been his only exercise. He had just made it to sixty, which was probably the primary reason for Grant's neurosis with exercise.

'Why would Lydia shoot Henry?' he asked.

'All I know now is she shot him sometime last night in his office, Grant,' Maggie said.

'Could it have been some gun accident?'

'It doesn't look like an accident, Grant. She's admitting it anyway. I've got to get down there.'

'Right. I'll cancel my morning appointments and meet you,' he said. 'I'll be there as soon as possible, Maggie.'

Grant buzzed Fay and told her to reschedule his morning appointments.

'Just tell everyone an emergency has come up,' he said, and then sat back for a moment to catch his emotional breath.

Carl hadn't mentioned anything this morning, so he certainly didn't know. He, too, had worked with

9

Henry. Everyone in the psychiatric community was going to be so devastated and so confused.

Grant didn't even remember the drive to the police station. Along the way, he got caught in some early morning L.A. traffic, but he didn't notice or care. He was remembering all the good times with Henry, the socializing, the celebrations, the weddings of Henry's children, Henry's twenty-fifth wedding anniversary party nearly five years ago. It all passed through his mind like a series of dreams printed on soap bubbles and popped the moment he drove into the police station parking lot to face this ugly, illogical reality.

Maggie was waiting with Phil Martin, one of the other junior partners at her firm.

'Phil's here to handle Lydia's legal needs,' she told him quickly. 'I didn't think I could do it, Grant, and after I spoke with her, I know for sure that I couldn't do it.'

'Then you've already spoken with her?'

'Just a few words ten minutes ago. Phil has asked them to keep her in the conference room for you.'

He turned to Phil Martin, a six-foot-one-inch, dark-haired man of thirty-six, more on the cute side than handsome because of his impish smile and dimpled cheeks. Phil's wife Susan often voiced revealing remarks about the way Phil flirted.

'Yeah, we need your quick evaluation, Doc,' Phil said.

'I don't do quick evaluations,' Grant responded.

He looked at Maggie. Her eyes were glassy, tearful. She shook her head.

'She's not making an ounce of sense, Grant.'

He nodded.

'All right. Let me talk to her. Alone,' he emphasized.

'Great,' Phil said. He turned to the police detective nearby and moments later Grant was led to the conference room where Lydia Flemming sat calmly sipping hot tea. She looked up at him and smiled.

'Hello, Grant,' she said. 'How are you?'

'I'm fine, Lydia.' He kissed her on the cheek and sat adjacent to her. 'What happened?' he asked after a beat. She sipped some more tea.

'I did what I had to do, Grant.'

'You did what you had to do?' She nodded. 'You shot him, Lydia.'

She smiled as if he had said the stupidest thing.

'Of course.'

'Lydia,' he said, leaning over. 'Do you realize you killed him? You killed Henry,' he said.

She widened her smile.

'That wasn't Henry,' she said.

They conferred in the hallway. Maggie was sitting on the bench talking to her office on her cellular when Grant emerged from his session with Lydia Flemming. Phil was standing nearby, leaning against the wall, looking like a wise guy gunslinger with his coy smile, like Jack Palance in *Shane*, eager to bait

11

some unsuspecting dirt farmer. Grant directed himself to Maggie, who got off the phone the moment he appeared.

'She's lost all sense of reality,' he said. 'A form of autism, I'd say. She's preoccupied with illogical ideas, fantasies, schizophrenia.'

'Perfect,' Phil Martin said.

Grant turned to him.

'Perfect? She shot and killed the man she married and lived with for nearly thirty years. They have children, grandchildren, and he was one of the most highly respected psychiatrists in the country. Perfect?'

'I meant to develop a way to defend her,' Phil said, holding his smile. He shook his head. 'I certainly didn't mean I approve of what happened. I'm just looking . . .'

'I couldn't get through to her,' Grant said to Maggie. 'I couldn't make any sense of what she said, either. When she looked at him, she apparently didn't see Henry. We haven't seen them for months, so I don't know what to make of it. Didn't you speak with her recently?'

'No. I haven't spoken to anyone, really. I came off the Hobson case and went right into the Todres matter. You know what our lives have been like this year.'

'Yeah,' Grant said a little too dryly. 'I know.' He looked at Phil. 'I'm not your man for this. First off, I'm sure my relationship with Henry and Lydia would discount any testimony, and second,' he continued, looking at Lydia, 'you know what I think of forensic psychology these days. You lawyers,' he added, turning back to Phil Martin, 'have your teeth sunk into it so deeply, I don't even recognize what's being said in the courtroom.'

'It's all right. I'll find a reputable psychiatrist for her,' Phil said, missing Grant's point or ignoring it.

'I've got to get back to the office, Maggie. Let me know when Henry's children arrive and we'll see about visiting with them later.'

'I better go back in there and get some of the paperwork moving,' Phil said, nodding at the entrance to the police station.

'Right. Sic 'em, counselor,' Grant said.

Phil laughed.

'Hey, it's like anything else. You hate us until you need us, and then you love us,' Phil said.

'God help me from ever needing you,' Grant replied.

Phil laughed harder.

'I'd love to be in on some of your private discussions at home.'

'I know you would,' Grant said.

'Grant. Stop it,' Maggie said, standing. 'This is not the time or the place for this discussion. It's too horrible what's happened.'

Grant nodded.

'You're right.' He kissed her quickly. 'I'll talk to you later.'

He hurried away, chased by the images Lydia Flemming had spun for him in the conference room as much as by anything else. Late that afternoon, Maggie called to tell him that Henry and Lydia's son Thackery and his wife Camille had arrived from San Francisco. She suggested they meet at the Flemmings' residence and visit with Thackery and his sisters when they arrived.

Grant hadn't realized how long it had been since they'd been to the Flemmings until he pulled into their driveway and parked behind Maggie's red 325I BMW convertible. He admitted to himself that it wasn't only her fault. He hadn't spoken to Henry or Lydia, either. Time had a way of slipping by, rushing past like some stream after a sudden burst of a dam. When you finally realized how much had gone, it was too late to draw it back.

Inside, Maggie sat with Henry's son and daughter-in-law, both looking too stunned to speak. Thackery was a tax attorney. Physically, he took after his mother more than his father and was barely five feet five, slim to the point of looking fragile, with small wrists and hands.

'I should have paid more attention to what my mother was telling me these past months,' he complained. 'But who ever thought it would come to this?'

'What was she telling you?' Grant asked. Maggie had made some coffee and the four of them sat in the living room.

'She complained about my father a lot. She said he was becoming a stranger.'

'How?' Maggie asked.

14

Thackery shook his head.

'We haven't been down here for a while,' he said, now guiltily preparing some rationalization.

'Neither have we,' Grant said quickly, glancing at Maggie.

'That was part of how my mother claimed he had changed. It was Dad's doing. She said he didn't want to see any of his close friends.'

'I wish she had called me,' Grant said softly.

'I told her to, but she said she had made the mistake of telling one of his associates at the group about his personality changes. Dad became enraged, accusing her of betraying him,' Thackery said.

Maggie looked at Grant.

'That doesn't sound like Henry at all.'

'No, it doesn't. But it might have been part of her own problem,' he said softly.

'Her problem?' Thackery asked.

'I just saw and spoke to her for a few minutes today, Thackery, but it looks to me like she's lost hold of reality. She's evincing symptoms of a form of schizophrenia, but there has to be a fuller examination and diagnosis.'

'But wouldn't my father have noticed that?' Thackery asked.

'Of course,' Grant said.

'Then how . . . why?'

'I don't know,' Grant said. 'Henry might have felt he was handling it. I just don't know.'

Some of the associates from Henry's group began to arrive to commiserate with the family. As more

15

people learned of the tragedy, the phone rang and others arrived.

Henry and Lydia's daughter Cassandra and her husband arrived from Tucson, soon to be followed by the Flemming's second daughter, Beatrice, and her husband, in from Santa Fe. They, too, had been away from their parents for a while, and also talked about their mother's complaints concerning their father, but like Thackery, his sisters had no idea how serious things had become.

Finally, Grant and Maggie decided it was time to leave. Late in the day, Maggie called him to say she had fallen so far behind because of the loss of her morning, she would have to stay at the office and send out for dinner.

'I forgot about this pretrial hearing in the morning,' she explained. 'Sorry.'

Grant found himself alone at home, preparing leftovers and muttering to himself about how the modern American scene had reversed itself. Used to be the wife waited home alone while the husband went into overtime at work, he thought.

The Flemming murder was the number one story on the local news. Every channel carried it and highlighted it with pictures of the Flemming home and interviews with other psychiatrists, some patients, and especially members of the bar who commented on Henry's expertise at murder trials and rape trials. Grant had forgotten how much forensic work Henry had done recently. It was difficult to resist. The money was good, the exposure was great, and the impact on one's career and reputation enormous, especially in a high-profile case. Carl Thornton's group had been specializing in expert witness testimony lately, sending associates as far as New York to testify in criminal proceedings. But Grant remained adamant. His treatments would stay behind his closed doors where they belonged. He was aware that some were sarcastically referring to him as the 'gentleman psychiatrist,' the one who wouldn't dirty his analysis, but he ignored it. He was comfortable and happy with himself. What was more important?

It was nearly eleven o'clock before Maggie returned. Grant was already in bed with a book. He heard her come in and heard her high heels clicking as she marched down the tile corridor to their bedroom.

'Hi,' she said. 'I just want to get something cold to drink. Anything new?'

'Blue chips are up three points.'

She smirked.

'You know what I mean, Grant.'

'Nothing on the news that we didn't know. I saw your Clarence Darrow giving his sound bite, calling Lydia a seriously disturbed woman. What do you attorneys call that, setting a foundation, influencing prospective jurors?'

'What would satisfy you, Grant – seeing Lydia sent to hard time, maybe even the gas chamber?' She walked away before he could respond. He folded the book and lay back on his hands to gaze up at the ceiling. What did he want? Henry was dead; it was bizarre. Lydia was suffering from something. If ever there was a case of diminished responsibility . . . but how, why?

Maggie returned and silently got ready for bed.

'I keep going over it,' he said. 'How did we lose touch so completely?'

'It sounds like Lydia was living in abject terror, damned if she didn't do anything and damned if she did. You can't remember anything unusual about Henry the last time you two spoke?' Maggie asked.

'No. We had some of our typical philosophical arguments, but he was always the calm, clear-thinking man. I didn't see anything coming. He mentioned something about working on a new book and I just assumed that was taking up much of his free time. He certainly didn't say anything negative about Lydia. And we were all close enough so that he would have, I'm sure.'

She crawled under the covers and put her head on his shoulder.

'It's terrifying,' she said. 'I tried working hard to keep from thinking about it, but every once in a while I would stop and see Lydia's face, that strange smile that made her look like someone else. You know what I mean? It's as if . . . she was possessed and what she said about Henry is even truer about her.'

'What?' he asked.

'That's not Lydia.'

He nodded.

'Yes, schizophrenics often take on such distinctly

different features, gestures, even voices that it's possible to think of them as being possessed. Maybe psychiatry is just a fiction. Maybe we're trying to put medical and scientific concepts on supernatural events,' he said.

She lifted her head.

'You don't believe that?'

'No, but after today, I won't laugh when someone else proposes the idea,' he said.

He reached over to turn off the light and in the darkness, more to confirm their own sanity and safety, they kissed and held each other until they both surrendered to fatigue and let sleep shut off the shock of what they had witnessed and learned.

Twice a week and sometimes once on the weekend, Grant ran on the beach. It was only about a fifteen-minute ride down Sunset to the Will Rogers Beach, where he parked, stretched, breathed in the raw, misty sea air, and then began his jog toward the pier in Santa Monica. Usually he was at the beach by seven and found it deserted. Today, as he ran, he hoped more than ever that the ocean breeze would wash the cobwebs of sadness out of his mind and help him to be clear-thinking. Sometimes he ran with his eyes closed, striding as if in a dream. Today, he did that.

He felt his feet lift and fall in the sand, his ankles straining with the effort, with pain traveling up his calves and into his thighs. He wanted it; he wanted to suffer to purge himself of his nightmares and dreary thoughts. It was working. He felt his lungs clearing, his mind stimulated. Then he caught the whiff of a familiar redolent fragrance and opened his eyes to see her pass only inches from him.

She was wearing skintight white shorts that pinched her buttocks so just an inch or so of them were exposed. Her shapely legs lifted and fell rhythmically. She wore no socks or sneakers and he could see the red-tinted toenails in the sand. His gaze went to her back. She wore an abbreviated halter, really no more than a fancy bra. Her shoulders were tanned and smooth. When she turned, her cerulean eyes were dazzling with lust. Her smile was taunting.

'What's the matter, Doctor,' she said in a voice barely above a whisper, 'can't you keep up?' Her laughter trailed behind as she picked up the pace.

So did he. He dug his sneakers into the sand and pushed on his thighs until he drew within a foot or so from her. Her dark brown hair floated, the strands so close he could reach out and touch them. His breathing quickened and he felt himself hardening as she titillated him with her childish laugh, her teasing eyes.

'I have a blanket out here,' she said, turning on the sand toward the ocean. He slowed, but followed. She collapsed on her blanket, laughing.

'What exactly do you think you're doing, Mrs Leyland?'

'Morning exercise, what else?' she said, leaning back on her hands and smiling. 'You don't think I came out here just because you do, do you, Doctor?'

'That's exactly what I think, Mrs Leyland.' He stood there gazing down at her. She turned her shoulders suggestively and ran her tongue over her lips.

'Beats your office, doesn't it?' she said, holding her arms out. 'Sunshine, fresh air, the ocean.'

'Yes,' he said, nodding. 'I'd like to hold all my sessions here, but there are distractions.'

'I know,' she said, teasing him with her smile. 'But I thought you should know something I haven't told you during any of our sessions.'

'Oh?'

He knew he should just walk away, return to his jog, but that halter was so loose and her cleavage was so deep and inviting, he was drawn for a moment. He rationalized that learning about a patient any way possible was a worthy endeavor.

'Whenever I'm in the sunshine and fresh air, I get aroused even more. I could make love with anyone. My heart starts to pound; I just want to open myself,' she said, spreading her legs a little.

He felt his own heart begin to palpitate even more than it had from the jog.

'Why do you suppose that is, Doctor? Am I Nature Girl?'

'In natural surroundings, our basic instincts emerge more clearly, vividly,' he said.

'Basic instinct,' she said. 'I like that.' She batted her eyelashes.

'Yes, well, this is a discussion we should continue in the office.'

'Can't we continue it here?'

'No, Mrs Leyland. We can't,' he said, but it almost sounded as if he were really sorry, as if he wished he could. He was surprised at his own tone. It frightened him and he stepped back. 'I've got to finish my jogging,' he said, and backed farther. She started to laugh. He turned and quickened his pace, her laughter following and chasing him like a sharp, embarrassing whip.

He ran harder than usual and finished the run sooner than he expected. When he arrived back at the parking lot, he wondered if he was breathing harder from the run or the sexual arousal. He glanced down the beach and saw she was gone. He hadn't treated many patients with nymphomania. He had always been a little afraid of it and was beginning to regret taking on this one.

He stretched, cooled down, and got back into his vehicle to go home to shower and change for work.

The sight of his mother's Rolls took him by surprise. It was just a little after eight a.m. Patricia Blaine up, dressed, cosmetically together, and properly scented by this early hour? What's happening to the privileged classes? he wondered with amusement.

'In here,' Maggie called when he entered the house. They were having coffee in the sunroom, a recent addition to their Beverly Hills hacienda. The room was three-quarters glass and offered a view of their banana trees, flower garden, fountains, and pool with the water cascading over the blue- and white-tiled whirlpool.

Maggie was dressed for work, stylish in her light green suit. His mother wore her black leather toreador outfit. For a woman of sixty, she had a remarkable figure. Of course, he knew her breasts were implanted nearly twenty-five years ago, she had had a tummy tuck five years ago, a butt tuck four years ago, various facial surgeries, and even cosmetic work done on her hands. Her plastic surgeon built a house on her body work, Grant thought.

'Mother, what are you doing up and at it before noon? I thought you told me that's uncivilized.'

'It is,' she said, 'but I got talked into heading the fund-raiser for the new pediatric wing at the hospital and these idiots planned a meeting at nine a.m. Maggie was kind enough to provide me with a jolt of caffeine. How do you manage to get up and get all sweaty before breakfast, Grant?'

'It's not easy, Mother.' He looked at Maggie, all smiles. 'I'll just shower and come down,' he said.

'Grant, I don't understand this business with Lydia Flemming,' his mother said before he could turn away.

'Business? She shot and killed him, Mother.'

'That's what I mean. Obviously, she's not in her right mind. Maggie tells me you were asked to evaluate her and testify in court.'

'Oh?'

'I didn't exactly say he was asked to testify, Mom.'

23

'Well, if he's examined her and can make a diagnosis . . .'

'I didn't spend enough time with her, Mother.'

'Nevertheless, dear, look at what's going on. Do you know the murder is on the front page of the *L.A. Times* this morning?'

'I didn't look at the paper yet.'

'Well, it is. Everyone's wondering about it. A noted psychiatrist's wife shoots him in cold blood? Really, Grant, it will be on *Hard Copy*, for sure. Think of what your testifying could do for your career. I'm sure you're more capable than anyone Maggie's associate can get and –'

'Mother,' Grant said slowly, 'I'm not crazy about being involved in a case concerning someone who was almost a father to me.'

'That's exactly why you should involve yourself, Grant,' she continued, undaunted. 'You should have more concern.'

'Mother,' he said, closing and opening his eyes to illustrate his battle to remain patient, 'when you are too close to a patient, you can't be properly objective.'

'Oh, that's –'

'That's the truth and my decision about this is final,' he said firmly.

'Just like his father,' she said, shaking her head. 'Stubborn to the point of irritation. When he was a little boy, he would fold his arms and close his eyes and pretend not to hear me until I gave up.'

Grant folded his arms and closed his eyes. Maggie roared.

'That's not funny, Grant,' his mother said. 'How do you put up with him, Maggie?'

'She closes her eyes,' Grant said, and shrugged. 'Got to get dressed. Have a good committee meeting, Mother, and try to listen to other people when they talk.'

'What?'

He hurried away, very self-satisfied. As he showered, his thoughts went back to Deirdre Leyland's short shorts and that bulge beneath the bottom, the bulge of promise. He found himself getting hard again and deliberately turned the water colder.

'Check your libido at the door, Doctor Blaine,' he warned himself.

His mother was gone by the time he went down for breakfast. Maggie was just finishing her coffee.

'That's dirty pool, using my mother like that,' he said as he poured himself a bowl of Swiss muesli and cut in a banana.

'I didn't. I told her what happened and she came to her own conclusions.'

'Maggie, I couldn't testify anyway, knowing Lydia and Henry as I do.'

She nodded.

'If you want, you can visit with her some more and be sure Phil gets the right diagnosis,' she suggested softly.

'I'm sure he'll find a competent psychiatrist who will provide what Phil thinks is the right diagnosis.

He'll call Carl's group or he has by now.'

'I only want what's right and true and good to happen. I feel just as bad about Henry as you do. I just can't make any sense out of it and that makes it so much harder to accept, Grant.'

'I know,' he said. He softened. 'All right. Let me see what they come up with and maybe I'll talk to her again this week.'

'Good,' Maggie said. 'I'll call you lunchtime,' she sang as she started out. 'Have a good day.'

'You, too.'

The house was quiet and then suddenly he heard the sound of blowers as the gardeners began clearing debris on the grounds of the house next door. Very symbolic, he thought. Here we don't get rid of our dirt, we just move it into someone else's life.

In a real sense that was what Lydia Flemming had tried to do. What in hell was she trying to blow away?

2

It couldn't have been a more appropriate day for a funeral. The late April southern California sky was completely overcast with heavy-looking, bruised clouds and a cool wind coming from the northwest that actually had people buttoning jackets and putting their hands in their pockets. The church service had been long and, to Grant, too impersonal. None of the Flemming children were able to speak, of course. They sat stunned, reality settling in like a bad migraine.

Carl Thornton asked to say a few words and spoke eloquently about Henry's major contributions toward psychiatry, but that only made the mad thing that had occurred seem even more ironic. Grant thought that the minister, like any showman, played longer to a larger audience. The church was packed with other psychiatrists and doctors,

27

former patients, lawyers, distinguished government officials, some movie actors Henry had treated, and members of the media.

There were cameras everywhere outside, and some people were pulled aside to offer comment, especially the actors and actresses. Everyone spoke highly of Henry, of course, but no one could offer any explanation as to what had happened. Few had met Lydia or knew Henry on a personal basis. None of the psychiatrists cared to speak, except for Carl Thornton, who offered the cryptic promise that everything would be understood in due time.

'We owe it to Henry,' he said, 'to find an explanation for this seemingly illogical tragic act. But after all, that's what psychiatry does: finds logic for the illogical.' His last statement was the sound bite.

Most of the mourners who had attended the church service didn't come out to the cemetery, but a good-sized group of fellow doctors and some patients did attend the service at the grave site. Grant and Maggie and Carl Thornton and his wife Joan stood with the family as the minister said the final words over Henry's coffin. Afterward, when Carl and Grant were talking, Carl pointed out some of those he described as Henry's newest patients.

'That woman on the right's family owns Grandos Jewelry on Rodeo Drive, and the short man to her left . . . that's Jeffrey Brookman, the Bagel King. He's in his own television commercials. You've seen him.'

Grant nodded. Big-money patients. From the way

they spoke softly to each other and remained close together, it seemed they all knew one another. One man in particular stood out, not only because he was tall, but because he had a very confident demeanor. He was good-looking, too, dark, distinguished. Grant noted how the others seemed to treat him with deference, turn to him to ask questions or listen to his remarks and then nod.

'I'll meet you at the car in a few minutes,' Maggie said when the minister finished. 'I just want to talk to Camille.'

'Okay,' Grant said. He and Carl watched her walk away.

'What a nightmare,' Carl said. They shook hands. 'I'll call you.'

'Right. Bye, Joan. Hope we meet at happier occasions soon,' he said.

As Grant started toward his car, the tall gentleman Grant had noticed before stepped out from behind a tall oak tree. To Grant it seemed as though the man simply materialized out of thin air. One moment he was across the cemetery and the next . . .

'Excuse me,' he said. 'You're Doctor Blaine, aren't you?'

'Yes,' Grant said, turning.

'How do you do? My name is Bois, Jules Bois. I was one of Doctor Flemming's patients,' he said. 'Very recent patients,' he added.

Grant nodded.

'It's a great loss,' Bois said, his eyes shifting toward the grave and then quickly back to Grant.

'Yes.'

'He spoke very highly of you when we spoke about psychiatrists who practiced in Los Angeles.'

'He was my mentor,' Grant offered. The overcast sky was threatening to let loose with a downpour any moment.

'I won't take up any of your time now, but I wanted to tell you that I intend to continue my therapy and I would be grateful if you would consider taking me on as one of your patients. It would mean a lot to me. As you know, it's hard enough to develop a comfortable relationship with your therapist, comfortable enough to be productive, and just when I had done so . . . this,' he said, gesturing at the graveyard.

Grant nodded.

'Of course. Call my office and speak to my secretary.'

Bois nodded and smiled. 'We've all lost a good friend,' he said.

Grant watched him turn and walk away. He saw Maggie at the car and hurried to meet her.

'Sorry,' he said. 'I was held up by one of Henry's former patients. He wants to continue his therapy with me.'

'Strange place to make an appointment,' she said.

'Not any stranger than some of the places my patients choose these days,' Grant muttered.

They got into their vehicle. When they arrived home, they found a message Grant's mother had left on the answering machine, raving about how the Flemming case was capturing everyone's imagination.

'It could be bigger than O.J.,' she wailed, 'and you won't be a part of it.'

He didn't return the call. The rain that had started earlier grew heavy. He and Maggie went to bed soon after a very light dinner, eager to curl up in each other's arms and watch some television. Maggie fell asleep first and he clicked off the television set following the evening news, which had a segment on Henry Flemming's funeral with pictures of some of the celebrities who attended and Carl Thornton's sound bite. It took Grant longer to fall asleep, which made it harder for him to get up the next morning. Maggie was nearly dressed and finished with breakfast by the time he appeared.

As usual, she outlined her schedule, but she promised to come home early enough to prepare something special for dinner.

'I suddenly feel a need to be Suzy Homemaker,' she said.

'Fine with me.'

Their lives fell back into their normal schedules over the next few days. Maggie kept him up on what was happening with Lydia Flemming and promised to show him the psychiatric report by week's end.

Grant went to his regular racquetball session on Thursday, but Carl Thornton didn't attend. Everyone was still quite disturbed by Henry's death, but Grant felt it was better to stick with his routine and sublimate all his anxiety, sorrow, and anger in his exercise.

When he left the Club that morning, he could have sworn he saw Jules Bois, the man who had approached him in the cemetery. He thought he was standing at the far corner, but when Grant got into his car, the figure was gone. Later that afternoon, he had what he called another Bois sighting in the Stage Deli, where Grant had gone for lunch. The place was always jammed and noisy, but had the best roast turkey sandwiches in town. He saw Bois get up from the counter and go into the men's room. However, when Grant stopped in on the way out, Bois wasn't there.

That night at dinner, he mentioned his Bois sightings to Maggie and told her the man had made an appointment and he would be seeing him the next day. She didn't know who Jules Bois was.

'The man at the cemetery, the one you thought a little strange for asking me to be his doctor while at the funeral,' he reminded her.

'Oh, yes.' She half smiled. 'Why do you call them sightings?'

'I don't know. I thought I saw him, but . . .'

'But?'

'He wasn't there. Thus, like sightings,' he quipped. 'You know, seeing Elvis, James Dean . . .'

She started to laugh, but stopped.

'What's the man's problem?'

'I won't know until tomorrow.' He shrugged.

'Stop looking so worried. I'm just imagining things. Who's thinking clearly these days?' he added.

She nodded and smiled, but still looked uneasy.

Bois had a morning appointment. Grant thought the man moved with an almost liquid, easy grace when he entered the office and sat in the chair in front of Grant's desk. He had a full head of auburn hair, brushed back neatly with just a slight pompadour, and striking dark eyes.

'Before we start,' Bois began, 'I have a few questions.'

'Fine.'

'As I understand it, you, like Doctor Flemming, are a Freudian, correct?'

'Yes.' Grant sat back.

'Oedipus complex, Electra complex . . . you subscribe to all that?'

'Yes.'

'So you place a great emphasis on the importance of sexuality in psychological development?'

'I do, but I have room in my thinking for other schools of thought,' Grant said.

Jules Bois leaned farther back so that the shadow deepened on his face and Grant could no longer see his dark eyes, which Bois fixed on him with a directness that demanded he be heard.

'Good, because you may have a little problem with the Freudian approach as it applies to me. My mother died when I was born, so I never had an opportunity for an Oedipus complex,' he added with a small smile.

'That's not really a problem for me,' Grant began.

'And my father and I don't get along. In fact, he threw me out when I was in my late teens.'

'I see.'

'Are you sure this doesn't present any problem with the approach you take?' Bois asked. Grant felt the man was humoring him, but he kept a serious expression, calm, refusing to be baited. It wasn't unusual for a patient to begin with a combative demeanor. Therapy was a hate-love relationship at best. The voluntary patient wants to be cured, but a part of him wants to resist as well. It was Henry Flemming who first told him people are often afraid of being what we call mentally healthy.

'Not a problem, no. I'm not one to pigeonhole people in comfortable little psychoanalytic slots.'

Bois nodded.

'I hope you don't mind my inquisition. I just want to know what sort of scalpel you'll be employing on my personality,' he added.

'I don't mind.' Grant smiled. 'Is the inquisition over?' he asked after an appropriate pause.

'For the time being. But I reserve the right to cross-examine you at any time I feel it's necessary. If that's all right,' Bois said.

'You sound like an attorney.'

'I have a law degree, yes. But I wasn't satisfied with that.'

'So what do you do now?'

'I'm a consultant.'

'Consultant? Legal?'

'Legal, financial, even engineering . . . whatever. I am, in all modesty, a man of many talents.'

'I see.' What Grant really saw was that details and personal information would be slow in coming. 'All right. So, why do you believe you still need the services of a psychiatrist, Freudian or otherwise?'

Bois hesitated and then leaned forward, his eyes brighter, a smile on his lips.

'I have a compulsion. To state it simply, I enjoy causing, stimulating, encouraging others to perform illegal, immoral, self-destructive, and destructive acts. When I was a child, they used to call me an instigator. I need to explore the reasons for it and decide whether or not I should put an end to it. Can put an end to it, I should say.' He sat back. 'If it's a compulsion, I will need your help, correct?'

'Yes, if it's truly a compulsion – something that's truly obsessed you and something you can't control. When did it occur last?'

'About five weeks ago.'

'What did you get someone to do?'

Bois smiled. 'Recently, I talked someone into killing his wife,' Bois told him.

'Killing his wife?'

'Yes.'

'You talked a man into murdering his wife?'

'He went ahead and hammered on her head until she was dead,' Bois replied. 'I suppose you could call that murder.'

*   *   *

35

Grant wasn't overly troubled about Bois' revelation he had encouraged someone to kill his wife. More than one patient had confessed to doing things he had not really done, or at least things he had imagined he had done. But it remained on his mind when he joined Maggie, Phil Martin, and Phil's wife Susan for dinner. He was nearly twenty minutes late, which normally in Los Angeles was on time. But they had all actually arrived a few minutes early, anticipating Grant's usual promptness.

'The normally reliable Doctor Blaine, I presume,' Maggie said, holding up her wineglass to show him she was nearly finished with her first glass.

'Sorry. I had to hang around to make some phone calls.' He kissed her and sat down. 'Hi, Susan.' He gazed with less warmth at Phil. 'Counselor.'

'Hi, Grant,' Susan Martin said. She looked like she had already had two, maybe even three glasses of wine. Grant knew Phil's wife was into the sauce. He had commented to Maggie about it on more than one occasion.

'Doc,' Phil said. 'We've just been celebrating.'

'Oh?'

'District attorney decided to plea-bargain the Cronenberg case. I got a probation deal.'

'Cronenberg. That's the one where the stoned teenager drove his father's Jag through the front window of a department store in Westwood, nearly killing a clerk and a customer?'

'Yes,' Maggie said.

'And the public interest the district attorney is sworn to ensure and protect?'

'Served,' Phil snapped. 'It was a victimless crime. Fortunately, no one did get hurt. We have a chance to rehabilitate this kid, a chance we wouldn't have if he went to hard time. I can assure you of that.'

Grant smiled.

'You know, you might very well be the fastest gunslinger in the court. I didn't even see that coming.'

'What's the matter with you, Doctor Blaine?' Phil asked. 'You look a little on edge, and for a psychiatrist, that's a serious thing, right?'

'Stop teasing him, Phil,' Susan said.

'It's all right, Susan. I am on edge. I saw one of Henry's former patients today.'

'Oh? I guess most of Henry's patients are having great difficulty dealing with his death, huh?'

'I imagine so, Phil. Yes,' Grant said.

'What's this guy's problem?' Phil asked. 'If you can say, that is.'

Grant eyed Maggie.

'As long as I don't mention names. He believes he is compulsive.'

'So who isn't?'

'His compulsion is a bit unusual. He encourages, stimulates, advises . . . got to be careful about the choice of words around you people . . . causes other people to do immoral and illegal things.'

'Really? A coconspirator, an accessory?' Phil lit up. Susan giggled.

'Thought you might say that.'

'Did he do anything worth mentioning?' Phil pursued.

'He said about five weeks ago he convinced some man to murder his wife and the man crushed her head with a hammer. Is that worth mentioning? What do you guys get for a crime of passion these days? What's the going rate or . . .' He paused because he saw the way Maggie and Phil were gazing at each other. 'What?'

'This supposedly happened in L.A.?' Maggie asked.

'I don't know. I didn't get into details. With new patients, it's like walking on thin ice. Especially in this case. Why do you ask?'

'Phil's defending a husband who beat his wife to a pulp with an ordinary hammer.'

'How do you defend that?' Grant quipped.

Phil shrugged.

'Everyone's entitled to a defense, remember?'

'How could I forget?' He looked at Maggie. She seemed very pensive.

'What is it, Maggie?' She sipped her wine and glanced at Phil again. 'Mag?'

'I was going to tell you after a while. With Henry's tragic death and all, I just . . .'

'Will you just spit it out, for God's sakes? Phil?'

'His name is Dunbar, Clarence Dunbar. He claims his psychiatrist influenced him, actually encouraged him to do it, even suggesting the means.'

Grant just stared until Maggie dropped the infamous second shoe.

'His doctor was Henry Flemming.'

Grant smirked.

'You of all people know how ridiculous that assertion is,' he said. Maggie nodded.

'But if someone would have come to you with the assertion that Lydia was going to shoot Henry, you would have thought that ridiculous, too. Wouldn't you, Grant?'

'Yes, I suppose so.'

'Phil confirmed that Dunbar had been seeing Henry. He looked at Dunbar's file. Henry had diagnosed Dunbar as paranoid.'

'Oh. I see.' He smirked. 'Dunbar believed his psychiatrist was out to hurt him, too, and Phil is thinking of using that as a defense? Is that it, Phil?'

'Hey, if the psychosis fits, use it.'

'Did it ever occur to you that maybe we're all hopelessly mired in the excuse-abuse syndrome? Too many hardened, cold, and calculating criminals are slipping through our fingers, fingers we've greased ourselves with our distorted views of what's right and what's wrong?'

'In your profession that's close to blasphemy,' Phil said. Grant nodded.

'I stand accused.'

'Does this new patient of yours claim he suggested Dunbar use an ordinary household hammer?'

'I didn't get into that and he didn't mention any name. I spent the remainder of the session discussing his father and his relationship with his brothers and sisters.'

Maggie thought a moment.

'Could he have had contact with Dunbar, Grant, being they shared the same psychiatrist and all?'

'Maybe.'

'If that's true, why wouldn't Dunbar put the blame on your patient rather than on Henry?' Phil asked quickly.

Grant thought a moment.

'I can only guess.'

'Go on.'

'Henry was probably making enough headway to challenge his paranoia. The irony here is Dunbar's paranoia caused him to believe Henry had an ulterior motive. So, the healthier he started to become, the more he felt threatened.'

'Complicated, the work you psychiatrists do,' Phil said, sitting back.

'We just unravel mental knots. Whereas you guys tie them.'

Phil laughed. Maggie remained thoughtful.

'Still, it's odd this patient of yours referred to Dunbar,' she said, 'and was that specific.'

'Not so odd. Dunbar was available for his delusion, if he is delusional. I need a little more time before I make a diagnosis, of course, but it could very well be that the guy just follows news stories and imagines himself a player.'

'Don't be afraid to bring this one home,' she advised.

'I won't be. But for now, let's drop it. I suddenly feel like I'm obsessing.'

'You ought to know,' Phil quipped. Susan giggled.

'My husband's so witty, isn't he?'

'So much so, he overwhelms us. Let's order while I still have an appetite,' Grant muttered, and Phil signaled for the waiter.

The noise in Brewmeisters in West L.A. was deafening compared to the upscale restaurant in which Grant, Maggie, Phil, and Susan sat. Four men in plaid flannel shirts were arguing heavily at the dartboard, the juke was wailing, men and women around the horseshoe bar were shouting to be heard, and waitresses were screaming orders at the two burly bartenders. Above the bar, two twenty-five-inch television sets played a fight on ESPN. The forty-year-old woman sitting in the rear and hovering over a pint of beer didn't seem distracted by the noise or activity. She stared ahead, waiting, apparently lost in her own thoughts.

She was still in her light brown raincoat. Her dark brown hair was down, straggly along her cheeks, the bangs uneven. A cigarette smoked in the ashtray. She picked it up and nervously held it in her fingers for a moment before taking a quick puff and putting it back into the glass ashtray. Then she gazed at her watch, took a deep breath, a swig of her beer, and another puff on her cigarette.

The stout bald-headed man at the table to her right smiled at her, revealing missing back teeth and an almost purple tongue. She swung her eyes toward the front door, but the stout man continued to stare, continued to smile. He looked like he was about to get up and approach her when she suddenly smiled and he turned to see Jules Bois stroll into the tavern, walking between the couples and groups of men as if unaware they were inches away. Those in his way parted to let him pass, few taking any real note of him even though he wore a jacket and tie and looked like he had made the wrong turn on the freeway.

'Hello, Mrs Mosley,' he said when he reached her table.

'Doctor,' she said.

The stout man, disappointed, turned to look at a thin woman bent over the jukebox.

Jules sat and signaled the waitress.

'I'll have that Moonlight Amber,' he said, nodding toward the sign that advertised it. 'Pint.'

'Right,' the waitress said.

Bois turned back to Janet Mosley.

'How are you today?'

'Not good, Doctor. Things are getting worse. Allan is so distraught, he's like another person. Our marriage is very strained. He no longer seems to care about my needs, our needs. All he talks about is his mother.'

'From what you've told me and from what I've observed, he's obsessed. We call it the Oedipus complex.'

'I heard of that,' she said.

'Yes, it's very popular these days,' Bois said. The

waitress brought the beer. 'Let's look at your problem logically, intelligently, Mrs Mosley.'

'I appreciate your help, Doctor. I don't have any money.'

'Yet,' he said.

'She'll eat all of it up,' Janet muttered.

'Yes, she will,' Bois agreed. 'I've seen it a hundred times if I've seen it once. But getting back to what I said . . . logically, we have identified the problem. Now we have got to eliminate it.'

'Eliminate?'

Bois drank some beer and looked around.

'Look at these people, Janet. Most of them have a lot more problems than you do, yet they play and live as if they're carefree. Some people can do that. It's as if a piece of their conscience has been under-developed. Others, like yourself, are plagued with too much conscience and therefore suffer unnecessarily. It's not fair.

'Does your mother-in-law even know where she's at these days?' he followed quickly.

'No, the Alzheimer's is worse. There are days she eats lunch twice. I swear,' Janet said, sipping her beer. Bois drank more of his and nodded.

'Almost a crime to keep her going this way. It's like someone who's already left her body behind. Janet, your solution is as simple and as obvious as the nose on your face. It's time your mother-in-law was relieved of her agony, a by-product of which will be relief of your own. You and Allan will become a couple again. Life's too short to waste it like this.'

Janet nodded.

'You've heard about that doctor who helps people commit suicide to relieve them of their misery?'

'Yes.'

'Janet, this is not much different. Another beer?'

'What? Yes. Thank you. But how, I mean . . .'

'It's easy, Janet. An Alzheimer's patient could easily overdose on her heart medication. Waitress,' he called, and smiled at Janet. 'Relax. Would I tell you to do anything that wasn't good for everyone, even for Allan?'

She shook her head. He downed his beer and ordered another for himself as well as for her.

Suddenly, as if returning to this world, Janet Mosley heard some of the noise around her. She was happy when he finally suggested they leave.

Less than an hour later, Jules Bois stood in the shadows across the street from Janet Mosley's mother-in-law's apartment house. It was a little chilly. He had his collar up.

'It's a good time now, Janet,' he said.

She moved from his side and crossed the street. He watched as Janet, with her hands in her pockets, head down, entered the building. She paused once inside the glass door, looked his way, and then continued.

His eyes moved up the building to the windows he knew were her mother-in-law's. And then he smiled, took a deep breath, and turned to walk away, whistling his favorite tune from *Damn Yankees*.

3

As the day of Bois' next session drew closer, Grant found he was actually nervous, fidgeting with things on his desk, watching the clock, reading and rereading his notes from the first session.

Fay Moffit, who had been Grant's secretary for the past fifteen years, was as professional and efficient an employee as he could want. She never asked him about a patient. At times she appeared to be working in a bank, so he was surprised when she said, 'Mr Bois is coming in today, isn't he?' The question was superfluous. She knew Grant's schedule better than he did.

'Yes, why?'

'Did I tell you I spoke to him for quite a while the other day before he went in to see you?'

'You mentioned thinking he was a sincere man, yes.'

'Don't you think he's sincere?' she asked, fishing.

Fay was just forty, divorced, with a fourteen-year-old daughter. Her ex-husband was a homicide detective. Grant had done quite a bit of work with policemen and knew the pressures under which they lived and why their domestic lives were so complicated. Fay's husband had been an adulterer. She had, with Grant's counseling, forgiven him once; when she discovered a second and then a third and a fourth instance, she filed for a divorce. It had been four years since. In the interim, Fay had dated other men, but still hadn't found anyone in which she wanted to invest her trust. Although they had never sat down and discussed it formally, she and Grant had had a number of conversations concerning her fear that she was being too demanding on every man because she had been hurt deeply by one in particular. However, Grant was satisfied that she was capable of having another significant relationship.

'Tell me exactly why you made that conclusion, Fay. You didn't speak to him very long, did you?' he asked.

She thought a moment. Fay always claimed Grant made her choose her words more carefully than anyone she knew.

'Well, he was polite, but not ingratiating. As I said, when I talked, he looked like he was interested, like he was really listening. Most people ask questions just to make conversation. They nod or grunt, but you know they're not really listening.'

'A-huh. But you felt he really listened?'

'Yes. Just like you do, only . . .'

'Only what, Fay?'

'Only with his eyes so fixed on me, I felt . . .'

'What?' Grant asked, now fascinated.

'Important. What I said mattered to him. I hope I'm not wrong about him.'

Grant nodded. Fay didn't expect him to say anything about his patient, but she lingered a bit this time, obviously hoping he would. Of course, he didn't and she returned to her desk.

Bois arrived promptly.

'You look surprised to see me, Doctor,' he said with a wry smile. 'Didn't you expect I would return?'

'Most of my patients are quite unpredictable,' Grant replied, feeling the need to be clever, 'so I don't expect anything. Would you like the lounge or the chair?'

During the first session Bois had sat in the chair in front of Grant's desk, but most of his patients were more comfortable not looking at him when they spoke to him and released the thoughts and events they had kept secreted most of their adult lives.

'Today I think I'll take the lounge. I believe I can free-associate better on my back,' Bois added. His eyes twinkled impishly.

'So,' Grant began, pulling his chair up beside Bois. Bois lay with his eyes closed and Grant studied his face. It was a handsome face, the features carved with perfection, from his straight nose to his even

47

lips and smoothly shaped chin. His cheekbones were high and his forehead not too big or too small. He had firm shoulders and a slim figure with long arms and rather long fingers, upon the right pinkie of which he wore what looked like a ruby set in white gold. Grant remembered Bois said he wasn't married, nor, according to what he had told him, ever had been. In fact, he hadn't mentioned any significant relationship with a woman, although he was quick to add that he wasn't gay.

Grant opened with, 'How did you feel after coming here and making the sort of confession you made?'

Bois turned toward Grant, opening his eyes and smiling with surprise.

'Confessing, as I understand it, implies guilt, remorse, and as you should recall, I don't feel that.' Bois relaxed again, and with his eyes closed added, 'You're not sure whether I'm for real or not, are you, Doctor?'

'You wouldn't be my first patient to confess to crimes he didn't actually commit,' Grant replied.

'The husband's name was Dunbar,' Bois said, turning to him. Grant felt a heat in his face, but he kept rather cool.

'You could have read that in the newspaper,' Grant said quickly, perhaps too quickly. It brought that small smile to Bois' lips.

'Why so anxious to have me delusional, Doctor? Is it because you wouldn't have a moral dilemma?'

'No, but I have to be skeptical to be objective,' Grant said.

Bois shook his head as if Grant had given the wrong answer.

'Clarence Dunbar has suffered from impotency this past year. That won't be in the news,' he said, and lay back again. 'We met in the lobby of Doctor Flemming's offices. I saw this vulnerability in him and I couldn't pass it up. My compulsion took over,' he said. Then he lay back again and closed his eyes. 'I must say he was easy to manipulate. I just fed the paranoia, reinforcing his belief that his wife was to blame for his condition.

'He began calling me on the phone all the time, relating these silly stories, blaming her for the most mundane things. He likes salt on his salad,' Bois said, imitating a disturbed man's whine, 'but she always put an empty saltshaker on the table. When she put his socks in the drawer, she deliberately put a black and a dark blue one together so he would put them on and look foolish later.

'I told him if he didn't do something about her soon, he'd be totally dysfunctional.' Bois paused to see Grant's reaction. Grant simply nodded. Bois continued, 'Dunbar had one of these home shops. Used to be quite handy before he became quite paranoid. You know the type: he could build anything they needed in the house, fix anything. It was just natural to recommend he use a hammer. It was something with which he felt comfortable.'

His smile widened and his eyes brightened with a deep and clear sense of self-satisfaction.

'You see, Doctor,' he explained, 'my compulsive behavior has an intelligence to it. It's what makes this sort of evil interesting, don't you think?'

Bois glanced up at Grant.

'You look skeptical, Doctor Blaine,' he said. 'Do you still suspect I might be one of those people who imagine and hallucinate?' Bois rolled his eyes and laughed. 'Do you think I'm making all this up in my madness?'

'As I said, you wouldn't be the first,' Grant replied coolly.

Bois roared.

'I like you, Doctor. I really think you're going to help me, despite yourself.'

'Despite myself? Why despite myself?'

'Because you've had similar experiences.'

'What?'

'Don't act so innocent, Doctor. Wasn't there ever a time in your life when you instigated someone to commit an illegal or immoral act? Kids especially like to say, I dare you, and challenge one of their friends to something forbidden.

'Ever challenge a friend to throw a rock through a school window?'

Grant felt himself blanch.

'Ah, you have, I see.'

'Look . . .'

'What about your college days? I'm sure you coaxed someone, a girl perhaps, to smoke some

50

pot with you, right? Didn't that lead to something else . . . a little hanky-panky in the sack?'

Grant just stared, the crimson in his face deepening.

'It's all right, Doctor. I'm not condemning you for it. I think what makes it possible for us – not just you and me, but all mankind in general – to understand an obsessive compulsion is the fact that we have all experienced something like it. I mean, we have all deliberately started something burning, even if it was just a piece of paper in an ashtray . . . fascination with fire and our power to make it . . . goes back to our caveman days . . . but that doesn't make us pyromaniacs until we can't stop, right?

'You lit something on fire once, didn't you, Doctor? Did it get out of hand? Were you frightened? Did you 'fess up when you were asked how it happened or did you lie and pretend innocence?

'Am I getting warm?' Bois concluded with a thin smile on his lips.

'Even if I admitted any of those conjectures were true, the big difference is I felt guilt about something that was bad. At your own admittance, you seem to flourish or feel ambiguous at the worst. You don't experience any real remorse.'

'Yet I came here to have you analyze me. Most evil people avoid discovery,' Bois countered. 'They don't want to have themselves scrutinized. Doesn't that imply I am eager to be more like you?'

'Of course, that bodes well . . . your desire to stop the compulsion.'

'Or perhaps enjoy it without remorse. Just think of the freedom that brings, Doctor. Perhaps you could indulge a sexually active patient, for instance, and not feel guilty about it afterward.'

Grant raised his eyebrows.

'Have I touched a fantasy?'

'Let's stick to your problems, Mr Bois.'

'I suppose when you get down to it, it's all about control, isn't it, Doctor? Doctor Flemming and I often talked about this.'

'Oh?'

'We're all out there trying to control events, people. The more control we experience, the more confident and safe we feel about ourselves. That's why people do evil things,' Bois said, his eyes brightening. 'Yes. Murder, robbery, rape, embezzlement . . . you name it, it involves the criminal having control over the victim.

'When you get to the core of the issue, then, we find we are all driven by the urge to have power. That's what drives me,' he concluded, nodding.

'Is it?'

'Yes, and you know what, Doctor, that's what drives you, too. You're trying to control your patients, change them, aren't you?'

'I don't know if I would attribute my motives to a drive for power, Mr Bois.'

'Of course it is,' Bois retorted. 'That's all it is.' Bois leaned forward, his eyes penetrating. 'Why deny it? Why not admit it and finally and purely enjoy it, Doctor? Just as I do,' he said in a soft whisper. 'Doctor Flemming was just starting to do that when . . . he was unfortunately terminated,' Bois said with a smirk.

Grant stared at him silently a moment. Then Bois lay back again, smiling.

'Fortunately, he had begun to write it all down. He and I were actually collaborating on something, did you know that?'

'No.'

'We were, and we felt it was a very important work. Now that he's gone . . . I'm sure he would want you to continue the work.'

'I'm afraid I have enough to do and –'

'Don't decide now, Doctor. I'll give you a copy of the partial manuscript and you'll decide then. Henry would want you to have it, I'm sure. He would want it to be yours.'

'Doctor Flemming collaborated with you on a work?' Grant asked, not hiding his skepticism now.

'Well, not collaborating so much as using me as the source for his material.

'Doctor,' Bois said, smiling widely again, 'you are going to have to face the fact that I am real. The people I influence commit real crimes. They're in the papers, in police reports, on the evening news. I've made them infamous. I'm a signifi-cant subject for a new work, a new and exciting theory.'

Grant nodded.

'I see. Have you done anything between our first session and now?' he asked.

Bois stared at him, deciding. Then he relaxed, folded his arms over his chest, and closed his eyes.

'I couldn't help it,' he admitted. 'The opportunity presented itself.'

'What opportunity?'

'I convinced a woman to kill her mother-in-law before she wasted all her resources on her health care. Her mother-in-law lived alone, but was sinking into that quagmire of confusion known today as Alzheimer's disease. It was only a matter of short time before she would have to be institutionalized, and as you know, that would be at great cost, consuming her assets, assets our sweet little housewife had been counting on.

'So,' he continued, 'as you can see, I didn't have to do all that much instigating. The seed had already been well planted by her own need,' Bois added. 'I merely assisted on this one, gave her support and helped convince her she was doing the best thing. I helped her throw off the shackles of guilt.'

'What did she do?' Grant was almost afraid to ask.

Bois shrugged.

'Overdosed her dosage of nitroglycerin. That, I'll admit, was my suggestion,' Bois added with pride. 'She had the will, the intention, but she lacked imagination. If you want to confirm it, Doctor, the victim's name is Mosley.'

'I see. Was her daughter-in-law one of your clients, someone you give financial, legal consultation?'

'That's not the sort of question you should be asking as a doctor, Doctor. As a policeman, maybe.'

'I'm just trying to understand how you get into these so-called opportunities.'

'I told you. I'm compulsive. I go looking for them. And you know what, Doctor?' he added with that wry smile. 'I'm never disappointed. How about you?'

Grant smashed the hard, small racquetball with a fury that made Carl Thornton shake his head. Carl lunged and missed because the ball ricocheted with surprising speed. He caught himself before he slammed into the wall, and turned to watch Grant retrieve the ball.

'Terrific,' Carl said. 'Whatever you're eating, give me some. That's game point.'

Grant wiped the sweat from his brow and looked through the glass wall at a rather shapely young woman in a tight gym outfit. Carl saw the direction of his gaze and smiled.

'Libido going into overtime, Doctor?'

'Please,' Grant said. He walked to the side to put his racket in its case.

'What?' Carl was at his side.

Grant paused and looked at the wall for a moment. Then he turned to Carl.

'We sit there and we listen to their fantasies, sometimes in vivid Technicolor, graphic, and we're supposed to be neutral, asexual, objective, so unaffected that we can analyze them, prescribe therapy or drugs, and then go off to other appointments, our own lives as if none of it happened.'

'So?'

'I'm having trouble with my schizophrenia, Doctor,' Grant said. 'My split personalities are beginning to merge.'

Carl laughed.

'Occupational disease.'

'You, too?'

'All the time. I've even had the same nightmares some of my patients have had.'

Grant shook his head.

'This is more. It's really getting to me.'

'That why you're so hyper?'

'Probably,' Grant replied. They walked out together and paused to get some bottled water. Then they sat in the lounge. The Club, as it was known, was one of L.A.'s most prestigious. Entry fee was fifteen hundred dollars and the monthly fee was two hundred and fifty dollars, miles above any of the gym club chains. But the cost restricted the clientele to an array of successful producers, actors, lawyers and doctors, businesspeople, and those who had inherited fortunes. And that was what these people wanted – to be with their own economic, social, and political kind.

The truly wealthy in L.A., as everywhere else, moved from one cocoon to another, wrapped in their luxurious automobiles or limousines, draped in their designer clothes, protected and pampered. For them there was another level to everything, a higher, privileged level, whether it be medical treatment, justice, or even psychiatric evaluations. Running through their philosophy was the underlying, demonstrable principal that anything and everything was achievable or possessable for a price, even a clear conscience.

'I have this new patient, one of Henry's former patients,' Grant continued.

'What's his name?'

'Jules Bois.'

Carl thought a moment and then shook his head.

'Don't recall Henry mentioning him. What's he do?'

Grant laughed.

'He . . . instigates people to commit immoral or illegal acts.'

'For a living?' Carl smiled.

'You know,' Grant said, turning to him, 'I can't pin him down on that. He claims he has a law degree, but doesn't practice law.'

'That definition fits lawyers. Sorry, Maggie excluded.'

'It's all right. He only says he's an adviser, financial, et cetera. He obviously has money.'

'Jules Bois?' Carl said.

'He was part of that group you identified as Henry's newest patients, remember? Tall, dark man, good-looking.'

'I was probably in a daze by then and never noticed him. What about him?'

'He's uncanny, very sharp. It's almost as if he's analyzing me sometimes, know what I mean?'

'Yeah. I get that feeling when I go home and talk to my wife,' Carl said.

Grant laughed but then grew serious again. 'He has a way of making me think about things.'

'What sort of things?'

'Like I started to say . . .'

'Promiscuous things?' Carl asked. Grant nodded. Carl shook his head. 'No big deal. I'm telling you. We've all had that happen time in and time out. You recognize it for what it is and get past it.'

'I don't know. I've never had this happen so often or so strongly before.'

Carl smirked.

'Maybe you're just a bit frustrated, Doctor. Has Maggie been very busy lately?'

'Very.'

Carl shrugged.

'So. Solutions are often more obvious than we think. Go home, Doctor. Get laid.'

Grant laughed.

'Is that what you do?'

'I prescribe it for myself. Instead of two aspirins,' Carl said. He stared at Grant a moment. 'Maybe you want to give more thought to my offer. I can use you and you'd be a full partner, Grant.'

'Thanks, but I still like being on my own. It's less complicated.'

'Doesn't sound like it.'

'No,' Grant said, nodding, 'it doesn't.' He sipped some more water. 'Carl, you had no idea that Lydia and Henry were having serious problems, did you?'

'He never mentioned it to me, but Henry could be like that, hold in his own troubles so well you never knew they were there.'

'When was the last time you spoke to him?'

'Day before he died,' Carl said.

Grant looked up.

'Did he mention writing a new book, developing a new theory?'

Carl thought a moment and then shook his head.

'No. Why?'

'This patient claims he was the star subject.'

'Oh. Well, you know how secretive we all can be when it comes to original ideas,' Carl said.

'Um. You're friendly with Henry's associates, too. Did any of them ever mention Lydia being upset about him?'

'Not a one,' Carl said. 'It was something Henry had kept well contained in his own house. He thought he could handle it, I guess.'

'I'm sure his son Thackery told me Lydia had complained to one of the associates about Henry. Apparently he was upset she went out of the house with it.'

Carl smirked.

'You believe that, something Lydia said? Look at her, for God's sake.'

'Yes, her symptoms cry out. Henry must have noticed, had to have noticed. The funny thing about that is Henry always emphasized how important it was to recognize your own limits and seek additional help and advice,' Grant muttered. 'Why didn't he do so? He was too involved to be objective about his own wife's problems, right?'

'Ain't that always the case,' Carl said, smiling. We're the last to follow our own good advice. Got to get going, buddy,' he added, and gave Grant a playful punch on the shoulder before heading for the lockers.

Grant sat there a while longer, thinking. While he did so, a very attractive brunette, wearing a body suit so tight that the only secret left was for her gynecologist to discover, paused at the watercooler. She leaned over and plucked a cup from the sleeve, her cleavage deepening as she did so. His eyes never left her and she knew it, throwing him a flirtatious smile that sent a warm feeling up his inner thighs.

'Beautiful, isn't she?' Bois said. Grant whipped around. There was his patient in a sweat suit, wiping his brow with a towel.

'What are you doing here?' Grant fired.

Bois looked puzzled for a moment. He shrugged.

'Getting a workout. What else do you do here, Doctor?' Bois asked, and then turned to watch the sexy brunette cross the lounge.

'I meant . . . you joined this club?'

'No, but maybe I will. A friend of mine, an attorney, brought me along as his guest.' Bois jerked his head toward the weight room. 'He's pumping iron. I thought it might be you sitting here and then, when I saw how fixed you were on what was at the watercooler, I knew it was you.'

'Anyone with testosterone would have looked at that,' Grant said.

'Sounding defensive, Doctor. Not good for a psychiatrist,' Bois said, laughing.

Grant rose.

'Sometimes it's good to forget who you are and what you do for a while.'

'Oh, I agree. Absolutely, and practice that religiously.' Bois looked at another young woman, this one in shorts as abbreviated as the ones Deirdre Leyland wore. Grant looked, too. 'So many attractive women here, Doctor. The pickin's are certainly not slim, eh?'

'I happen to be a married man, Mr Bois. My pickin' days are over.'

'Nothing wrong with window-shopping, Doctor. It stirs up the appetite for a real sale.'

Grant just stared.

Bois laughed.

'I better get back to my exercise or my friend will send me to Cleveland. I'll see you soon, Doctor.'

Grant watched him leave and then he glanced at the girl in the abbreviated shorts. He gazed after Bois again, his heart pounding as hard as it had during racquetball, and then he hurried to the lockers like a man fleeing from a truth he didn't want to face.

4

Grant was surprised but happy to see Maggie's car inside when the garage door opened. He drove in and hurried into the house. The hum of a blender drew him to the kitchen. When he looked in, he saw her wearing an apron and reading a cookbook. She looked up and smiled.

'Hi. Got finished early today and thought I'd try again to be Suzy Homemaker.'

Grant folded his arms and leaned against the jamb. As he watched her work, he envisioned the girl back at the gym and then thought about Deirdre Leyland, recalling her describing how she liked to be naked while she worked in the kitchen, with her lover of the moment sitting at the table watching.

'It makes everything I make more delicious,' she had told him during her last office session. Her gaze had slid softly over his face, making him feel self-conscious about the flush her images had brought to his cheeks.

Maggie turned and smiled. 'What?'

'You turn me on when you do domestic things,' he said.

'What?' She put her hands on her hips. 'Since when?' She held her smile. To Grant her face looked polished, like glass.

'Since a moment ago,' he said.

She laughed, and the way she turned her head and revealed more of her soft, inviting neck sent a warm flow up his thighs. He stepped up behind her and put his arms around her waist before bringing his lips to that neck, following the line of it to her shoulders. She squirmed as the tingle rushed down her spine.

'Grant, how am I supposed to make dinner?' she asked, her own breathing quickened.

'Forget food,' he said. 'We'll live on love.'

She laughed and turned around to meet his lips. It was a long, passionate kiss, his tongue thrusting against hers, something he rarely did. She pulled back to look at him. His eyes were intense, piercing.

'Are you all right?'

'No. I think I have horn-o-mania,' he jested, and scooped her up before she could retreat. She shrieked with surprise as he carried her out of the kitchen, through the living room, to the bedroom, and dropped her on the bed, unraveling his tie the moment his arms were free.

'Grant, what are you doing?'

63

'You've heard of matinees? Well, this is a double feature,' he bragged. His shirt was off. She backed away, still half smiling, still half stunned.

'Grant, I've never seen you like this.'

His smile deepened, but Maggie thought the look in his eyes was different. It was lustful, ravenous rather than loving.

'Prepare yourself for an erotic experience you won't soon forget,' he said.

'I left something on the stove.'

'Let it burn. No, let us burn,' he added. He was practically naked. When he lowered his briefs, she saw he was fully aroused.

'Grant, you're mad,' she said as he crawled toward her.

'Doctor's orders,' he replied, and was at her. She realized he was not going to postpone it, but he was so impatient with her pace taking off her clothes that he tore off a button. She started to protest, but he brought his mouth down over hers, driving her head back and against the pillow. Then he sat between her legs and began kissing the inside of her thighs, working his way to her vaginal lips.

She moaned with the unexpected pleasure, complacent until she heard him laugh, but a laugh so unlike him, she had to brace herself on her elbows to look at him.

'I know what you like,' he said, smiling up at her, his eyes practically luminous. His expression resembled more of a sneer than a smile, full of arrogance. Before she could object, he was at her again, this time with such vigor and energy, her heart pounded with fear and surprise more than it did with erotic stimulation.

'Wait,' she cried. 'Move these pillows and –'

'No time for that,' he said.

He rose over her and brought his erection up with such force and accuracy, she lost her breath for a moment. He laughed again and then pressed his mouth over hers, sucking and driving his tongue into hers as he churned and pumped, holding her arms down and then reaching back to scoop under her thighs, lifting her legs so tightly she couldn't move. He pressed on, grinding, moaning. When she looked up at him, she saw his eyes were practically turned inward. He looked like he was about to pass out. She waited until he came, groaning, falling over her, gasping.

Then they were quiet. Maggie's heart was pounding against his, which was pounding just as fast and as hard.

'Now I know what it feels like to be raped,' she said after she caught her breath.

He didn't reply. He turned to roll off her and lay there on his back gazing up at the ceiling.

'You didn't like that?' he finally said.

'No. I never had the chance to like anything. You were pinning me down and twisting me like I was made of clay.'

'Sorry,' he said.

'What got into you?' she asked.

'I don't know.' He looked at her and smiled. 'I

guess it was watching you at the stove in your apron.'

'It's not funny, Grant. You frightened me and you hurt me,' she said, rubbing her thighs. 'You should have seen yourself; you wouldn't have recognized yourself.'

'Really?' he said. He gazed at himself in the mirror as if to see if it really was him.

She sat up and began to get dressed. Her anger made the veins in her temples more prominent. Her jawbone was taut, her teeth clenched. He felt remorseful and reached out to touch her softly, but she pulled away as soon as he made contact.

'I am sorry,' he said. 'I guess I've been having a bad day.'

'Why take it out on me?'

'I said I was sorry.'

She paused and looked down at him.

'What's wrong? What happened today?'

He shook his head.

'I don't know.'

She stared at him a few moments, thinking.

'You saw that patient again, didn't you?' she asked. His eyes widened. 'Well?'

'Yes.'

'That's part of it, isn't it? Isn't it?'

'Maybe,' he reluctantly confessed.

'Can you talk about it or . . .'

'Yeah, I can talk about it, if you really want to hear this stuff.'

66

'Something tells me I had better make myself a drink first,' she said. 'Let's go out to the bar.'

'What about your Suzy Homemaker recipe?'

'It can wait. The hungrier we are, the better it will taste,' she said.

He laughed, rose, threw on his robe, and followed. Now that he was calmer, he felt contrite.

'I'm sorry I was so aggressive. You're right. It's not like me.'

He sat on the settee. His face was still quite flushed, his hair over his forehead, but he looked more like himself.

'You want a drink?' she asked him.

'Please.'

She made him a cocktail and brought it to him.

'Go on, Doctor,' she said stepping back, her left arm folded under her breasts.

Grant laughed to himself, recalling what Carl had said about his wife analyzing him. That was the way Maggie looked at the moment, like his analyst.

He shook his head, took a sip of his drink, and sat back, gazing toward the ceiling rather than at her.

'I have described this patient's perceived problem . . . this compulsive obsession to get people to do wrong things, harmful, immoral things.'

'Yes.'

'Patients often try to get their doctors to admit they have similar problems. It makes them feel less insecure to know that others, even doctors, have committed comparable actions or have like thoughts troubling them. It's part of what builds

trust between the psychiatrist and his patient. It
alleviates guilt, the fear of being freaky –'

'I get the point,' Maggie said.

'Yeah, well, everyone has some evidence of compulsive behavior. We all might count our money
occasionally, maybe even twice the same day if we
forgot or thought we lost some, but if we did it every
ten minutes . . .'

'It would be obsessive.'

'Right. Anyway, my patient was trying to make
the point that I, like him, instigated someone to do
something wrong or did something wrong myself.'

'So?'

'To do so he brought up three examples, specific examples of acts I might have committed in
my past.'

Maggie stared for a moment, her eyes narrowing.
'So?'

He didn't reply.

'What are you saying, he accurately described
something you actually had done?'

'Yes,' Grant said.

'More than one thing?' He nodded. 'So it wasn't
just a lucky guess?'

'I don't think so.'

Her body tightened as if a chill had passed through
her, too.

'Who else would know about these bad things
you had done in the past?'

'Well, all psychiatrists go through analysis themselves, but the chances of someone learning the

intimate details of that analysis are quite remote. I think I once mentioned some of it to Henry after we had a few drinks together, but it's very unlikely, impossible to suspect he would tell a stranger intimate things about me.'

'How else would you explain such a thing, Grant?'

'I don't know.'

'I've never seen you so obsessed with a case, Grant,' Maggie said.

He hesitated and leaned forward. 'There's more,' he said. 'He just happened to turn up at the gym today.'

'He's really following you? You didn't imagine it?'

'I don't know. He claimed an attorney friend of his brought him there and he just happened to spot me.'

'Do you believe that?'

'I don't know.'

She stared a moment, sipped her drink. He sighed deeply and sat back.

'What else, Grant?'

'There's something about this patient, something ... intangible. He gets to me, gets inside me. I sorta lose my gracefulness, if that makes any sense. No patient since interning has made me feel as nervous and made me so careful about what I say and ask.'

'I don't like any of this, Grant. Why don't you refer him to someone else?'

'I can't do that.'

'Sure you can. You told me sometimes a patient and his psychiatrist have a personality problem and it's best to have another doctor involved.'

Grant shook his head.

'You're too proud to admit you can't handle it, is that it, Grant?'

'No. I'm too . . . intrigued. Maybe that's the same sort of sin,' he added softly.

'You once referred a patient to Henry for other reasons, didn't you, Grant?'

'That was different. Henry has become known as the expert in functional dyspareunia.'

'Had become,' she reminded him.

He sat back, shaking his head.

'It's hard to believe he's gone, and gone that way, Maggie.'

'I know.' She stared a moment, sipping more of her drink. 'At this last session, did this patient Bois give you another example of his instigating?'

'Yes.'

She paused almost as if she didn't want to hear about it and then nodded.

'Can you tell me?'

He described the Mosley situation just the way Bois had presented it to him.

'Grant, it's becoming eerie. You had better go to the police.'

'What? I can't do that. This is privileged information between me and my client.'

'But what about his following you about?'

'I can't say for sure he's doing that, and besides,

patients often develop fixations on their doctor. I said I can handle it,' he said.

'But . . .'

'Come on, Maggie.' He shook his shoulders as if throwing off a cold feeling. 'You've got me talking nonsense. The man's delusional. He's finding stories in newspapers.'

'You're sure?'

'What else could it be? You want me to go to the police and tell them I have a patient who has the power to make others do evil things? What's the charge, counselor? Being a bad influence? Psychiatrists have enough problems these days being taken seriously thanks to some of the crap that goes on in the courtroom. I'm not going to become part of all that,' he said firmly.

'Okay, Grant,' she said, not wanting to stir up old arguments. She took another sip of her drink. 'Maybe it's better we put all this aside and concentrate on Suzy Homemaker,' she offered.

He brightened immediately.

'Love to.'

She rose.

'Give me another twenty minutes and maybe I'll surprise you.'

'Wrong psychology. You should diminish my expectations so when I sit down, I am impressed.'

'I,' she said, standing tall, 'however, am confident.'

He laughed as she marched back to the kitchen.

Twenty minutes later she called him to the dining

room. She had the lights low, the candles lit, and wine on the table. A flick of the switch on the stereo produced the already set up disc of love songs.

'Doctor Blaine,' she said, pulling out his chair. She had prepared the chopped salad he loved and for the main course she had made her own sauce for the pasta.

'I'm impressed,' he said after tasting it. 'I really am. This is as good as Antonio's.'

She brightened; they finished off one bottle of wine and then started on another. Before coffee, they were both giggling like teenagers. They had a cappuccino machine they had used only once. Maggie admitted not knowing how to use it, so Grant reread the directions and started to make the cappuccino, but they had been gazing at each other lustfully throughout dinner, giving each other side glances, letting their eyes linger, until they both felt the heat. When she moved beside him, ostensibly to watch how he made the cappuccino so she could do it next time, his arm went around her waist and then his hand moved down until she was smiling, her breath hot on his neck. They kissed.

'I'd like another chance,' he whispered. 'To get it right.'

'What about the cappuccino?'

'Fuck the cappuccino,' he said.

He scooped her up far more gently this time and carried her back to the bedroom.

This time their sex reassured them of their commitment; they were more eager than ever to please
each other, and Grant was far more gentle and
caring. When he pulled back from her after his
climax, he saw there were tears streaming down
her cheeks. She smiled through them and he kissed
them and stroked her hair lovingly. Then he turned
on his back and caught his breath. Neither spoke
for a long moment.

'Did you ever tell me?' she suddenly asked.

'Tell you what?'

'Any of the evil things you did in your past?'

'Of course not. I wanted you to think of me as
Mr Perfect.'

She turned and leaned on her elbow to gaze into
his face.

'You are Mr Perfect. But . . .'

'But what?'

'Is the trust a patient has with her psychiatrist
the same trust a woman has with her lover?'

'No,' he said quickly. 'It's one thing to open your
mind; it's another to open your heart.'

She smiled.

'I like that. You can be romantic, Grant Blaine,
and for an analyst, that's not an easy task.'

He laughed. Then he grew serious.

'So what about children, Maggie? We keep putting off the decision.'

She lay on her back again. After a moment of
silence, she spoke.

'Maybe I should get the partnership locked up

first and then get pregnant and take the leave of absence,' she said.

'And after you get the partnership and they present you with the greatest case the firm ever had, will it be after that case and then the next?'

'Unfair, Grant.'

'Yeah, I guess it is,' he said, and started to rise. 'Let's have our coffee.'

She seized his arm.

'I can do both if you'll help; if you really want me to do both.'

'Maggie, I have no doubt if anyone can do both, you can. I just don't want you to lie to yourself about it. You're the one who has to believe she can do both.'

'Yes, Doctor,' she said, smiling. 'You don't mind having a schizophrenic for a wife: a relentless, conniving defense attorney during the day who becomes Suzy Homemaker, housewife, and mother at night?'

'Sounds like Cat Woman. Anyway, we're all a little schizophrenic.'

He laughed at the surprised look on her face and then put on his robe.

'Back to the cappuccino.'

They had it on the patio and sat listening to the sounds of traffic on Sunset Boulevard.

'Don't forget tomorrow night,' she said.

'I forgot. What?'

'Your mother's ball . . . at the Hilton?'

'Oh, yeah. I guess we had better show up for that one.'

'Grant, I was wondering about something.'

'Go ahead,' he said. 'Make my day.'

'No, really. Why did this Bois give you the name of one of his victims this time? He didn't give you Dunbar's name, right?'

'He thinks I'm going to go out there and check on it, I suppose.'

'Why?'

'Sometimes a patient can't get himself or herself to tell you the truth about himself or herself, but they want you to know it, need for you to know it, and so they leave clues, deliberate and obvious lies. Like a serial killer who wants to be caught,' he explained, 'and leaves just enough for the police to track him.'

'Great,' Maggie said. 'Serial killers.'

He laughed.

'Stop worrying so much.'

'I keep thinking that's what Henry did: stopped worrying until it was too late,' she said.

'I don't know what Henry did.'

'He did nothing,' she replied. 'And that's not the Henry Flemming you and I knew.'

Grant was silent. From somewhere east, they could hear the sound of a siren. It suddenly seemed closer than ever.

'Grant?'

'Yes, Maggie.'

'Does this Bois ever talk about Henry?'

'No, not really.'

'What did Henry think of his problem?'

'I don't know.'

'What do you mean, you don't know? Didn't you get his records sent over from Henry's group?'

'Bois insisted I don't.'

'Why?'

Grant shrugged.

'He wanted a fresh and objective analysis. He was very adamant about that.'

'Really?' She thought a moment. 'But he must have respected Henry if he continued to see him.'

'So?'

'So why wouldn't he want you to know what Henry thought?' she followed, with that cross-examination speed for which she was so famous in the courtroom.

Grant was a little annoyed by her tone. He didn't like feeling he was on the witness stand.

'It's not an unusual request, Maggie. I've had other patients who've come to me after being with another therapist and not wanted me to be influenced by their previous doctor's findings.'

She sipped her coffee. He could see the wheels turning.

'Maybe he wasn't ever one of Henry's patients. Maybe he made it up.'

'Then how did he meet Dunbar, Maggie? And why would he do that? Come on. You're getting paranoid. I'm not going to tell you any more about him. That's a promise.'

76

'That's a mistake, Grant.'

'I thought you said I was Mr Perfect.' He smiled. 'I don't make mistakes when it comes to my patients.'

'Maybe that's what Henry thought, too,' she said, and wiped the smile from his face.

5

Despite Grant's facade of self-confidence, Maggie remained worried. His situation with this patient Bois was the first thing that came to mind when she woke the next morning. When she got to the office, she asked Phil for a copy of the Dunbar case facts and put aside her own work to read them.

Clarence Dunbar was a salesman for a dental equipment company and quite successful at it. He and his wife had bought a home in Westwood five years ago. She had been a receptionist at ITF, an independent film production company, for nearly four years. They had no children. Dunbar, because of a psychosexual dysfunction, had been seeing Henry Flemming. According to the record, he had been in analysis for over six months.

One night, Dunbar had risen from bed, quietly gone out to his workroom, fetched a hammer, and returned to bludgeon his wife while she slept. After the murder, he went back to bed and didn't call the police until eight o'clock in the morning. They found the hammer beside Janet Dunbar on the bed. Dunbar himself was quite disoriented when the police arrived, babbling more about the hammer than his wife. Dunbar's sister was the one who had called Phil to ask him to take the case.

Maggie digested the material and thought for a while. Then she made an impulsive decision, called Phil, and asked him if he could make arrangements for her to visit with Dunbar.

'I was just going over to talk to him myself,' Phil said. 'What's up?'

'I'll explain in the car,' she promised.

As they rode to the jail together, she described her fear that the man Grant now had as a patient could very well be doing the evil things he claimed to be doing and may, in fact, have influenced Dunbar.

'Shouldn't Grant recognize that, Maggie? I mean, he kids me a lot and I kid him, but I have a great deal of respect for his abilities and intelligence. Anyway, if he needed anyone else's input, wouldn't he ask? Maybe go to Carl Thornton?'

'I think he's too close to this one, maybe because this patient was one of Henry's. He feels an obligation to solve it himself.'

Phil glanced at her and she shifted her gaze quickly.

'There's more to this,' Phil said. 'Isn't there?'

Maggie was silent.

'Trouble between you? Just tell me it's none of my business,' he added.

'It's none of your business.'

Phil laughed.

'Let's just say, I just don't like the effect this patient is having on him,' Maggie offered. 'It worries me.'

'Okay.'

'I'd like to talk to Dunbar alone first, Phil.'

'Fine,' he said.

When they arrived at the jail, she entered the conference room with Phil, who introduced her as his associate.

'She needs to ask you a few questions, Clarence. I have to do something and I'll be back in a few minutes, okay?'

Dunbar nodded. Phil looked at Maggie.

'All yours, counselor.'

'Thank you,' she said.

She sat across from Dunbar. He was about five feet eight, easily fifteen pounds too heavy, with a round face and dark brown eyes. His brown hair was cut neatly and brushed back, but he had a rather fancy pompadour.

'You know why you're here?' Maggie began, recalling Lydia Flemming's behavior after she had killed Henry. Dunbar nodded. He followed it with a shrug.

'I don't remember doing it,' he claimed. 'But I don't deny I did because I remember thinking about doing it on and off for days.'

'Do you know why you did it?'

'Sure,' he replied quickly, but with a matter-of-fact tone that implied everyone knew. 'It's because of what she did to me.'

'And what was that, Mr Dunbar? What had your wife done?'

'She took away my . . .'

'Go on. Please.'

'Manliness,' he said, and quickly shut his lips, as if releasing the word were blasphemy.

'And how did she do that?'

'In lots of ways.' He looked up, his eyes finally animated, only now they were bright with anger. 'I didn't even realize what she was doing. My psychiatrist explained it.'

'Doctor Flemming?'

'Yes. Once I told him everything, I could see he was just as angry about it as I was.'

'I knew Henry Flemming very well, Mr Dunbar. He wasn't one to show anger so easily. That's not something a psychiatrist is supposed to do,' she added softly.

'He did this time,' Dunbar insisted. Maggie noted how he was becoming more agitated, shifting in his seat, opening and closing his fist, nibbling on his lower lip.

'Okay,' she said calmly. 'Why did your wife do this to you?'

'She's was getting back at me.'

'For what?'

'For not making her a baby.'

'Why didn't she ask you for a divorce? Wouldn't that have been easier?'

'Her parents and she are devout Catholics. They thought permitting meat on Fridays was a sellout.'

'So instead of asking for a divorce . . . ?'

'My wife wanted me to go mad and then kill myself. That's what Doctor Flemming said, too,' Dunbar replied, his face red with anger.

'He told you that?'

'Yes. Yes, he did. He was very worried about me. He even called me on the phone from time to time to ask me what she was doing to me at the moment. We had a code. If he called and she was nearby, I always said we don't accept solicitations by phone.'

'Doctor Flemming called you at home?'

'That's right. He was very interested in what she was doing to me.'

'What sort of things was she doing? Give me an example that you gave him,' Maggie said.

Dunbar blushed and looked down.

'I just want to know the facts, Mr Dunbar.'

'I already told Mr Martin.'

'You're going to have to tell it again and again, and in court, too,' Maggie said.

Dunbar swallowed and looked at her. Then he looked down at his fingers, tugging gently on his right pinkie.

'She used to tell me it was too small, that she didn't know it was in her. She wouldn't move or nothing and she would never moan. She would just lay there with her eyes open and say, "Well? Well? What are you doing?"

'I was doing the best I could,' he protested. 'I was sweating, grunting. After a while I couldn't do that and then she laughed at me.'

Maggie thought for a moment. Could Dunbar be telling the truth? What was she doing here? This wasn't her territory, and yet she couldn't stop now.

'I understand,' Maggie continued, 'that you told Mr Martin Doctor Flemming encouraged you to kill your wife. Is that correct?'

'Yes,' Dunbar said without hesitation.

Maggie stared at him for a moment.

'Tell me about Doctor Flemming. You liked him, trusted him?'

'Sure. He told me he had problems with his wife, too,' Dunbar said, his face more animated.

Maggie leaned forward, her heart pounding.

'What sort of problems?'

'Similar problems. She made him feel . . . small.'

'Doctor Flemming told you this?'

'Yes,' he said firmly. Maggie sat back and contemplated him a moment.

'Please, describe Doctor Flemming,' she said.

'Describe? You mean what he looks like?'

'Yes. Please.'

Dunbar thought a moment. Then he pinched his temples with his right hand and rubbed his forehead as if he were conjuring up images.

'I don't know. He's a tall man, slim, red hair. He's a good-looking man, I suppose.'

'Red hair?'

'Well, it's kinda reddish blond, I suppose.'

'And you say he's slim?'

Dunbar nodded.

'I think so. I wouldn't call him skinny, if that's what you mean.'

'This is how you remember him now?'

'Yes,' Dunbar insisted.

'I want you to think for a moment about someone else, someone you might have met at Doctor Flemming's office, another patient.'

'I never met another patient there,' Dunbar said quickly, obviously sensitive to anyone having known he was seeing an analyst.

'Not even someone walking out when you arrived?'

'No.'

'Do you know a man named Jules Bois?'

Dunbar thought a moment and then shook his head.

'Can't recall anyone by that name.'

'You're sure?'

'Yes. Who is he?'

Maggie thought for a moment.

'Doctor Flemming doesn't have reddish blond hair, Mr Dunbar, and he's certainly not slim. He's stout. He was a football player in college, a defensive linebacker.'

Dunbar's face folded slowly into a cold smirk.

'He said someone might try to do that.'

'Do what?'

'Try to trick me.' Dunbar leaned over, keeping his

cool smile. 'Maybe you're not an attorney. Maybe you're just a cop. I'm not answering any more of your questions,' he added, and turned away.

Maggie stared.

If it was Jules Bois who had spoken to Dunbar and influenced him, how did Bois successfully impersonate Henry Flemming? Could he have disrupted Henry and Lydia Flemming's lives as well? Why had he chosen Grant to be his psychiatrist?

The answers to those questions hung like a bruised storm cloud, oppressive and foreboding, but she recognized that this was out of her ken. This was fodder for psychiatrists, not lawyers. She was over her head, swimming in confusion. She practically fled from the room.

When she emerged, Maggie found Phil talking with Carl Thornton. Phil had retained him for the case.

'So, Maggie,' Carl said, turning, 'what's your interest in Phil's client?'

'It's personal,' she replied.

Carl and Phil exchanged looks and she knew Phil had confided in him somewhat.

'He make any sense to you?' Carl asked. 'Do you find him competent to stand trial?'

'I wouldn't assume to be able to diagnose him, Carl, just because I'm married to a psychiatrist.'

Carl laughed.

'Dunbar,' he said, turning serious, 'is suffering from some from of psychogenic amnesia, of course, because he can't remember the actual events of the murder. How did he react to your questions, Mag?'

'He accused me of being a police spy.'

'Police spy?' Phil started to laugh. 'To do what?'

'I don't know.'

'That's his paranoia,' Carl said. 'Henry's diagnosis was accurate. Dunbar blames his wife; he blames his psychiatrist; he blames everyone but himself.' Carl gazed into Maggie's eyes like a mesmerist. 'And now that he's met you, Mag, he'll probably find a way to include you in the blame.'

'The man's bonkers,' Phil said happily.

'Yes,' Carl said, turning to him. 'The irony is that if he did accept responsibility and not blame his wife, his psychiatrist, and everyone else, and if he did recall the actual gruesome details of the violence, he would probably commit suicide or go into a deep, perhaps irretrievable depression. It's tricky; he's going to have to be treated carefully.'

'You'll testify to those conclusions?' Phil asked.

Carl nodded and smiled.

'Of course.'

'At least I have a solid line of defense,' Phil said, sighing with relief.

Maggie thought of Grant.

'Doesn't bring his wife back, though, does it?' she said softly.

'You're getting to sound like your husband, Mag,' Phil said, and laughed.

'It really isn't funny, though, is it?' she asked, gazing back at the conference room and then at Phil. 'He murdered that woman brutally. Did you read the medical examiner's report? He was still pounding her twenty minutes after she died.'

Phil shrugged.

'Hey, I'm not raising the dead. That's not our job,' Phil said. 'Look, we're just like Carl and Grant – hired guns. They kill the demons in the mind. We kill them in court.'

'Perhaps Maggie is here to help kill them in the mind as well,' Carl said prophetically.

She gazed back at him.

'Why did you say that, Carl?'

'Grant's been a little tense these days, hasn't he? I'm asking as a doctor as much as I am as a friend.'

'Yes,' she admitted with reluctance, but she was at the point where she couldn't keep it all bottled up.

'We're only human. Our work can get to us,' Carl said.

'Maybe I should talk Grant into a vacation,' Maggie said, nodding softly. 'We're both risking burnout.'

'But that's not what I hear about you, Maggie,' Carl said. 'According to Phil, you're the flavor of the month, maybe of the year. Everyone wants a piece of you these days.'

'Maybe Maggie means she's going to have to slow down because she has no choice,' Phil predicted with a smile.

'Oh?' Carl said. 'Something you two have been keeping secret, Mag?'

Maggie blushed. 'First of all, I'm not pregnant, and

second, if I were, I could strap the baby on my back and do opening arguments.'

The two men laughed.

'I bet she could,' Phil said. 'Seriously, though,' he added with a note of jealousy, 'word is out. Ken Simms is going to make her an offer she won't be able to refuse.'

'Oh?' Carl raised his eyebrows. 'Full partnership in the wings?'

'Talk's cheap,' Maggie said.

Carl shook his head.

'Not when your husband and I do it,' he retorted, and he and Phil laughed.

'I have to get back, Phil.'

'Right. Okay, Carl, after you see him today, give me a call.'

'Fine. Nice to see you again, Maggie. We should all get together soon for something other than sad occasions. It's been a while.'

'Yes,' she said without as much enthusiasm as she usually had. 'We should.'

She stood beside Phil as Carl headed for the conference room.

'So tell me, what did you really come away with after speaking to Dunbar?'

'A bad feeling,' Maggie said.

'Maybe you're the one developing paranoia, Maggie,' Phil quipped. 'I guess being a psychiatrist's wife is not all it's made out to be. Which is something poor Henry Flemming found out, huh?'

When she looked at him, he stopped smiling.

'That's not funny, Phil. Especially in light of the fact you're the one who's supposed to look after Lydia Flemming's interests now.'

'I know. I'm sorry. I was just trying to lighten you up. Really,' he said in a softer, apologetic tone.

'All right. Let's get out of here. I have something else I want to do before I get to the work I get paid to do,' she said.

'Uh-oh,' Phil said. He raised his eyebrows. 'What happens when Grant gets wind of this?'

'He's not going to, unless I tell him, right, Phil? Right?'

'Hey, you have the word of a member of the bar,' he said, raising his right hand.

'I'd rather have the word of a friend.'

He laughed.

'Me, too,' he whispered, and they were off.

6

When Grant arrived at his office in the morning, he was surprised at the changes in Fay Moffit's appearance. Not only had she gone ahead and bleached her hair and changed to a golden blond, but she was wearing a lot more makeup – eyeliner, rouge, a bright, wet lipstick – and a far tighter-fitting dress than she normally tolerated. It was especially snug around her bosom, and the V collar showed more cleavage than Grant thought she had. He suspected she was wearing one of those so-called Wonder Bras.

'Fay?' he said, widening his eyes. 'Are you my secretary, Fay Moffit?'

Normally Fay was quiet and demur, especially in the morning, but this morning she giggled like a teenager and without a hint of bashfulness or self-consciousness stood up to model her new look.

'Do you approve, Doctor Blaine?' She fluffed her hair and put her hands on her hips as she twirled on her high heels.

'At the moment I'm too overwhelmed, Fay.'

She laughed again. And then she wiped the smile off her face quickly and shifted her eyes toward his inner office door.

'She insisted on going in to wait for you, Doctor. She arrived only minutes after I had,' Fay said in a voice just above a whisper.

'Oh?'

The right corner of Fay's mouth lifted, her lips sinking into her cheek.

'I can't believe what she's wearing,' she said, 'even for L.A.'

'Uh-oh,' Grant muttered.

Suddenly the door to his office looked like the portal to a room containing forbidden fruit. But it was titillating. He tried to hide his interest, but Fay wore an uncharacteristically sophisticated smirk. It was as if she could see through his normally inscrutable psychiatric mask.

'Be careful, Doctor,' she warned as he reached for the doorknob.

'I always am, Fay,' he said. He nodded. 'I like it, the new look, the new Fay Moffit.'

'Thank you, Doctor.' She beamed and he pulled in his stomach, inflated his chest, and entered his office.

Deirdre Leyland was sprawled on the leather sofa in a crucifix pose, her legs spread apart. She wore a loosely fitted halter and those infamous short shorts, which were a good two inches below her belly button. Her sandals were off. It was just the way he had envisioned her in a recent fantasy, as if she had been conjured from his own imagination.

'Good morning, Doctor,' she said softly. Then she leaned forward a bit so the halter fell away from her bosom, revealing the curve of her abundant breasts. 'You weren't on the beach this morning. I was disappointed.'

'Not my morning for the beach,' Grant said, walking quickly to his desk. He set down his briefcase, keeping his back to her. 'You're a little early,' he said, flipping through some mail.

'Just trying to get the worm,' she quipped.

He nodded, still with his back to her, pretending not to understand the innuendo. When he raised his eyes from his papers and looked across his desk, he suddenly imagined Jules Bois sitting there, smiling. He could almost hear him instigating:

Go on, Doctor. Take advantage of the situation. You don't have these opportunities all that often. It's easy. Think about it. You can enjoy this beautiful woman and not only won't she complain, she'll thank you. And no one will know, no one will ever know. Later, if she told anyone anything, they would be skeptical because they would know what she was. How can a nymphomaniac cry rape? It's perfect, made to order. Go on. Don't be a fool. Do it.

He closed his eyes and took a deep breath. When he opened them, Bois was no longer sitting there. It was simple mental projection, Grant told himself, nothing more. Just a leak in his subconscious.

'Are you all right, Doctor?' she asked.

'What? Oh. Yes. Okay, let's start,' he said, turning to her.

'Let's,' she said, sitting back. She played with the zipper in front of her halter, pulling it down an inch and then up and then down an inch and a half and then up only an inch. Grant picked up his notepad and took the seat beside the sofa. It was set so he was just about parallel to her head. When she turned or leaned forward, the halter buckled again to reveal most of her breasts. They were like magnets playing to his iron eyes.

'How was your evening?' he began.

She pouted for a moment, crossing her arms over her breasts like a spoiled adolescent.

'Frustrating. I just couldn't seem to get enough. I left the house about seven, went to a singles bar, got picked up, and was in bed by eight-thirty. My first lover was one of those slam-bam, thank you ma'am deals. I didn't even approach an orgasm before he was spent. I had to masturbate while he was in the bathroom recuperating. I was back on the street a little after nine and went to this dance club in Melrose, where I picked up two bikers and went to their cottage for an orgy-porgy, but they were more interested in themselves than me.'

She turned back to him.

'Most men are very selfish when it comes to sex, Doctor. Did you know that?'

'No, I didn't know that, but I don't have your experience,' he replied, and she laughed.

'Come, now, Doctor. You don't expect me to believe that, do you? You're a good-looking man, intelligent, charming, and a man with a creative imagination. You could make a woman very happy; you do make your wife happy, don't you?'

'Let's try not to talk about me, Mrs Leyland. You're the one who's come for help.'

'We can help each other. There's nothing terribly wrong about that, is there? You have fantasies to fulfill, don't you? You're a Freudian. You see phallic symbols everywhere and you are forever trying to return to the womb.' She laughed.

'Who told you such a thing, Mrs Leyland?'

She laughed and then she grew serious, almost angry.

'Nothing you've suggested has helped. It got so bad I went into the department store yesterday and tried on pants that were two sizes too tight just to feel the tingle in my crotch. It's driving me mad,' she said, moving her hand to her crotch. 'Even now, just talking about it.'

'Mrs Leyland, if you don't want to take any medication, you've got to concentrate –'

'I am, Doctor.'

'On what I've been saying,' he added quickly, but his eyes were glued to her hand as it moved up and down. She moaned. 'Mrs Leyland, I want you to try to relax now. Come on. Close your eyes,' he urged, but she brought her hands to her breasts and pressed her palms against them.

'You said you could show me how to distract myself, how to sublimate these passionate cravings. You said I have to learn to give more of myself instead of demand more from my lover. You said it's just like any other appetite. But you don't show me, Doctor,' she complained. 'How do I give more and demand less when I make love? Can't you demonstrate?'

'That's not exactly what I'm here for, Mrs Leyland.'

'Isn't it?' she asked, turning her eyes to him as she continued to massage herself, one hand moving back to her crotch, the other remaining on her breast. He stared and then she reached for him. 'Doctor, please . . . help me,' she pleaded softly, so softly he couldn't swallow. His heart had begun to pound. 'My previous doctor did,' she said. 'He said he could get me to see everything clearer if I would try to subdue my drives, if I would try to surrender to his . . . instructions,' she added.

'What are you talking about, Mrs Leyland? What other doctor? You never mentioned another doctor.'

'Didn't I?' She laughed. 'Just an oversight, I guess. Or maybe I wanted to block him out because he didn't cure me. Yes, that's it. But you're different, Doctor Blaine. You're sincere. You really want to cure me. Don't you?'

She tightened her grasp on his hand and pulled him toward her.

'I've got to learn to think of other things, distract myself,' she said. 'Isn't that what you said? Doctor, show me how. I'll meditate as you show me, just the way you instructed, but you've got to help me calm down,' she said. 'You've got to help me cap this flow of raw desire, and then I'll do what you instruct,' she promised.

She placed his hand on her breast and then zipped down the halter quickly to shove his palm under the material. He felt the coolness and then her erect nipple. She had turned her face to him, her lips inviting, the halter falling to the side to expose her bosom.

'Please, Doctor,' she said. 'Help me. It won't take long and we'll be able to concentrate. All the distraction will be gone. That's just sensible therapeutic treatment, isn't it?'

She tugged on his wrist, urging him to get off the chair and come to her.

He heard his notepad fall to the floor. He felt himself rising. When he glanced to his right, he envisioned Bois again, sitting behind the desk, nodding, smiling, coaxing.

He gazed at Deirdre Leyland and her exposed breasts, her beautiful skin, her lustful eyes. All resistance was melting away under the heat of rationalization. She was right: there was a therapy, a line of thinking, that could justify this. It called for putting the patient at ease. And that's exactly what he would be doing, right?

That's right, he thought he heard the imaginary Jules Bois say as if he could hear Grant's thoughts. *You're putting the patient at ease. Nothing more. It's good therapy, Doctor. Force yourself to help her.*

He was on his knees and she was taking his head in her hands and guiding him toward those short shorts that she had undone.

When he gazed toward his desk again, he imagined Bois standing in front of it, leaning against it, his arms folded across his chest, scrutinizing like an objective observer.

The scent of Deirdre Leyland's sex hooked him and, like a poor, dumb fish he swallowed and felt himself jolted out of the security of his own identity.

'Relax,' he heard himself saying, 'just try to relax, Mrs Leyland. This won't take long and then you'll be relieved and we'll be able to concentrate.'

'Yes, Doctor,' she moaned. 'Yes, that's right.'

Afterward, after she had left the office, he stood by the window and gazed down at the street. He saw her emerge from the building and cross the street to a waiting black automobile. He couldn't see the driver's face, but the shape of the head was familiar. Before he could think any more about it, he heard the door open and turned to see Fay, all flushed, her hand at the base of her throat, her eyes wide.

'Doctor.'

'What is it, Fay?'

'It's . . . Mr Gordon,' she said. 'He deliberately came a half hour early to sit in the waiting room.'

Grant stared, anticipating. Peter Gordon was a forty-five-year-old man who had been arrested and convicted for obscene exhibitionism. The last time was his third arrest. Part of his punishment was a commitment to psychotherapy. This was only the second time Grant had met with the man and there was still a wall of distrust, anxiety, and resentment to scale.

'What?'

'He's sitting there on the sofa facing me . . . with his penis out!'

Grant rushed past her and stopped.

'There's no one here, Fay.'

'What?' She turned. 'He was sitting right there, Doctor,' she said, pointing to the sofa.

'I guess he left,' Grant said, but the door opened and Peter Gordon entered. He froze at the way they were both staring at him.

'What?' he said. 'I'm late?'

Grant turned to Fay. She shook her head.

'It's all right, Fay,' he said softly. 'Go on back to your desk. Right this way, Mr Gordon,' Grant said, stepping back.

Peter Gordon's forehead crinkled. He considered and then he walked through the waiting room, not glancing at Fay, who was looking down. She looked up the moment Gordon was inside the inner office.

'You all right?' Grant asked her.

'Yes. I guess I have to get used to this sort of thing if I'm going to work for a psychiatrist.'

Grant smiled.

'No one ever really gets used to this sort of thing, Fay.'

He closed the door and turned to Peter Gordon, who was sitting on the lounge. He didn't like lying back on it.

'So,' Grant began, 'were you just in my office, Peter?'

Peter Gordon looked up.

'What do you mean?'

'I mean, were you sitting out there and did you do something you weren't supposed to do?'

'I just came in,' he claimed. 'I just came into the building! I wasn't sitting out there.'

Grant stared at him.

'You don't believe me?' Peter Gordon shoved his hand into his pants pocket and produced the parking ticket. 'Check it out,' he said.

Grant narrowed his eyes and took the ticket from Peter Gordon. It was stamped literally two minutes earlier. How could he have been in the office a half hour early? Unless he had parked someplace else, committed the act, and then left and parked in the garage. This was maddening.

'You gotta give me that back,' Peter Gordon said, 'or they'll charge me for the whole day.'

'What? Oh, sure. Sorry,' Grant said, and handed the ticket to Gordon, who stuffed it in his pocket and stared at the floor sullenly.

'Everyone blames me for doing things I don't do,' he mumbled.

After the session, Grant followed Peter Gordon

out to Fay's desk and watched her paste on the validation stickers to cover his parking fee in the building. Peter Gordon took the ticket without saying thank you and left, still in a quite sullen demeanor. Grant hadn't had a very productive session with him. The man barely uttered more than two polysyllabic words.

'Did you notice the time stamped on Mr Gordon's parking ticket, Fay?' he asked.

'No, why?'

'According to the ticket, he pulled into the building only about two minutes before he walked in.'

'He's never been very early, Doctor.'

'But . . . no, I was referring to what you said had happened before,' Grant explained.

'He was here, Doctor. It happened. I wouldn't lie about it, would I?' She smiled at him with an all-knowing, sophisticated look quite uncharacteristic of her.

He stared a moment. Should he continue this? He decided to retreat into the office and closed the door.

He was sweating and he was feeling very confused. His head was actually spinning. He went to his desk and sat a moment, thinking and then looking at his desk to find anything that would prove Jules Bois had indeed been sitting there, watching.

What, am I going mad, too? he wondered.

Physician, heal thyself, he heard, and went for a Valium.

7

Maggie was more upset than she had revealed after her visit with Dunbar. She was twisted with contradictions. First, she told herself she had no right to go there. As she had told Carl, just living with a psychiatrist gave her no ability to evaluate anyone. She was sure that Carl Thornton and even Grant could easily explain away Dunbar's confusion about Henry Flemming.

And yet, she had the instinctive feeling there was more to this. Maybe years of practicing criminal law had made her somewhat paranoid, but she found the coincidence of Grant's patient Bois claiming responsibility for the criminal activities of one of her firm's clients a bit too much. Grant was having an unusual reaction to this patient anyway. He as much as admitted that to her. She had to look into all this for Grant's sake, and for her own.

She decided she would do one more thing before she did anything else in her office. Grant had said Bois claimed another victim, someone named Mosley. A simple phone call to the coroner's office revealed that a sixty-eight-year-old woman named Lillian Mosley with a Santa Monica address had arrived at St John's Hospital DOA. She had been brought in by ambulance when her son found her in the apartment, collapsed on the kitchen floor. So that part proved true, she concluded. Of course, Bois could be, as Grant had said, simply scanning newspapers for delusions.

Maggie knew that a person brought to a hospital emergency room dead on arrival was automatically reported as a coroner's or medical examiner's case. The coroner would investigate for possible foul play and determine if a complete postmortem examination was needed. Not all cases would require an autopsy, however. Only those truly suspected of foul play would even have blood drawn for toxicology tests, especially with the workload the coroner's office had these days.

Maggie spoke with a coroner's secretary, who, annoyed with her questions, nevertheless agreed to read her the coroner's conclusion.

'"It is my opinion that Lillian Mosley, a sixty-eight-year-old female, died as a result of cardiac arrest. She had a history of heart disease,"' she recited in a monotone.

'That's it?'

'That's it. Okay?' she whined with impatience.

She was about to cut her off.

'No,' Maggie said quickly. She explained who she was and asked to speak with Doctor Benson, the medical examiner who had handled Lillian Mosley. After putting her on hold for nearly ten minutes, the secretary managed to transfer the call to Benson. Once again, Maggie explained who she was and then asked if there was any possibility the Mosley woman overdosed on her nitroglycerin.

Doctor Benson had trouble recalling the corpse. Maggie could hear him sifting through paperwork before he finally responded.

'Oh. Yes. Well, that was a possibility because she had some evidence of Alzheimer's and was living alone. So what's new, huh?' Benson said dryly. It always amazed Maggie how everyone from one end of the social structure to the other accepted the plight of the elderly in America as inevitable.

'Well, if that's a possibility, shouldn't you have done a toxicology?'

'No, not necessarily. I had no reason to believe there was criminal activity involved. Do you know something? Because this was four days ago. I'm sure the body's either been buried or cremated.'

'Can you give me the son's name and address?' Maggie asked. Doctor Benson did so and then Maggie considered her next step. If she somehow convinced Grant to go to the police with the information Bois gave him and it turned out Bois was delusional, they would have wasted their time and caused innocent people some deep emotional trauma. Grant would be furious with her for getting him to do it.

On the other hand, what if Bois was telling the truth? A woman was murdered. The police would want to interview Bois. Yet Grant had said he couldn't tell the police about Bois anyway. He had insisted that would be a breach of the patient-doctor confidence. What's more, she was sure he would be furious about the investigating she had already done.

To her way of thinking, Grant was trapped by the principles of his profession; but she wasn't. She buzzed her secretary.

'Get Jack Landry on the phone for me, Marsha,' she snapped.

Jack Landry was a private investigator often hired by the firm. She had had two previous experiences with him on cases and was very satisfied with his work and professionalism.

Landry was an ex-New Orleans police detective who had opted to leave the department when he was, as he put it, disgusted with the corruption, corruption he called insidious and infectious. He told Maggie he had eventually felt like Serpico and feared for his own life. It was best to effect an early retirement.

At forty-four, he wasn't really retired. He enjoyed private investigatory work, enjoyed being his own boss, and had developed a very good reputation, not only with attorneys, but among the well-to-do, who hired him to spy on their own children, as well as on spouses and business partners. For the most part, he said he found the work clean and easy. And he was well paid.

Maggie arranged for them to meet for lunch at a coffee shop not far from her office. Landry was a six-foot-one-inch lanky man, Lincolnesque, with deep facial lines that gave him a habitual look of sadness and worry. Even his smile was melancholy. Maggie attributed the sculpturing of the man's face and personality to the ugly exposures he had endured as a police detective in New Orleans.

'Good to see you again, counselor,' Landry said in his Cajun rhythms after they shook hands. They ordered coffee. Landry ordered a bagel and cream cheese and Maggie ordered a cob salad.

'Why is it you women eat healthier than us men?' Landry complained. 'Do women really have stronger willpower?'

'You're the detective, Detective,' she said, smiling. 'You tell me.'

Landry laughed.

'Maybe it's just because I'm too busy to think about myself these days. Everyone wants information; no one trusts anyone. Your husband would probably say paranoia has become an epidemic in America.'

'I might be another victim of it,' she said.

'Oh?'

'I hope you'll have time for one more assignment,' Maggie said, and explained what she wanted Landry to do: investigate the Mosleys.

Landry sipped his coffee and chewed his bagel,

listening. Then he sat back and after a moment shook his head.

'You have a witness who claims he knows Mrs Mosley's daughter-in-law killed her. Why don't you just get him to go to the police?'

'He doesn't just know she did it, Jack. Grant says the patient claims he encouraged her to do it.'

'Why?'

'He told Grant he enjoys getting other people to do harmful things to themselves and to other people.'

'So, he admits it to Grant, but won't to the police because he thinks he's an accessory?'

'I don't think that's what keeps him from telling the police. It's more complicated.'

Landry nodded.

'I don't know what's worse,' he said, 'the sewer in the streets I investigate or the sewer in the mind your husband investigates. I suppose his is less dangerous.'

'Supposed to be,' Maggie said. 'There's one other thing for now, Jack.'

'Oh?'

'Grant doesn't know anything about this.'

'Oh,' he said, rolling his eyes.

'If there's nothing to it, no harm done,' she said.

'Except to your pocketbook,' Jack reminded her.

'Right now I think it's a worthwhile and necessary expense, Jack.'

'Well, I'll do it fast and cut the costs. This doesn't seem too complicated.' He checked his watch. 'If I don't call you by the end of the day, I'll call you tonight.'

'No,' she said quickly. 'I'll call you.'

'Oh, yes.' He smiled. 'Paranoia is very good for my business,' he concluded.

Maggie returned to her office and dove deeply into her own work to keep from worrying about Grant. She nearly forgot she had to leave a little earlier than usual to get ready for the charity ball at the Hilton. Fortunately, her secretary reminded her about what was on her calendar.

'Oh, damn,' she cried, and hurried out, hoping Grant had remembered the affair as well. Her mind was put at ease when she turned her vehicle down their street and saw his Mercedes in the drive-way. But when she rushed into the house, she was surprised again, this time by finding Grant sitting quietly in a dark corner of their living room, gazing out the window, a healthy glass of scotch on the rocks in hand. He seemed not to have heard her enter.

'Grant?'

He turned slowly.

'Oh, hi, Mag.'

'How long have you been home?' she asked, moving cautiously toward him.

'I got home early. My four o'clock canceled. Louise Singer, the procrastinator,' he said, and laughed. It was a cold laugh. 'Sometimes I feel like that Dutch kid with his finger in the dike.'

'You've done good work, Grant, and you've had

some striking success with other patients. Don't put yourself down because of one or two failures.'

'One or two?' He laughed again. Then he sighed deeply and took a good swig of his drink.

'Something else is wrong, isn't it?' she asked. She was about to follow with, *Does it have anything to do with your new patient?* But she hesitated.

'The strangest thing happened in my office today,' he said. 'It's making me question my own relationship to reality.'

'Why? What happened?'

He gazed at her and then shifted his eyes guiltily away.

'Grant?'

'I had strange . . . visions today. While I was treating a patient.'

'Visions of what?'

He hesitated and then put his glass down.

'I kept seeing this patient, hearing his voice while I treated another patient and . . . it caused me to make some errors,' he said.

'What sort of errors?'

'Just some errors,' he snapped. 'Actually, I don't want to talk about it right now, Mag. I've got to work this out myself.'

'Grant, you're scaring me.'

'I'll be all right. It's just an occupational hazard,' he said.

'You should speak to someone else, Grant.'

'I have. I called Carl today and we had a good discussion.'

'Carl Thornton?'

'Yes.'

She was waiting to see if Carl had said anything about her visiting Dunbar, but apparently he hadn't.

'We have the affair tonight, remember? But if you're not up to it . . .'

'No, I should go. I should get out,' he said. 'I'll just take a hot shower.'

He smiled at her.

'How was your day?' he asked. She hated deceiving him, but now, more than ever, she was convinced she was doing the right thing.

'Typical,' she said.

'Any talk about partnerships?'

'Not today. Maybe that's just all it is, Grant, talk.'

He nodded and rose.

'Okay,' he said, and took a deep breath. 'Let's get ready to pay our respects to the Queen of Beverly Hills: my mother.'

'Grant!' she warned. 'You'd better behave.' She followed him to the bedroom to get herself ready, too.

The affair was as plush as any Grant and Maggie had previously attended. Besides the elaborate cocktail party and full-course prime rib or chicken Cordon Bleu dinner, there was a twenty-six-piece dance orchestra, magnificent flowers on the tables, photographers and society columnists everywhere. Grant had had to check the invitations to recall for which charity this had all been arranged.

'Just another excuse for the rich and famous to put on their diamonds,' Grant told Maggie on the way to the hotel. Maggie was driving. She thought he was still in quite a bitter and depressed mood and she knew he could be rather biting and sarcastic in conversation when he was like this.

'They get their tax write-off and feel so magnanimous. It's all bullshit, Maggie.'

'Why so down on the privileged class tonight, Grant? Is it because you're still down on yourself?'

'Everyone's a psychiatrist these days,' he muttered.

She looked at him, tears clouding her eyes. It was uncharacteristic of him to turn that sharp edge on her.

'I'm only asking because I'm worried about you, Grant.'

'Stop worrying. I'm fine. I'm sorry I even mentioned anything,' he added after a moment.

When they arrived at the hotel, he did seem to revert to his old self. He gave his mother the big greeting she expected and began to mingle, charm, and hold conversations with people. He smiled more, danced with Maggie before the dinner was to begin, and generally moved about freely, with ease. She began to think he simply had to get out among people, whether he thought they were all hypocrites or not.

Just before they sat for dinner, a couple approached Grant at the bar. They quickly introduced themselves as Marvin and Phyllis Becker. Maggie was standing beside Grant and had heard it all. Marvin Becker was a dark-haired man in his late forties, about five-eight. He had a soft, almost feminine face with eyelashes Maggie thought some women would kill to have. When Grant introduced her to Marvin and they shook hands, Maggie found his grip slippery, smooth, his fingers pudgy. She thought here was an example of the sort Grant was railing about on the way over. Becker personified the idle rich, wallowing in money, hiring people to do everything but move his bowels for him. However, Becker's wife did most of the talking.

Maggie noticed a fragility in her, a note of hysteria in her voice when she spoke. She was only an inch or two shorter than her husband, but almost as overweight. Bedecked in jewels, manicured and primed by the best Beverly Hills beauticians and hairdressers, she looked like a farcical attempt to turn Miss Piggy into Christie Brinkley.

But they had a problem, a serious problem with their teenage son, and Phyllis and Marvin Becker placed the blame solely on their son's present psychiatrist.

'I know this isn't the proper time and place to bring this up,' Phyllis said, 'but everything's just come to a terrible crisis today and when you were pointed out here . . . we've heard so many good things about you.'

Marvin nodded at the end of each of his wife's sentences.

'You can call my office tomorrow, Mrs Becker,'

Grant said politely, trying to effect a graceful escape.

But the woman started to cry.

'Stop it, Phyllis,' Marvin said, and nudged her, rather hard, Maggie thought.

'Well, it's horrible, absolutely horrible. This doctor has Gary believing there are things deep in his childhood memories he's repressed, disgusting things involving both of us,' she revealed.

Grant tried to look at ease. People were starting for their tables.

'He calls it memory repression,' Marvin said bitterly. 'He's blaming everything Gary has done on us.'

'It's so horrible,' Phyllis reiterated. 'Can you see Gary right away – tomorrow, perhaps?'

'Money's no object,' Marvin quickly added.

'Grant,' Maggie whispered. 'Your mother's waving at us.'

'I'll work him in. That's a promise, Mrs Becker. Call my office about ten in the morning, okay?'

'Thank you, Doctor,' she said, grasping his hand between hers.

'Yes, thank you,' her husband said. 'Sorry to bother you here.'

'It's all right. Just call,' Grant said, and followed Maggie's lead away from the bar.

'What was all that about, memory repression?' Maggie asked as they strolled arm in arm toward his mother's table.

'It's the flavor of the month in psychiatric circles,' Grant said. 'Remember that girl who claimed her father raped her and then years later claimed her psychiatrist put it in her mind? The rape. It never happened.'

'Like what supposedly happened with the children in the MacMartin case?'

'Exactly.'

'Maybe you psychiatrists should be registered like weapons these days,' Maggie said, half in jest.

Grant nodded.

'Maybe,' he said. 'We'll see.'

8

They were both tired at the end of the evening, but Grant seemed positively exhausted the moment they got into the car and started for home. Even his mother commented to Maggie that Grant looked drained, pale. Once they had sat at the table, whatever energy source Grant had relied upon when they had first entered the hotel ran dry. He barely spoke and he ate very poorly. Twice during the short speeches, he dozed off and she had to nudge him, especially when it was his mother who was talking.

'Are you all right?' she asked him as they waited for the valet to bring up their car.

'Fine,' he said, but as soon as they got in, he lay his head back and closed his eyes, not opening them until they had pulled into the garage and she literally told him they were home. He groaned and got out. Skipping his usual humorous review of one of his mother's charity affairs, he then undressed and went to bed. By the time she emerged from the bathroom, he looked dead asleep. She stared at him a moment and then went to the kitchen and quietly called Jack Landry.

'Sorry if it's too late,' she said, 'but I didn't have any other opportunity.'

'It's not too late; it's never too late to a professional insomniac. Okay, here's what I have,' he said. 'The background was easy and when I visited Lillian Mosley's apartment building, I came up with some information you might find interesting.

'First,' Landry continued, 'Mosley's son Allan is what you would call a plodder, simple, indistinguishable, almost anonymous. He works for a big accounting firm, has for nearly twelve years, but hasn't been promoted to anything or had the courage to go out on his own. No one dislikes him, but no one really cares about him. You know the type, ripe pickings for a dominatrix.'

Maggie laughed.

'You know more about that than I do, Jack. What about his wife, then?'

'His wife Janet is a beautician, early forties, been working in an upscale salon in Beverly Hills for nearly ten years. Exposed to the rich and richer, probably wondering all the time why the bitch in the chair has all the money in the world and she doesn't, if you'll permit me a little license to guess motive,' Jack added.

'Maybe you should be writing detective stories, Jack,' Maggie said.

'Maybe. Maybe my clients' paranoia is catching. Anyway, the story is she often went to the old lady's apartment to do her hair and just happened to go the evening the old lady OD'd on her nitro, if that's what she indeed did.'

'Is that your interesting information?'

'That and one other thing . . . neighbor told me the old lady had run out of the medicine and the old lady told her that her daughter-in-law was bringing it to her. Puts her at the scene of the crime, if it was a crime. We have good motive – they inherit all; there is no other sibling.'

'How did you get a neighbor to tell you this sort of thing, Jack?'

She was really worried about someone tracking him back to her.

'I did my usual routine, pretended to be an insurance investigator. They love talking to insurance investigators. Everyone thinks other people are scamming their insurance companies, probably because they would, too, if they had the chance.'

'What did they inherit from the old lady?'

'She had about eight CDs in four different banks, besides a few blue chips I bet she forgot she had. We're talking about a quarter of a million. This neighbor also confirmed that Mrs Mosley was losing it. A nursing home was surely in the wings, and with it, loss of the money. A fortune to Mr and Mrs Nobody. Bottom line is Janet Mosley could have done what your patient claims she did, and it would appear to be a medical accident. You want me to do more?'

Maggie considered a moment. She was tempted to put Landry on Jules Bois.

'Let me think about it, Jack. There's a lot to digest. Thanks. In the meantime, send me the bill.'

'Maybe I should just build up a line of credit with your husband. The way things are going, I might need analysis myself soon.'

'I don't want Grant to know about this,' she quickly reminded him. 'You told me you would respect that confidence, Jack,' she fired.

'I'm just kidding, Mrs Blaine.'

Maggie took a deep breath.

'I'm sorry. This has all put me on edge. I'll call you in the morning, Jack.'

'Fine. Try to have a good night,' he said.

After she cradled the receiver, she stood there a moment thinking. Who was this new patient of Grant's? If all that he did was scan newspapers for possible delusions, how could he know that people had motives for possible crimes? Did he visit with them after he found their names in the obituary column? Or preyed upon them in psychiatric offices, like he preyed upon Dunbar? How ghoulish and insane, and yet, that might be all it was. And if that was so, he certainly belonged with Grant and it would be Grant's professional problem, not hers.

She didn't realize how long she had been standing

there in deep thought, but suddenly she had a cold feeling moving up the back of her neck. She turned sharply to see Grant standing in the kitchen doorway. The chill flowed down her shoulders, over her chest, and into her heart.

'Who were you talking to?' he asked.

How much had he heard? She wondered before she responded.

'I forgot something I had to tell Phil about tomorrow's sentencing hearing,' she said. He continued to stare at her. He was wearing only the bottom of his pajamas and he was barefoot.

'I heard voices. I thought someone had come to the house,' he explained.

She smiled.

'Sorry. I didn't think I was speaking that loud.'

'Couldn't you have called him in the morning?' he asked, his eyes narrowing with suspicion just when it looked like he was going to accept her explanation.

'Phil's going right to the courthouse in the morning. I didn't want to miss him,' she said. 'I'm sorry, Grant. I thought you were dead to the world and wouldn't hear anything, especially if I came out here.'

He nodded and went to the sink to get himself a glass of water.

'Are you all right?' she asked.

'No. I thought I was tired, but minutes after I closed my eyes, they popped open and I suddenly feel wide awake.'

'Interrupted sleep. You told me that's a sign of anxiety, Grant.'

'Serves me right for giving you a little knowledge, which, as you will recall, is a dangerous thing,' he replied, and gulped a pill.

'What's that?'

'Something to help me sleep,' he said, and started out of the kitchen. She stood there a moment, wondering. Had he heard her conversation? Was he just pretending?

She turned off the lights and started after him, but stopped when she saw him standing in the living room, gaping at the window, his eyes wide, his lips stretched in a grimace.

'What is it?'

'I thought I saw someone looking in our window,' he said in a deep whisper.

'What?'

He moved into a crouch and turned off the lamp.

'Grant. Is it him, that man?'

'Quiet,' he said moving to the window. She stood there, watching him, her heart pounding. He peered out at the edge of the window. 'Did you arm the alarm after we came home?' he asked.

She thought a moment.

'No, I forgot.'

'Go do it,' he said.

She hurried up to the pad by the front door and punched in the numbers. Then she held her breath, waiting to see if one of the doors or windows would trigger the siren. None did. She let out the hot air in her chest and returned to the living room. Grant was still at the window, crouched.

'Who did you think you saw?'

He didn't respond.

'Grant?'

'A man, looking in at us,' he said quickly.

'A man? Did you recognize him? Was it your patient Bois? Grant?'

'No,' he said, but he sounded like he was lying.

'You're scaring me, Grant.'

'It's all right,' he said, straightening. He flipped on the lamp again and he smiled at her. 'It was just a shadow, I'm sure. No point in not being cautious, though right? And you did forget to arm the alarm, so it was good.'

She stared at him. His whole demeanor seemed to have changed in seconds. There was a brightness in his face; the groggy look in his eyes was gone.

'Relax,' he said, starting toward her.

'Relax?' she started to laugh. 'After this?'

'I'm sorry. Are you tired?' he asked with a strange glint in his eyes.

'I was. Now, I might need whatever you took to help you sleep,' she replied.

'I have something better,' he said. 'Come on.' He turned off the lamp and put his arm around her shoulders as he led her back to the bedroom. 'All of us have built-up tensions in our bodies from the day. We're like charged batteries; a crisis here, a conflict there, some problem to consider . . . everything,' he lectured, 'puts some static into our system. Meditation helps, of course, but at this time of night, especially if you're married to a beautiful woman, and she's married to a handsome man . . .' he added when they reached their bed. He turned her so they faced each other. 'Sex can be a terrific panacea.'

'What?' She started to smile, but he remained deadly serious, intense.

'I'm talking about two people focusing all their energies on their sexual involvement. It's a way of channeling the static, putting it to good use and at the same time relieving yourselves of the tension,' he explained.

She tried again to smile, but looking into his face, she felt she was gazing at a stranger. His lips, his eyes, even the way he moved his nostrils made him look different. She wondered if this wasn't the face Grant put on when he treated his patients. She had never seen him in action, of course, but there was something very aloof, very analytic about the way he gazed at her.

'Are you using psychology on me, Grant?'

Now he was the one who smiled.

'We all do that, every day, to everyone we meet,' he said, and then he brought his lips to hers and held her tightly as he moved his tongue into her mouth and moaned. His hands slipped down her thighs and groped to raise her nightgown and get under it. Once he did, he clutched her buttocks firmly and pulled her toward his erect penis.

She was overwhelmed with the urgency and firmness in him. She did feel as if he were using sex as therapy. He surprised her by not moving them to the bed, however. Instead, he lifted her and drew her back with him to the settee by the window.

'Grant . . .' she started to protest.

He kissed her neck and her shoulders and brought his mouth to her ear.

'Just listen to the doctor,' he whispered. He drew her nightgown over her head and sat, guiding her onto his phallus. 'Maggie, Maggie,' he said softly. She was very confused. One moment he was rough and urgent, and the next he was gentle, loving, crying for her, needing her, wanting her. As they moved faster and faster, she realized the curtain on the window was wide open and the light behind them in the room surely silhouetted them in the pane.

Normally, there wasn't much of a risk of being seen. It was late. Streets in Beverly Hills were quiet. Rarely would there be a pedestrian, and the windows in the house adjacent to theirs were all dark. The neighbors were asleep.

Grant's hands were kneading her breasts, his mouth was on her stomach. He pulled her down and lifted his face so that his mouth found her nipples. He was like a breast-fed infant in a feeding frenzy. It excited her and frightened her at the same time because he was so unlike his well-controlled self again. When she opened her eyes to get more comfortable, she gazed out the window.

She gasped and pushed down on Grant's shoulders. There was someone there, by the wall, a man, clearly silhouetted.

'Grant,' she cried. He moaned and pressed his face into her. 'Grant, there *is* someone out there. He's watching us. Grant.'

Grant was too far gone to hear or care. His thrusts were deeper, harder, faster. She held on like a rider on a bucking horse and waited for him to spend himself. As soon as he had, he clutched her and wheezed through his teeth.

'Great,' he muttered. 'Great.'

'Grant.' She lowered herself until their eyes met. 'There's someone standing out there, watching us.'

'What? What's this, a joke, revenge for what I did?'

'No, Grant. There really is someone. Look for yourself. See if it's Bois,' she said. She moved off him and he turned and gazed out the window.

'Where?'

'By the wall,' she said, leaning on him and gazing out. There was no one there. 'He was there. I saw him.'

Grant laughed.

'I did, Grant.'

'Okay. So one of our neighbors is a mad voyeur. Who could it be – the movie producer . . . the dancer, the singer, the owner of the pizza chain? Maybe, it's the orthodontist. I don't trust anyone who makes a living in people's mouths,' he quipped.

'Very funny. You saw someone looking in the

window but made believe you didn't because you didn't want to frighten me. You know I saw someone, too, Grant, and you told me about Bois following you. Why couldn't it be him?'

'All right. All right. I'll check it out,' he said. He started to get up and reach for his robe.

'No. Don't go out there,' she said, grasping his arm firmly. 'That's exactly how people get hurt. I'm going to call the police.'

He flopped back on the settee.

'And what are you going to tell them, Mag? Someone was spying on us while we were making love? And it might be one of my patients?'

'No, I won't tell them that, but I'll tell them someone's looking in our windows. They'll keep an eye on our house,' she explained. 'Grant?'

'Okay,' he said. 'Maybe that's not a bad idea.'

She went to the phone. Grant went into the bathroom as she described the problem.

'They promised a patrol car immediately,' she said when he emerged. They both gazed out the window.

'I don't see anything now,' he whispered.

'Maybe he's hiding.'

'Maybe it's all our overworked imaginations.'

'People don't imagine the same thing at the exact same time, do they, Grant? Well, do they?'

'I don't know,' he said, and sat.

She remained at the window, watching and waiting.

'They're here,' she said, seeing the patrol car

turning its searchlight on the area. Moments later, the phone rang. It was the police. They called to tell her no one was found, but they would keep an eye on the house. She thanked them and reported it to Grant.

'Okay,' he said. 'Let's go to sleep. I'm exhausted.'

'I don't know if I can fall asleep.'

'Take a pill,' he suggested, and went to the bedroom. She lingered a while by the window with the lights off behind her, watching, waiting, wondering. By the time she went to bed, Grant was already asleep.

She took one more look out the window. There was no one there, but she was positive she had seen someone. He looked to be about as tall as Grant, but there wasn't much else she could discern. All of this made her feel she and Grant were descending into some maelstrom that was sweeping them into a world of madness.

Lydia Flemming, a woman no one would ever dream could become so violent as to shoot and kill her psychiatrist husband Henry, did so. One of Henry's strangest patients seeks out Grant and claims to have influenced people to do evil things. Grant starts behaving weird and her preliminary investigation of the people Bois was supposed to influence reveals very strange and very credible possibilities. Grant described Bois appearing out of nowhere, perhaps developing a fixation for him. Now someone who could be Bois was watching their house. Paranoia or justifiable fear and caution?

In the morning she would call Jack Landry and have him do more. As long as Grant didn't know what she was doing, the only harm was to her pocketbook, and right now that seemed the least of all her problems.

9

Grant burst into his run more as would a sprinter than a jogger. Maggie had appeared to still be in a deep sleep when he woke this morning, and she didn't stir when he leaned over to kiss her shoulder. When he kissed her neck, she groaned with complaint.

'I'm so tired,' she had muttered, and turned away from him. He shrugged, rose quietly, and got into his sweat suit. He got himself a glass of juice and then returned and peeked into the bedroom. Maggie hadn't moved a muscle. He had smiled to himself, imagining he was an exhausting lover.

It was heavily overcast at the beach and he thought it might actually rain before he finished, but he had run in the rain before, and he was determined, driven, to do a full-throttle jog today. He had woken with a knot of energy in his chest unlike anything he had experienced. He felt powerful, energized. Like a wonderfully conditioned race-horse, he fell into an easy rhythm, every part of his body coming to full life, the blood pumping rich and easy, his muscles extending, his lungs nowhere near straining.

As he moved over the beach, he saw two figures a good thousand yards ahead of him. The one on the left was clearly female. Drawing closer and closer because he was running faster than them, he soon realized the one on the left was Deirdre Leyland. He slowed down, debated turning and running in the opposite direction, but the man running with her slowed down, too, and she pulled ahead and away from him. The man fell into a quick walk back toward Grant and then he stopped and sat on a bench. Grant maintained his pace, but as he drew closer, he slowed even more. The man on the bench was Jules Bois.

He was smiling up at him.

'Good morning, Doctor.'

Grant paused.

'What are you doing here, Mr Bois?'

'Now that I've joined a gym, I thought I'd try this jogging business. If I want to live in southern California, I guess I'm going to have to become an exercise fanatic. Otherwise I'll feel like an outsider,' he said smiling. 'Actually,' he said, gazing down the beach at the receding figure of Deirdre Leyland, 'Mrs Leyland talked me into it. You know Mrs Leyland. She can talk any man into almost anything.' Bois said, his eyes glittering.

Grant felt the heat rise from his chest and into his neck and face.

'How do you know Mrs Leyland?' Grant asked.

'Oh, let's just say we have a mutual acquaintance. Why don't you sit and rest a moment, Doctor?'

'I have to complete my run,' Grant said.

'Okay. If you don't mind, I'll run along with you,' Bois said, and stood up.

Grant started away, deliberately running faster than he had planned. But to Grant's surprise, Bois easily kept up.

'Invigorating,' he said. 'I never realized how reassuring exercise could be.'

'Reassuring?'

'It's good to feel healthy, alive, strong. Gives one confidence, self-esteem, eh, Doctor? Not to mention the therapeutic value as a treatment for depression, tension.'

'You continually surprise me with your knowledge, Mr Bois. I know you said you have a law degree. What other intellectual experiences have you pursued?'

'If one is to practice law, in this country especially, he or she had better be a student, ready at a moment's notice to become somewhat expert in almost anything. There isn't any subject I haven't investigated one time or another, I suppose, even psychiatry.'

They ran side by side, stride for stride, almost breathing simultaneously, their arms swinging out in similar rhythm, their heads so perfectly aligned that anyone looking at them from the side might very well not realize there were two of them. It was as if Bois were absorbing Grant into him or vice versa.

Deirdre Leyland was gone from their view, having turned into another parking lot and disappeared.

'You're either in good shape for someone who doesn't do much exercise or I'm not in as good condition as I had thought,' Grant said, glancing at Jules Bois, who appeared to have no difficulties with his breathing or his muscles.

Bois laughed.

'I have this uncanny ability to take on the personae of people I get to know,' he said.

'Pardon?'

Bois laughed.

'Occasionally – actually, nearly always – I imagine myself to be the people I influence. I take on their personae. I see myself acting out the very crimes I've encouraged them to commit.

'I was there with Clarence Dunbar, wielding that hammer, striking his wife repeatedly on her skull until I felt it crumble like an overripe melon.

'I overdosed Mrs Mosley's nitro and watched her gasp and struggle for precious breath.'

He smiled.

'I even seduced Deirdre Leyland in your office,' he added.

Grant slowed his pace.

'Now, now, Doctor, no worries. I'm not a gossip.'

'Mrs Leyland has problems with reality,' Grant said. 'She fantasizes.'

'Don't we all. Please, Doctor. Don't become defensive. I'm not trying to blackmail you. Just like you, I never make anyone do anything he or she doesn't really want to do. That's the beauty of it,' Bois said, smiling.

Grant picked up the pace again and so did Bois.

'When you are these people in your fantasy, how do you feel after the act has been committed?' Grant asked.

'If you mean do I feel remorse, the answer is no. I feel replenished. I don't wither; I don't moan and groan, break out into a sweat and feel my heart pounding. I feel resplendent. My skin is so hot I appear sunburned. My eyes are dazzling. The muscles in my body are full, vibrant. I'm gigantic. I think this is what interested Doctor Flemming so much and why he made me the subject of his new work.'

Bois looked at him.

'Isn't that like you've felt when you've succeeded with a patient?'

'Forget how I feel. When you first came to see me, you claimed ambiguity. Something else must follow these vicarious experiences,' Grant suggested.

'Yes, it does,' Bois replied unhappily. 'I crash like a drug addict and go into a depression, which is revived only if I find another victim. And, like a drug addict, it seems to take more and more to satisfy me these days. That was one of the reasons I went into analysis,' Bois confessed.

'With Henry Flemming?'

'Oh, even before Henry.'

'Was he making progress with you?'

'That's something only Henry could answer. Unfortunately. I can't be the judge of it, can I?'

Grant slowed.

'I've got to turn back,' he said.

'Fine. Turn back,' Bois replied, and followed him around.

'You don't mind if I keep talking while we jog, do you, Doctor? It's almost like getting a free session.'

'I don't mind.' Grant gazed at him. Bois didn't even appear to be sweating. 'I'm just amazed at your physical condition.'

'That's nothing,' Bois said, waving it off like a bothersome fly. 'Getting back to my fantasies and dreams, Doctor . . .'

'Yes?'

'I can actually feel my body metamorphose sometimes,' he said, holding up his hands as he ran. 'These fingers become the fingers of a woman, old, young, breasts emerge in my chest, my facial features soften, and my penis falls off. I see myself poisoning my lover or my husband, cutting their throats, blowing their heads off with a high-caliber pistol, pushing them out of high-story windows . . . whatever.'

'Doesn't that frighten you?' Grant asked, more out of fascination than psychiatric interest.

'It did in the beginning, but it doesn't anymore. Now it's just . . . my nature,' Bois said. 'After the act is committed, my body returns to whatever state it had been in before.'

'What do you mean, whatever state it had been in before?'

'Just that,' Bois said, smiling. 'If I was young when it happened, I was young again. Remember, Doctor, I've been doing this a long, long time.'

'And still are,' Grant said.

'And still are.'

Grant slowed down because of a sharp pain in his side. Without realizing it, Grant had let Bois set the pace and the pace was nearly twice his usual.

'How about a five-minute rest here?' Bois suggested when they reached a bench. Grant nodded and they stopped.

'It threatens to rain; yes, it threatens to rain, but it doesn't. The heavens tease us,' Bois said, gazing up. Grant took deep breaths and closed his eyes for a moment.

'You all right, Doctor?'

'Yeah. Just a little winded.'

'If you would do what I do, Doctor, you would never be winded, you would never be tired. You would never be depressed again. It's like being on a constant high. I think Doctor Flemming was coming to that conclusion.'

Grant opened his eyes and gazed at Bois.

'Really?'

'Yes. I'm going to give you the pages soon. I think you're nearly ready for them,' Bois said.

'Ready for them? For what? I thought you didn't want me to see Flemming's notes.'

'This is different. It's the book Doctor Flemming and I had begun. At a point where you can appreciate me more, you'll learn more.'

Who is the one in control here, Grant wondered, me or my patient?

'You were at it again, I take it,' Grant said.

'Of course. I'm addicted, compulsive, remember?'

'What did you do this time?'

'You mean how have I exercised my obsession?'

'Yes. Describe it to me.'

'I actually found myself hesitating this time, doing what you asked me to do, trying to impose my own will, resisting, really make a choice. But that lasted only for a few moments,' he added.

'You know, Doctor,' Bois continued, nodding, 'some of my previous analysts had been convinced that what I did, I did to get back at my father. Doctor Flemming helped me to realize that that is not the whole story. No, I'm not getting back at my father, so much as I am doing what makes me feel good, and in the final analysis, isn't that what it's all about, Doctor: pleasure, whether that pleasure comes from sex or power, greed or lust?'

'So what did you do this time?'

'Are you interested as my doctor or as a voyeur? Do you want to live vicariously through my experiences, my power, Doctor?' he teased. 'Can you admit that to yourself and perhaps to me as well? It's a start,' Bois said, smiling gleefully.

'Who's the therapist here?'

Bois laughed.

'Yes, who is? I'll tell you what, Doctor, I will describe this recent incident, one that you will really enjoy. It has all the makings of a good psychological murder story, but first, a little quid pro quo, eh?'

'What do you want?'

'Your fantasies. I want to share one of your fantasies, Doctor.'

'Why? Do you want to live vicariously through me? Are you the voyeur?'

Bois roared.

'That's good. You are a lot more like me than you care to admit, Doctor. But soon, very soon, you might stop resisting yourself and become . . .'

'Become what?'

'Free,' Bois said, his eyes wide.

Grant felt himself caught up in the man's luminous eyes for a moment. Bois smiled and his gaze shifted toward the ocean. Grant turned and looked.

Deirdre Leyland was jogging through the water, splashing and laughing as she ran.

Totally naked.

'Jesus.'

'She's rather incorrigible, isn't she?' Bois said.

Grant turned back to Bois.

'I don't understand. How long have you known her?'

'It's not important, the length of time. It's the quality of the time you spend with someone, right? Forget her for the moment,' Bois insisted. 'Let's get back to our trade. You want to trade, don't you? Really. Go on, Doctor. We can help each other,' he said.

Maggie had risen immediately after Grant had left the house. She had pretended to be groggy and asleep. She didn't shower. She threw on a sweat suit herself, located Grant's second set of office keys in the den desk drawer, and rushed out to her car. In minutes she was on her way to his office. She wanted to get there well before Fay Moffit. As soon as she did, she went to the file cabinet and located Jules Bois' folder. She copied out the address and then hurried out of the office and drove home, hoping she would be there before Grant. If he did return before her, she was going to tell him she got the urge to join him on the beach.

He wasn't home yet when she arrived, so she called Jack Landry.

'Man, I was only kidding about that insomnia stuff, Mrs Blaine,' Jack said, his voice cracking.

'I'm sorry I woke you, Jack. But I wanted to get this to you before I left for work. I'm going to be tied up in court all day today.'

'Why are you whispering, Mrs Blaine?'

'I'm whispering?' She laughed. 'Sorry, Jack. I'm not used to this clandestine activity.'

'Everyone thinks it's like it is in the movies. What d'ya got?'

'I've got privileged information,' she said, punching hard on *privileged*.

'That's all I ever get, Mrs Blaine,' Jack said dryly.

'I have the name and address of Grant's strange patient.'

'Okay? What d'ya want?'

'I want to know everything you can find out about this man, Jack. What does he do for a living? Where did he live before he lived here? Who are his friends? Does he have a police record? Especially that,' she said.

'Something else happen?' Jack asked.

'I think he's been following Grant and he's now spying on us. I think he was looking in our windows last night.'

'Sounds like the patient from hell. Sort of *Fatal Analysis* or something.'

'That's why I'm so worried.'

'Okay, give me the information,' Jack said.

She told him Bois' name and gave him the address.

'You can try me at my office very late this afternoon; otherwise, I'll call you.'

'Gotcha, Mrs Blaine,' Jack said.

Once again, Maggie felt ambiguous about what she had done and what she was doing. She knew she was violating every ethical code between a doctor and his patient. Grant would be very upset if he found out. But if there was something there, she would prevent more serious trouble, and if there wasn't, she would be relieved and Grant wouldn't know.

137

She went to shower and was lost in her thoughts when suddenly the stall door was thrust open. She gasped and turned to find Grant standing there naked, a wide, licentious smile smeared across his face.

'You frightened me half to death, Grant,' she cried.

He didn't apologize; he didn't say anything. He stepped into the shower and put his arms around her waist.

'Grant!'

'The garage door was open,' he said. 'I thought I closed it. Didn't you realize it?'

'I didn't notice. I . . . just got up,' she said.

'A prowler could easily get into the house. He could easily have come down the hallway to the bedroom and noticed you were in the shower. He would have opened the door just as I had and stepped in.'

He pushed her gently toward the tile wall. The water streamed down his head and over his face. His smile looked distorted and his eyes were beady.

'Grant?'

'You would have been at his mercy, Maggie. Just like this,' he said, and kissed her hard on the mouth as he groped her breasts. She squirmed. Grant laughed and lowered her to the tile floor, the water cascading over his shoulders and onto her face. She struggled as he lifted her legs.

'Grant, stop it. It hurts on this tile. Stop it!' she screamed. She started to push him away.

He hesitated and then he rose, turned his head to the water, and began to wash himself as if she weren't even there. She crawled around him and got up.

'That wasn't funny, Grant,' she cried, and stepped out of the stall. She caught her breath and checked her back in the mirror. It was beet red around her shoulder blades and so was the base of her spine. She wrapped a large towel around herself and left the bathroom. She was nearly dressed before Grant emerged. She glared at him.

'Sorry,' he said. 'I guess I got carried away.'

'What were you thinking of, for God's sake, Grant? What were you trying to do, teach me a lesson?'

'No. It was just a little joke that got out of hand. Sorry,' he repeated, and went to his closet. She marched out of the bedroom and got herself a glass of juice. She was running late and would skip breakfast. Her heart was pounding too hard and fast for her to eat anyway. She still hadn't calmed down and she was afraid it would carry over to her work.

Dressed only in his socks and pants, Grant appeared in the kitchen doorway.

'Hey, I said I was sorry,' he pleaded, but kept that small smile on his lips.

At the door to the garage, she turned to look at him.

'It's getting so I don't know who you are anymore, Grant,' she said, and left.

She was halfway down the street before she realized that was essentially what Lydia Flemming had been saying right after she had shot and killed Henry.

10

'Mr Simms wants to see you right away,' Maggie's secretary told her as soon as Maggie had come down the corridor toward her office late in the afternoon.

Most of Maggie's day had been spent in negotiations rather than in actual trial because the district attorney's office had floated a possible plea bargain, which Maggie's client, Samuel Kitman, a forty-year-old insurance agent on trial for embezzlement, decided to let Maggie explore. Maggie had told him that some of the evidence was compelling, and these days her tolerance for guilty clients was diminished. The give-and-take with the assistant district attorney was difficult and exhausting, but in the end she settled for what she considered the best possible deal under the circumstances.

Some, she recognized, might think she had settled too quickly and for too little. With all that was going on in this city, the district attorney didn't want to tie up his resources on a white-collar crime, especially when it was pointed out to him and to Maggie that Kitman had the financial wherewithal to return the allegedly stolen funds. When her secretary told her Kenneth Simms wanted to see her immediately, Maggie imagined she was going to be called on the carpet for her decisions.

Maybe, she feared, they had been made aware of her distractions these days and thought that it was detracting from the quality of her work.

All the full partners had grand offices, but Maggie considered Kenneth Simms' office the best because he had the most awesome view of the Hollywood Hills on the north, and on his west side, the ocean. The curtains were all drawn open, the late afternoon sunshine filling the office with natural light. The crystal triangles on Kenneth Simms' desk glittered. The fifty-four-year-old attorney sat back in his over-sized, leather-cushioned desk chair, which, combined with the long and wide dark mahogany desk, looked like part of a set for the movie *Gulliver's Travels*. Despite his five feet eleven inches of height and one hundred seventy-five pounds, Simms looked diminished by his own furniture.

Maggie's mind was cluttered. She had tried to keep herself focused all day, but every time there was a break in negotiations, her thoughts returned to Grant, to Jules Bois, and to Jack Landry. She had

142

hurriedly entered the office building and down the corridor in hopes of hearing she had a message of some sort from Jack Landry, but instead she was immediately redirected to her boss's office. Troubled by what was to come and by what had already occurred, she entered slowly, her eyes down, her gait depressed.

'What happened?' Simms asked. He held a fresh number five pencil in his hand like a conductor's wand.

'As usual, they waited until the last possible minute and then floated an offer to plea-bargain. I bluffed my way through for quite a while, and twice I thought they were going to just walk out on us, but I guess I wore them down. I think so, anyway,' she added quickly. 'They had some good stuff,' she continued when Simms just stared. She started to open her briefcase.

'That's not the problem at hand,' Kenneth Simms said. He leaned forward so his elbows rested on his desk. 'The problem at the moment is what are we going to do with you.'

'Pardon?' Maggie said.

'My partners and I have been discussing it all morning,' he said, and nodded to his right.

Maggie turned. Jack Krammer and Sheldon Beadsly were sitting on the black, soft leather settee, smiling up at her.

'You see,' Kenneth Simms continued, 'we're all married to very jealous women. Right, Jack?'

'The worst. My wife has a forensic detective

on retainer to scour my clothing for evidence of women's makeup, perfume, hair.'

The three men laughed. Maggie stood there looking from one to the other.

'What these two idiots are trying to say, Maggie,' Sheldon Beadsly continued, 'is we want to offer you a full partnership in the firm, but we're worried that our wives will think that because you're rather attractive, we're doing it for the wrong reasons.

'However,' he added quickly as Maggie's mouth started to open, 'we are certain that once they meet you and Grant on more relaxed, social occasions, they will see how devoted you two are to one another, and they will realize there is no threat.'

'Besides, even women like the ones we married can appreciate the dynamo in court you are,' Jack Krammer said. 'More success, more clients, more money, more shopping.'

They all laughed. 'Just kidding, Maggie. Just having a little fun,' he added quickly, and nodded at Kenneth, who reached down to produce a bottle of champagne in an ice bucket with four glasses.

'Really?' Maggie said.

'Couldn't be more real than this,' Kenneth said. 'Right, gentlemen?'

They stood up to shake her hand and Kenneth Simms poured the glasses of champagne.

'To our new partner,' he said. 'May this prove to be the most profitable and successful decision

Simms, Krammer and Beadsly have made to date.'

'Here, here,' the partners chanted, and tapped glasses with Maggie before taking a sip.

'Now what's this nonsense about your caving in on a plea bargain?' Kenneth said, and they all laughed again.

The news moved with computer speed across the desks of every secretary, junior partner, and associate at the firm. Maggie's office was a stage for constant applause and congratulations. She phoned Grant, but Fay said he was in a session with a new client and had asked not to be interrupted. She left word for him to call as soon as he was able. She had plans to celebrate. In the meantime, she called her parents, who were overwhelmed with pride. They promised to call her sisters. As usual, her mother asked when she and Grant would take some time off and come visit.

'Maybe soon,' she promised. 'We're both a little burned out.'

'Oh?' her mother said, instinctively tuned in to Maggie's moods. 'Is everything all right, honey?'

'Yes. It's just we've been very busy. I can't think of a more successful combination than psychiatrist and criminal attorney in Los Angeles, Mom. But don't worry.'

'Money's no good if you don't have time to enjoy it,' her mother warned.

Maggie promised to call again very soon and give her some concrete idea concerning when they would visit.

'So the little bird who twits around my ears wasn't all that premature with information,' Phil remarked when he stepped into her office a moment after she cradled the phone.

'You're next, Phil,' she said. He shrugged. She knew Phil thought he was just as good, if not a better attorney than she was, but that she was getting the promotion because of all the jazz around women's rights.

'If not here, then somewhere. I don't sweat it,' he said. 'But I am happy for you, Mag. Really. You're a helluva nice guy for a woman.'

'Thanks.'

'How about we have one together at O'Healies in, say, a half hour? We've been on enough raids together that we can take a special moment, huh?'

'Sure,' she said. 'Thanks.'

O'Healies was just down the block from their office building. It was an upscale tavern done in rich dark wood decor, featuring a line of microbrews, and had become a favorite watering hole for attorneys. There were so many who had offices in the vicinity. California was well known as one of the most litigious states in the Union, especially the city of Los Angeles. People sued each other, prosecuted each other, at the drop of a glass of Evian water here.

'You and Grant going to do something special to celebrate tonight?'

'I'm sure. I'm just waiting for him to call me back,' she said.

'Great. Oh, and good moves on the Kitman case. He's lucky the wheels of justice are overworked,' Phil said. 'See you in a while.'

Maggie sat back and turned her chair away from the door so she could close her eyes and take some deep breaths. What a day, considering how it had first begun. With all the excitement and noise, she had completely forgotten about Jack Landry. She checked her list of calls and saw, however, that Jack wasn't listed.

I've got to give him enough time, she realized, but she couldn't help being anxious. She was already much deeper into all this than she had ever envisioned, and that worried her more.

She returned some of her phone calls, dictated two letters and a memorandum before she realized Grant had still not called back. She tried the office again and was surprised to get the answering machine. Then she remembered it was Friday and Fay Moffit left a half hour earlier on Fridays because of her daughter's school dismissing earlier. She left another message.

'Grant, call me on the cellular. I have some good news. If you can't reach me on the cellular, try O'Healies. I'm stopping in there for a few minutes on the way home. Enough hints? Can't wait to talk to you. I love you,' she concluded.

Phil was at the door.

'Ready?'

'Yes.'

'Did you tell Grant? What was his reaction?'

Phil asked as she gathered her purse and brief-case.

'He's still in a session. I could only leave a message.'

'I wonder who the poor patient is. Doesn't he or she know about psychiatric overtime costs? They're just as bad as legal fees.'

'You had better stop teasing Grant about lawyers and psychiatrists being two sides of the same coin, Phil, or soon I'll be representing my husband on trial for murder.'

Phil laughed and they started out of the office. Maggie felt all eyes were on her. She was a celebrity. She was at the top of her form, the envy of most professional women, with a lot for which she should be grateful.

Please, she prayed privately, let nothing ruin this now.

Grant hadn't intended on going much longer than the famous psychiatric hour everyone in his profession treated as holy, but Gary Becker, Marvin and Phyllis Becker's fourteen-year-old son, fascinated him. Physically, which was good for him, the boy didn't appear to take after his parents. He was lean and already taller than both his mother and father. However, Gary wasn't exactly good-looking: his nose was a little long, his mouth a little small, and his chin too sharp, but he had a sophistication in his eyes that projected an intriguing, almost beguiling demeanor. He had a way of holding his twisted lips, suggesting he knew or suspected ulterior motives. But what was most interesting to Grant was this vague feeling that there was something familiar about the boy. He struggled to discover what it was.

Rather quickly in the session, because of the boy's willingness to talk, Grant addressed the subject of repressed memories.

'I'm sure my parents, especially my father, don't want me talking about them,' Gary Becker said.

'If your parents had something to hide, why would they bring you to me?' Grant asked him.

'They're just hoping that you'll change my mind. That way they don't have to worry about being blamed for anything. It's all right,' he continued coolly. 'I can deal with it.'

'So when did this sexual abuse stop?'

'When I was old enough to understand that that's what it was,' Gary recited.

'And nothing ever since?'

'Nobody would try nothing now,' Gary said, his eyes like two marbles of ice.

'How do you deal with such memories? Don't they disturb you now?'

'No.'

'No?'

'Actually,' he said with that crooked smile on his lips again, 'they make me feel better about myself.'

'Better? How's that?'

'Whenever I have this guilty feeling about something I've done, something immoral or illegal, I just

149

think about them and what they did to me and that . . .'

'Justifies what you've done?'

'Yes,' Gary said, nodding. 'A-huh.'

Grant smiled at him and Gary relaxed in his chair.

'I thought you would understand,' Gary said.

'Why were you so sure?'

'My doctor told me,' Gary replied.

'Your doctor told you?' When Gary nodded, Grant asked, 'When?'

'Just before I agreed to come here. I spoke to him first and he said it would be fine. He said you and I would get along very well.'

'Then he knows me?'

Gary shrugged.

'I guess.'

'What's his name?' Grant asked.

Gary smiled.

'I thought I wasn't supposed to tell you his name. I thought we weren't going to talk about him. That's what Dad and Mom said.'

'Okay. When you feel you trust me, you'll tell me. So,' Grant said, looking at his notepad, 'how do you really feel about things you have done, Gary? There's quite a list here, including the things that have happened in school.'

Gary shrugged.

'I don't know. I just . . .'

'Yes?'

'Had some fun. No big deal.'

'I understand you pal around with much younger kids. Why would you want to do that? You seem bright for your age. I'd think younger kids would bore you.'

'If you know the answers, why are you asking me the questions?' Gary shot back.

'I don't know the answers,' Grant said. 'I'd like to, though.'

'Why? So you could come up with a convenient psychological explanation that would make my parents feel better?' Gary said bitterly.

'Do you hate them?'

Gary looked away.

'It's all right to talk about it,' Grant encouraged him. 'You want to get your feelings out in order to truly understand them.'

'That's what he said, too.'

'Who? Oh, right. You don't want to tell me yet.'

'What, do you guys have such boring lives that you got to hear about someone else's all the time?'

Grant laughed.

'That's what we do for a living, hear about other people's lives and then try to help them.'

'By changing them?'

'If that's what has to be done. It's not always the solution,' Grant said softly. 'Maybe I don't want to change you. Maybe I want you to continue as you are but put your energies into more profitable endeavors.'

Gary studied him a moment. Then he relaxed again.

'It's just easier with younger kids,' he said.

'What's easier?'

'Getting them to do things.'

Grant hesitated a moment, his pen poised above the notepad.

'Then you admit that you do that?'

'Sure.'

'How do you come up with your ideas for things you want them to do, Gary?'

'They're just things I dream about,' he said. 'My other doctor called them my fantasies.'

'Okay.'

'Okay?'

'That's a good way to put it, I think. Then you're saying you fantasized about putting the poodle into a microwave oven?'

Gary nodded and then shrugged.

'I wondered what would happen.'

'But you couldn't do it yourself?'

'I could, but it was more fun getting them to do it.'

'Why was it more fun?'

'They were the ones who would get into trouble.'

'You liked getting them into trouble?'

'Yeah.'

'Why?'

'Because . . .' Gary hesitated and looked away. Another silent moment passed between them before Grant spoke.

'There has to be a because why, Gary,' Grant said softly.

Gary glared him.

'Because their parents think they're so goody-goody, so perfect.'

'And that bothers you?'

Gary turned away again, and when he turned back to look at Grant, he had a wide, gleaming smile on his face.

'Yes,' he said. 'It bothers me. Nobody is goody-goody. Not even you,' he said, and Grant realized why he was so fascinated with Gary Becker and why there was the sense of something familiar about him.

Gary Becker reminded him of Jules Bois. He was just like Grant imagined Jules Bois would have been when he was Gary's age. The realization put a flush of heat into his face and made his heart beat faster. He turned and looked at the sofa.

I'm hallucinating again, he thought. Jules Bois was lying there with his hands behind his head, smiling at him.

That's right, he imagined Bois saying, *you have a young one just budding. Nurture him. Don't do anything to close his wonderful imagination or anything that will lose him his power. Instead, enjoy him.*

'Can I go?'

'What?' Grant said.

'I'm getting tired.'

'Oh, right. Sure. We've had enough for today,' he said. He put his notepad down and came around his desk to shake hands with the boy. 'I enjoyed talking to you.'

Gary shook his hand and nodded.

'He said you would.'

Grant watched Gary walk to the door, smile at him, and leave. A moment later, there was a knock. It was Marvin Becker.

'We thought we'd wait the whole time,' he said. 'How did it go, or is it too early?'

'It's too early. I have a lot more to do with him,' Grant said.

Marvin nodded.

'But you think you can make progress with him?'

'Oh, without a doubt,' Grant said. 'Without a doubt.'

Marvin smiled gratefully and bowed a bit as he backed out of the office and closed the door.

When Grant turned, Bois wasn't on the sofa, but his words lingered in his ears. He just sat there for a while staring out of his office windows. Then he sighed deeply and gazed at the blinking light that indicated a message. He hit the button and listened to Maggie.

But he didn't call her. He just wanted to go someplace and have a drink by himself first. He wasn't in the mood for happy people, laughter, and music. There was a battle going on inside him and he was ashamed of it and afraid.

11

Jack Landry sat in his car across from the apartment building in an upscale neighborhood of Westwood in Los Angeles and studied the building for a few moments. It looked recently renovated, with a small patch of lawn in front, brass doors, ivy along one side. There was an underground garage and a small but elegantly furnished lobby with restored antique furniture and mirrors. But there was no doorman. Tenants entered with a key or buzzed in visitors and deliveries. Nevertheless, rents were surely high.

Jack wore his Air Postal Express outfit. He had hoped to get here earlier, but a complication with an investigation he was doing for a wealthy client who suspected his much younger wife of adultery had tied him up in Studio City for most of the morning. Then, after he had taken the freeway, he got caught in a traffic jam caused by a pickup truck colliding with a van. Neither driver was seriously hurt, but removal of the wreckage and the curiosity of passing motorists backed up the highway for miles. Still, it was only a little after one. Good chance Bois wouldn't be at home, which would give Jack a chance to reconnoiter the man's apartment.

Carrying an empty wrapped box, he stepped out of his vehicle, crossed the street, and checked the directory for Bois' name and apartment number. He pressed the buzzer for the video entry system and waited, but there was no response after a second and third attempt. Just what he had hoped.

He then located the nearest apartment and buzzed it. An elderly female voice responded.

'Yes?'

'Good afternoon, ma'am. This is Air Postal Express. I have a special delivery for a Jules Bois, but no one answers the buzzer. Could you accept the package?'

He stood in front of the video camera so she could have a clear view of him in uniform.

'Oh. Oh, yes. Just bring it up,' she said.

Jack smiled. Bingo on the first attempt. Usually it took four or five, these days. He heard the buzzer and opened the outer door. Bois lived on the sixth floor. Jack took the elevator and went directly to the apartment of the woman who had responded. She looked like she was well into her seventies, if not eighty, and apparently living alone.

'This is very kind of you,' Jack said.

'Oh, we often help each other out in this building,' she said, taking the package. Jack turned the clipboard so she could sign.

'My first delivery here. It looks like a nice building. You live here long?'

'Nearly twenty years,' she replied, smiling and handing him the clipboard. 'Mr Bois is one of our newer tenants, but he's been here more than six months and we've had some nice talks. He's a very nice gentleman. I'll see that he gets this.'

'Thanks again,' Jack said, and stepped back so she could close the door. He waited a moment, gazed down the corridor, and then went to Bois' apartment. It took him only a minute to unlock the door, which surprised him as well. Usually there was more than one lock, and few were this simple. Jules Bois was apparently not a person who suffered the same paranoia that had gripped most of the population, especially in urban areas, these days.

He paused after opening the door and listened.

'Hello?' he said. He could claim the door was just open, but there was no response. He entered, closed the door softly, and walked into the apartment, a very nicely furnished single-bedroom. Jack thought it was immaculate. In fact, it looked like the model for the sale of apartments in the building. The marble floor entryway glittered. The walls were done in soft pastels. Perfectly spaced out on them were watercolors depicting quiet country scenes, the art obviously chosen by a decorator who was looking for color coordination more than artistic value.

157

He gazed into the living room. Everything looked brand-new. The furniture was all in beige, with soft woods and glass tables. On shelves behind the longer sofa were glass figures, vases, and small ivory boxes. He saw no magazines strewn about, no unclean ashtrays, nothing to reveal anyone had been in the room recently.

The kitchen was the same way. Everything was in place, the table clear and clean, the sink empty. He began by opening drawers. All were well organized: one for table linen, one for silverware, one for kitchen implements, etc. Nothing was out of place. He found no papers, no books except for the phone book, and, rifling through that quickly, he saw no numbers underlined and found no notes on the inside of the covers. Actually, the kitchen looked as if it had never been used.

He shook his head in amazement and went through it to the single bedroom. It was a good-sized room with a California king-sized dark cherry wood bed, matching nightstands, and hutch. The telephone was on the table on the left and there was a miniature grandfather clock, same shade of cherry wood as the bed, on the other table. Next to it was a framed picture of a good-looking, tall man standing in front of what looked like a cathedral, maybe St Patrick's in New York, Jack thought. The man had a wide grin. Jack looked more closely at the picture. On the bottom in red ink was written: *To Jules, You look like you belong right there. Congratulations . . . L.* At least now I know what the subject looks like, he thought. He put the picture back and gazed up.

Above the bed was a print of Edvard Munch's famous painting *The Scream*. The picture depicted a very disturbed woman, someone who might be found in a mental institution, in the midst of a horrible scream.

Who the hell would want to sleep with that hanging over his head every night? he wondered.

Jack checked the drawers in the nightstands. Both were empty. He turned and looked, went to the dresser and began to search those drawers. Again, everything was perfectly organized: the drawer for socks, the draw for underwear, shirts, all items clean, and some even looking brand-new. But there was nothing else. He opened the closet and saw how all the garments were perfectly organized, color-coordinated as well. There was nothing unusual on the shelf above, or below with the shoes.

Except for the painting above the bed and the clothes in the closet and dresser, and that one framed photograph, there was no evidence anyone inhabited this apartment, Jack thought. And yet, the woman next door had told him Bois had lived here more than six months. He must be a fanatic when it comes to cleanliness, Jack concluded, and started out, not sure what he could tell Maggie Blaine. He had been in the man's home and he was even more of a mystery now.

He opened the door and peered out cautiously. All was quiet, so he slipped out, closed the door softly, and went to the elevator. When it opened on the lobby, he saw Jules Bois checking the mailboxes. There was no question he was the same man as the one in the picture. He didn't turn. Jack walked out quickly and went to his car.

Apparently Bois didn't go upstairs. All he had come to do was check his mail, because a few moments after Jack got into his vehicle, Bois came out and got into his late-model Lexus. He pulled away quickly, not so much as glancing Jack's way as he did so. Jack started his car and followed. Bois headed right for the freeway. Jack remained two car lengths behind and was quite surprised at the exit downtown Bois took. They were going right into the heart of South-Central L.A.

A wave of low clouds had begun to drag a dark curtain over the city's seedy, grubby neighborhoods, adding to the depression and gloom painted over the scorched structures, windowless buildings, all scarred with the scribbling of angry and psychotic minds. To Jack's way of thinking, the graffiti was a cry for help, a desperate attempt to be noticed by a society that chose to ignore that which revolted it. He felt as if he had passed through some boundary between earth and the netherworld. Even the toughest, most down-trodden areas of New Orleans had afforded him more comfort. But perhaps that was because he was more familiar with the grime and degradation in that city. He had been in it so long, he was practically at home with it.

Fortunately, he thought, he had decided to take

his field car this morning when he had left his West L.A. condo. Jack owned two vehicles. He nicknamed one the field car, which was a 1989 brown Ford Taurus, dented and nicked, with a right rear window that was filled with a large cobweb of cracks emanating from the center of a blow made with a tire iron. It wasn't the type of vehicle that would attract much attention or demand. His other vehicle certainly would have. That was a vintage red 1955 MG in prime condition, the love of his life. He reserved its use for what he considered milk runs and non-work-related trips.

Nevertheless, it was easy to become instantly paranoid here. Every look he received appeared threatening. His pulse quickened when he and Bois stopped at red lights, and he gazed cautiously from right to left. They were not any more than two blocks west of the epicenter of the most recent L.A. riots.

Minutes later, Bois turned down a street and stopped in front of a small house between two low-income apartment buildings. The pale, yellow-stained white stucco on the outside of the cottage-sized structure was chipped and gouged as if some creature had been nibbling on it. There was a tiny patch of lawn, but that was scraggly and filled with weeds, broken bottles, smashed beer cans, crushed cardboard boxes, and other litter.

A wrecked car looked planted in the short drive-way. Most of what was valuable on the vehicle had been torn off. It had no tires and even the door handles had been ripped away. It was battered, the windows smashed, the rear bumper fallen to the pitted macadam.

There was really no sign of life in the house or around it. It was easily something passersby would ignore or even miss; it blended into the blight and had lost its identity years and years ago.

Bois got out of his vehicle as casually and calmly as he would in upscale safe Westwood and walked to the front door of the house. Jack pulled to the curb and watched as Bois reached into his pocket, took out a set of keys, and unlocked the door. After he entered, Jack edged his car closer to Bois' and put it in neutral.

Suddenly there was a sharp rap on his window. It was so unexpected, he literally jumped in his seat. The two black girls, neither looking more than sixteen or seventeen, laughed when Jack spun around. The taller girl, her hair shaved closely to her scalp, earrings that looked made of steel dangling from her lobes, had a pipe wrench in her right hand. She wore a tank top and a pair of jeans. The tank top was thin and she wore no bra, so her small, perky breasts were well outlined beneath, the nipples nearly punching through the material. Her arms, right up to the shoulders, were covered with tattoos of snakes and dragons, something off the cover of an interactive CD-ROM game. Cautiously, Jack lowered his window.

'Hi,' she said. 'You here to pick me up, honey?'

The other girl laughed. She was stouter, bigger

boned, with a heavier bosom and shoulders. She was also dressed in a tank top and jeans, but she had what looked like a bicycle chain over her shoulder.

'Pick you up?'

'I like your car. So does my boyfriend,' she said, and nodded ahead. Leaning against a battered brown van directly across the street were two males who looked like they were in their twenties, although Jack wasn't sure. He thought they could be teenagers, too, prematurely aged by their lifestyles and living conditions. One was light-skinned and looked Latino, and the other was black. Black bandannas were wrapped around their foreheads and both wore earrings similar to those dangling from the tall girl's lobes. They looked cool, confident, amused. It was as if they had just appeared out of thin air, because when he had driven up, Jack had seen no one.

'If he likes this car, he doesn't have much taste. Lose him,' Jack said, and the girls laughed.

'Whatcha doin' parked in front of the doctor's office?' the taller girl asked.

'Doctor's office? A doctor uses this dump as an office?'

Is that why Bois came here? he wondered, and looked at the dilapidated house again.

'It ain't a dump inside,' the stout girl said belligerently. 'He fixed it up real nice.'

'And we don't like no one saying bad things about the doctor, neither,' the other girl said. She nodded at the two young men, who lifted their bodies off the brown van and started a slow, arrogant walk toward Jack and the girls. Jack opened his jacket and unclipped his pistol holster.

'How come there's no doctor's sign in front if it's a doctor's office?' Jack asked.

'He don't like people thinking of this as an office like that,' the taller girl said. 'Right, Charliemae?'

'That's right. It don't matter. Everyone who has to know, knows what it is.'

'He wants us to feel at home,' the taller girl added.

'What's the doctor's name?' Jack asked the girls, while at the same time keeping his eyes on the two young men. They parted as they reached the front of his vehicle. The Latino moved to his right.

'Why you asking so many questions?' the taller girl demanded.

'That's how you learn things,' Jack said. 'You ask questions. Didn't you do that in school?'

'I still go to school,' she replied, 'but I don't ask questions,' she added, and the two girls laughed. The Latino took a toothpick from his mouth and pointed at Jack.

'What's he want?'

'To know about the doc,' the stout girl replied.

'What for?'

'I'm looking for someone; it might be him,' Jack said. 'It's worth something to me.' He reached into his pocket and produced a fifty-dollar bill.

The two girls looked at it covetously, but neither moved toward him. Both watched and waited for the young black man's approval. After a moment of hesitation, he nodded and the taller girl stepped closer and reached for the fifty.

'Information first,' Jack said, pulling the money back.

'Whatcha want to know?'

'The doctor's name first.'

'Doctor Jules,' she said. 'That's what we call him.'

'Jules?' Jack gazed at the house. 'Jules is the doctor? Is his last name Bois?' He pronounced it *Bwas*.

'His name's Doctor Jules Boys,' Charliemae said, correcting him.

'What kind of a doctor is he?'

'He's a counselor.'

'A shrink,' the other girl said.

'Yeah, that's right,' Charliemae said. 'He takes your big headaches and he shrinks 'em into peas.'

The girls laughed and the young man with the toothpick smiled.

'This is his office?' Jack gazed at the house again. What was this? Maggie Blaine had told him Bois was one of Grant's patients, not fellow physicians. Was he a doctor who did some sort of charity work in the ghetto? Could it be that Maggie didn't know?

'He be the first one to use it for anything since the murder,' the taller girl said. ''Cept a few drunks and dope addicts from time to time.'

'Murder?'

'You ain't heard about the murder and the cookin'?'

'He don't read our newspapers,' the young black man said, and they all laughed.

'So, tell me about it,' Jack said. The girl's smile

165

faded. She gazed at the young black man again, but he just stared at Jack. The other young man was leaning against the window on the passenger's side.

'You can tell him,' the young black man said grimacing with cool amusement. 'Doc always says outsiders like to hear 'bout the bad stuff. It's a trip for them. What's he call it, Ricky?'

'Vicarious experience,' the Latino said. He leaned over the hood to smile at Jack through the windshield. His eyes were full of mad laughter.

'What's he, the one with the master's degree?' Jack asked, nodding at the Latino.

'He's smart,' the tall girl said.

'Great, I'll recommend him for a scholarship. So what's the murder story?'

'You tell him, Charliemae,' the taller girl said. The stout girl moved up to the window and straightened her posture as if she really were in school about to recite a passage she had memorized from a play.

'That there's where the man stabbed his wife 'bout a hundred times and then cut her up and started cooking away her body in the kitchen stove before anyone found out. He had only the legs left when the police come.'

'When did this happen?'

'Years and years ago. Nobody want to go in there afterward until the doctor come,' Charliemae said.

'He said he wanted to be where he was most needed, where he could do the most good, so he don't mind the murder bein' in the house,' the taller girl said.

'That's right,' Charliemae added. 'He knew the man who did the killing, too.'

'That's quite a story.'

'It's true. Now hand over the fifty.'

Jack started to hand Charliemae his fifty, but held on to it when she grasped it.

'I told you what I know,' she said. He released the bill and she stepped back.

'Any of you ever been to see Doctor Jules?'

'Maybe,' Charliemae said. 'What's it your business?'

'I just wondered how good he was.'

Everyone stared. Then the girls backed farther away from the car as the young black man moved to the window.

'Were you one of his patients, too?' Jack asked, that instinctive little siren sounding at the base of his brain. He kept one hand near his pistol. The young black man leaned in and pointed to his temple.

'He's been in here and I feel just fine,' he said, and like magic, the hand he held below the window came up with a snub-nosed revolver clutched in his fingers. 'Which ain't the way you're going to be feeling,' he said, and fired.

The bullet shattered Jack's skull and splattered fragments of bone, scalp, and brain tissue on the passenger-side window. The report died and all was quiet again, but the stench of burned gunpowder filled the air. Then the door of the small house opened and Jules Bois stepped out.

'Derek?'

'Yeah, Doc?'

'Everything all right out here?'

'Just fine now, Doc.'

The girls laughed.

'Okay. Theresa, it's time,' Jules Bois said, and the tall girl smiled, sauntered past the others, and walked toward the small house, still carrying her wrench.

12

O'Healies was crowded and lively. It was, after all, TGIF, and the tavern encouraged a celebration of the workweek's end by reducing its prices and putting out a free hot buffet. All of the attorneys who were here made good incomes – none needed to look for bargains – but the advent of free food and discount prices added to their glee and raised the level of their voices a half dozen decibels.

By the time Maggie and Phil arrived, the bar was jammed. The CD jukebox was playing, but the music was buried under the din of loud conversation and laughter. Some of the attorneys had already heard about Maggie's advancement and began buying drinks and toasting before she and Phil made their way toward any of the available tables.

The long, dark hickory bar was to the right of the entry. There were tables across from it with more tables in the rear, where there were also a half dozen private booths. All of the revelers wanted to be up front where there was more action. The population was mostly young and up-and-coming attorneys, both male and female, as well as paralegals. Some clients had been brought along, the whole crowd mixing in well with O'Healies regulars who were absorbed and soaked in the sea of suits.

Pulling herself away from the handshakes, kisses, and looks of envy, Maggie went to the pay phone and called Grant's office again, and once again she was immediately tied in to the answering machine, this time advising the caller of the emergency phone number. She actually debated calling it and having Grant paged. Where was he? Why hadn't he phoned? She kept her cellular in her purse on a string at her side, and it was the sort that vibrated when it rang, so if she couldn't hear it, she could certainly feel it.

Phil had gotten up from the booth and was in a quiet discussion with two attorneys from Beck, Levy and Taylor. From the way Phil was looking at her, Maggie sensed he didn't want her to hear the topic and imagined it might have something to do with his chances of making a partnership there. When someone you work with gets a promotion, it puts the pressure on you to think more about your own advancement. It was only natural, and no matter what these men said or claimed to believe, it bothered them to see a woman leapfrog over them, she thought. That might even be true for Grant.

Goodness knows, we've had our heavy little discussions about me being too ambitious, she thought. After all, it was her ambition that he blamed for their not having children. Was this why he wasn't around the day she got her promotion?

'Did you get him?' Phil shouted toward her.

'Not yet,' she said, forcing a smile. Phil shook his head and went back to his ménage à trois. Maggie slid into the booth and cupped her drink between her hands. Suddenly she was alone, really alone, even though the tavern was two or three bodies above its fire department limit. She gazed around sadly. Everyone was into his or her thing: unmarried female attorneys were eyeing possible beaus, and the beaus were doing the same; others were expounding on their recent successes, each trying to sound more successful than the other.

She wasn't like them; she was married, but where was her husband? Obsessing about his patient, off somewhere involved in himself. She felt tears burn under her eyelids and closed them just as Martin Saperstein entered the tavern, the uproar so loud she had to look up. A wave of admirers rushed up to him, pulling groups from the bar to gather in the circle that had formed. Saperstein represented the Kettleman twins, a nineteen-year-old brother and sister who had plotted the murder of their stepfather and their own mother, claiming she was too beguiled by him to see or even want to see how he had abused them both from ages five until now. It was the number one legal story on the news and the main event on Court TV.

Saperstein, who looked more like a soap opera star than a criminal trial attorney, played well to the cameras. He had already been on the cover of *People* and was scheduled to do *GQ* the *L.A. Times Magazine*, and *Gents*, as well as the lead interview in *Playboy*. Like some sort of media shark, he fed on the adulation and literally glowed as the center of attention in O'Healies.

Maggie shook her head and smiled to herself, but her gaze floated from Saperstein to a tall, handsome man who appeared to have accompanied him into the tavern. The distinguished-looking gentleman was even more handsome than Saperstein, Maggie thought, and certainly looked more intelligent. His charcoal Italian-cut suit complemented his strong, firm appearance. He radiated success and confidence and appeared remarkably cool and amused by the hullabaloo surrounding Martin Saperstein. Some-one handed him a tumbler of scotch and water on the rocks and he drifted back from the crowd, his eyes finding her.

She started to look away, but stopped when she saw his smile. It was friendly, calm, with a mature brightness void of the lustful or flirtatious look she was more accustomed to receiving from men. This man looked kind, gentle, and imbued with the sense of relaxation that accompanies a strong sense of self-confidence. In a room full of hungry, insecure ingratiators, this man was refreshing.

He started toward her. She sat back, sipped her drink, and looked up with surprise and interest when he stopped at her table.

'If anything illustrates the myopic vision of attorneys in America, it's the fact that a woman as beautiful as you sits here alone while they jabber about depositions, objections, judicial decisions, and financial settlements,' he said.

She laughed.

'You're not an attorney, Mr . . . ?'

'Becket, Thomas Becket. Yes, but I'm what you would call an attorney's attorney.'

'Defending them against charges of malpractice, overbilling . . .'

'Even unethical behavior,' he said. Maggie was taken with the way his dark eyes glittered and held her own gaze. Her grandmother used to talk about the power of Rudolph Valentino's cinematic eyes. In close-ups, he would mesmerize a theater full of women. Looking up at this man, she finally understood what her grandmother meant.

'May I join you?' he asked, nodding at the seat across from her in the booth.

Maggie gazed at Phil, who looked even more deeply involved with his conversation.

'I'm not staying much longer,' she said.

'Somehow,' he said, sliding in, 'I feel a few minutes with you is worth hours with them.' He gestured with his head toward the bar.

She relaxed her lips into a soft smile and admitted to herself that even though her feminist friends

173

would consider it blasphemy, she felt good being stroked just because of her femininity. There was a roughness, a coarseness and toughness she had to assume when she dealt in a world mostly governed by men. How many times had she been the only woman in a room? Too often she felt like brushing their eyes off her body as if they were stickers clinging to her breasts, her hips, and her pelvis.

'I have friends who would say you are making typical male chauvinistic shallow observations,' Maggie replied.

The man who called himself Thomas Becket laughed. Then, after peering at her over his glass as he sipped his drink, he grew serious.

'Something's wrong when a man can't talk as a man to a woman anymore. Things that are pure and natural in us have been given a bad rap. Everyone is so concerned about his or her identity.'

'Sounds like something a man would say,' she replied. His eyes widened at the fire that sparked in hers. 'For most of our history, only men were permitted a real identity. Women were part of the furniture.'

'Not true,' he said softly. 'Remember how it all began. Man was so incomplete, he had to have woman, and then, after she joined him, she ate of the fruit.'

'A-huh. Thought you would get around to that quickly.'

'But,' he continued, 'why did Adam eat the fruit?'

'I forget, but I'm sure you know.'

'Oh, I do. Once he realized Eve had broken the rules and would be excommunicated from the Garden of Eden, he decided he had to sacrifice himself and eat of the fruit so he would go with her. Now, there's a man who didn't care about losing his identity. And,' he said, shrugging, 'it's really been that way ever since.'

Maggie laughed. He really did have a warm, beautiful smile, and during the few minutes he had been with her, she felt the tension in her body dissipate. She felt like a teenager again, adventurous, virginal. There was that delicious sense of danger.

'It's romantic, isn't it?' he asked. 'You're not one of those women who ridicules romance, are you?'

'I hope not,' she said. Her drink was finished.

'Can I get you another drink? I understand you have something to celebrate.'

'How did you know that?' she asked, sitting back.

'As I made my way here, someone whispered it to me. A full partner. I'm impressed. I insist you permit me to get you another drink.'

'I don't know. I should . . .'

'Please. Consider it my attempt to get your business, should you ever have need of someone like me. I can write it off, too,' he added with a smile.

She had to laugh.

'Okay, I guess I have time for one more.'

'Oh, we all have time for one more, Maggie.'

'Wait,' she said as he stood up. 'I don't remember telling you my name.'

'Didn't you?' He thought a moment. 'Maybe the

little bird who whispered in my ear gave me your name, too. I don't blame you for being concerned,' he added. ' "Who steals my purse, steals trash . . . but he who filches from me my good name . . . makes me poor indeed." Iago in *Othello*. One of my favorite literary characters.'

'Yes,' she said. 'I remember that play.'

'Be right back,' he said. She sat back. What a charming man and what a nice diversion while she waited for Grant's call, she thought, and took out her cellular to make sure the battery wasn't dead. The tiny light blinked. It was working fine. Why hadn't he called?

She tapped out their phone number and waited as it rang into the answering machine message.

'Grant,' she said, imbuing her voice with signs of her frustration and annoyance, 'if you missed my message at the office for some reason, call my cellular as soon as you hear this. We have something to celebrate,' she added, but not with the same enthusiasm she had evinced in the first message. He knew what she had to celebrate. He's deliberately avoiding me, she thought, and felt a mix of rage and sorrow.

Becket returned, drinks in hand.

'Thank you,' she said. He noticed the cellular.

'Trying to reach someone?' he asked.

'My husband.'

'Don't tell me he doesn't know of your good fortune yet,' Becket said as he slid back into the booth.

'He's a psychiatrist and he was tied up with patients. We have yet to talk since my promotion,' she explained, finding her explanation bitter. She sipped her drink. 'Are you married?'

'No. I'm one of those who is still searching for the perfect relationship.'

'What is the perfect relationship?' she queried, a little more cynically than she had intended. Damn him, she kept thinking. Why doesn't he call?

'That's easy. One in which neither individual is afraid to share his or her most intimate secrets. In other words, total trust.'

She nodded, pensive, now even a bit melancholy.

'I hope that's been true for you,' he said.

'Somewhat,' she said.

'Spoken like a good attorney,' he said.

She stared at him a moment and then she laughed.

'Don't you like lawyers?'

'As a group they are generally my kind of people,' he said. She thought his eyes were absolutely luminous, glittering with glee. 'They have taught us how to equivocate, how to rationalize, how to justify our most selfish acts.' He turned to the crowd. 'There's nothing more exciting than finding the exception to the rule, the exculpating detail, the argument that provides reasonable doubt. What would we do without the jury system?' he concluded dryly, and drank.

'You sound a bit cynical about the people you admire,' she said.

'Let's just say I've been on both sides and I appreciate what they can do; but I also recognize their limitations.'

'I couldn't help but notice Martin Saperstein. Did you come in with him?'

'No, but I know of him,' Becket said. 'I think he could have successfully defended Judas.'

He laughed.

'Is that good or bad?' she asked.

'Depends.'

'On?'

'Whether or not you need him,' Becket said, and she nodded. She drank some more and then checked her watch.

'I've really got to get going.'

'Where are you going? Home?'

'I guess,' she said.

'To celebrate?'

'I hope so,' she said.

'You shouldn't waste this happy moment. It's not fair, Maggie. You've worked hard for it, been diligent, dedicated. You should be going to a fine restaurant, listening to music, drinking champagne.'

'Maybe I will,' she said. It sounded like she was accepting a dare, petulant.

'Maybe you won't,' he followed quickly. He looked at his own watch. 'Did you try his office?'

'He's no longer there.'

'Is he home?'

'I'm sure he will be when I arrive,' she replied.

'And if he isn't?'

She smiled.

'Why are you so persistent, Mr Becket?'

'Thomas, please. I'm just worried that you won't have your well-deserved celebration. Actually,' he said, 'I have something to celebrate, too. I won a big settlement today . . . six figures.'

'Really?'

'Yes. Wouldn't you like to hear about it?'

'Maybe some other time,' she said, and started to slide out. Sitting here with him was making her nervous. She actually was enjoying it too much and was tempted to stay with him. 'Thanks for the drink and the conversation.'

'It was all my pleasure,' he said.

'Thank you. Good night,' she said, and headed toward Phil. When she turned back, Becket was gone. She looked toward the bar, but she didn't see him. She was surprised at her own pang of disappointment. What was it she wanted from this man?

What you want, what you crave, Maggie, is good, intelligent company, someone doting on you, a little romance, a forbidden voice whispered. What you want is a husband who appreciates your accomplishments. He's a psychiatrist, for Christ's sake, he should know.

She started out, thanking people who reached for her to offer their congratulations. Even Martin Saperstein stopped holding court for a moment and leaned toward her to offer his praises, but in a condescending manner. She thanked him coolly and retreated. Closing the door, she left the laughter and loud chatter entombed. She took a deep breath. She should be feeling better than this; she should be feeling ecstatic, she thought, and headed for her automobile, a feeling like a small, tight fist in her stomach.

When she got in, she tried all the numbers: Grant's car phone, the house again, even the office, hanging up as soon as the answering service came on line. She sat back, disgusted. Where the hell was he?

A light tap on the passenger-side window quickly drew her out of her seething thoughts. It was Thomas Becket. She lowered the window.

'Hi again,' he said. 'I was sitting in my car over there and saw you using the phone. Any luck?'

'Look –' she began, her rage spilling toward him. He raised his hands immediately.

'I don't mean to pry. I just told myself, Thomas, you mustn't let that woman miss a high moment. If you're free, why don't we just have dinner together on my expense account? Call it research, if you feel funny about it, but let's celebrate.'

Her anger dissipated. His easy tone and soft smile made her feel silly sitting in her car raging.

'You have to eat anyway,' he continued. 'Can you imagine sitting home alone tonight, of all nights? Follow me in your car. I know this little Italian restaurant not far from here. Everything's homemade, the genuine thing, and they have an accordion player that will bring laughter and tears to your eyes.'

180

It did sound good. What did he say, research? Little lies we make to ourselves and others are sometimes the tickets to happiness, she thought. Could she do this? She glanced at her car phone, the dead car phone. It wasn't fair; it really wasn't. She had been working so hard for this and she had accomplished a great deal.

'Well . . .'

'Good,' he said, clamping down on her moment of least resistance. 'Just follow me. I have that Lexus,' he said, pointing.

She watched him walk back to his car and start his engine. When his lights went on, she started her car. What am I doing? she thought as she followed him down the street. Moments later, he turned into the driveway of a small restaurant called Grandma's Kitchen. She had been down this street before, but she didn't recall the place. She pulled alongside his vehicle.

'I don't know this place,' she said, stepping out of her car.

'You will now, and I'm sure you'll come back often.' He put his hand on her arm at the elbow and led her to the door. 'It's homey and authentic as the sign claims.'

The restaurant was decorated with flowers that appeared natural and fresh, prints of Italian country scenes, and low lights. The red vinyl booths looked like something out of a fifties diner. It was just campy enough to be fun. All the tables had candlelight, and a tall, thin man sat on a small stage in the far right corner and played soft tunes on the accordion. An elderly woman got up from a table on the left and came to greet them. She had her gray hair tied in a bun and wore a red dress with a plain white apron.

'Good evening, Mr Becket,' she said.

'Annette, I'd like you to meet Mrs Blaine.'

'Maggie,' Maggie said, holding out her hand.

'Pleased to meet you. Your usual table, Mr Becket?'

'Thank you,' he said, and indicated that Maggie follow her to the rear of the restaurant to the most private booth. There were only two other couples in the restaurant. Seated across the room, they ate quietly, almost like people under hypnosis. But the aroma of wonderful sauces, garlic, herbs, and pasta filled the air. Maggie's stomach churned in anticipation.

'We'd like a bottle of your best champagne, Annette,' Becket said. 'And, of course, the house wine with dinner. It's homemade wine,' he told Maggie.

'I didn't realize how hungry I was until we stepped into this place and I smelled the food,' Maggie said.

'Very few of us realize just how intense our hungers are,' he replied with a smile.

'I'm talking only about food,' Maggie countered.

'Actually, I am, too,' he said.

A younger, plain-looking woman brought them the menus and a basket of garlic rolls.

'These are delicious,' Maggie said.

He nodded and put down his menu.

'I usually go with whatever their special is for the evening,' he said.

'Why don't you order for both of us. You seem to be quite a regular here.'

'Antipasto for two, Mary,' he told the waitress, 'and tonight's special is?'

'Lobster *fra diablo*,' she said.

'Perfect.' He handed her the menus. Annette brought the bottle of champagne, which she uncorked and poured into the champagne glasses. 'The first toast of the night,' he said. 'To you, Maggie, to your wonderful accomplishment. May it bring you more success and much satisfaction.'

'Thank you.'

They touched glasses and drank, both of them gazing at each other over the rims of their glasses.

'I'm sorry. Do you feel funny having dinner with another man?'

'Actually, no,' she said. 'I have lunch and often dinner with other attorneys so often, I don't give it much thought,' she snapped defensively.

'This is different. We're not here to negotiate, to make strategy, are we?' he pointed out softly.

She gazed at the accordion player, who seemed now to be playing especially for them.

'It does look like you're trying to seduce me,' she said.

'Would anyone blame me?'

'My husband,' she replied.

'He's a psychiatrist. He'll understand,' Becket said.

Maggie laughed and had more champagne. She felt like being giddy and silly, and she felt like toying with seduction. The lawyer in her had blossomed. Now the woman demanded attention.

They finished one bottle of champagne and then another. The antipasto was wonderful and the *fra diablo* magnificent. She couldn't get over how wonderful the food was, and she especially was fond of the homemade wine. It was so smooth, she didn't realize the proof until she sat back to consider the tray of desserts and her head spun.

'Oh,' she said, 'I think I've had enough to eat and drink.'

'Not even a cannoli?'

'No way,' she said.

'Just a couple of cups of your coffee, Annette,' he told her.

'I can be a good cook when I really try,' Maggie said suddenly, sadly.

'You don't try often?'

'I don't have the time.' She thought for a moment. 'Why do I feel guilty for not cooking more often? Other women my age treat the kitchen like a vestigial organ, why can't I?'

'Does your husband complain?'

'No, not really.'

Becket shrugged.

'Were you brought up in what some people refer to as a traditional home?'

'Yes, definitely.'

'Your mother was a homemaker and still is. She's

a bright, very independent woman, but a woman who takes pride in the way she keeps house,' he recited. 'You saw your father admire her for that and you always sought your father's approval. It's not abnormal, nor is it neurotic. It's just . . . image identification. Big deal.'

Maggie stared at him a moment.

'You sound more like a psychiatrist than an attorney. And if anyone should know, it's me,' she said.

He shrugged.

'A good attorney has to be something of a psychiatrist, doesn't he, Maggie?' He put his hand over hers and added, 'Just being married to one isn't enough.'

'I think I had better go,' she said.

He nodded at the waitress, who brought the check. He paid it in cash.

'I thought this was supposed to be a write-off,' she said. 'Don't you want a receipt?'

'I wouldn't insult you,' he said.

She liked that. He reached out to take her hand as she stood and they walked toward the front of the restaurant. Annette was waiting at the door. Maggie noticed how she stared at her, her eyes the same dark shade as Becket's.

'I hope everything was all right, Mr Becket,' she said, her eyes still on Maggie.

'As wonderful as ever, Annette. Give Danny my compliments.'

'It was really very, very good,' Maggie said.

'Thank you. I hope we'll see you again,' Annette said.

'You will.'

As they headed toward the parking lot, Maggie caught her heel in between the squares on the walkway and stumbled. Becket caught her and held her firmly.

'You all right?'

'Yes, I just . . . I don't know why men don't have to wear high heels,' she said, and giggled.

'Some do,' he said. 'Anything to elevate their egos.'

Maggie laughed. He still held her. They were in the shadows under the neon sign. The street was quiet, empty, not even an occasional passing automobile, which for any street in Los Angeles was unusual. Maggie felt as if she had lowered herself into a warm dream. The lights around them were subdued. The building spun and she dug her fingers into his strong arms to steady herself. Vaguely at first, she heard him whispering.

'Maggie, you deserve more, better. You should be happier. Maggie . . .'

Just as vaguely, she felt his lips on her ear and then on her cheek. She turned. Her heart was pounding. His lips grazed hers and then pressed harder, his arms sliding over hers and his hands moving down to her waist to lift her into him, fit her comfortably against his chest. She felt as if she were going to faint and fought to maintain consciousness, at the same time resisting the urge to kiss him back, to hold him just as tightly.

'I can't,' she pleaded. 'Please . . . stop.'

His hands moved up and over the sides of her breasts and settled under her arms. Then he lifted her easily and gently brought her back down to his waiting mouth again, again pressing firmly. Her body felt limp, distant, out of her control.

'Don't do this,' she pleaded, and he lowered her until her feet found the ground.

'I just wanted you to know it's yours whenever you want it, Maggie. Don't be afraid to ask.'

She leaned against her car. He let go of her hand and backed away. Moments later, he was in his car and driving out of the lot. He gazed at her, smiled, and then, after a small wave, turned to pull into the street.

She took a few deep breaths and opened her car door. For a while she just sat there.

What happened? What had she done? It really did seem like a dream. She started the engine, tightened her grip on herself, and backed out of the spot. As she pulled out of the lot and onto the street, she gazed into the rearview mirror and saw the restaurant lights go off.

It was as if it had been opened just for them.

13

Grant was still not home when Maggie arrived. She was actually relieved, afraid that he might take one look at her and know what she had done. But what had she done? She had somehow been charmed into going to dinner with a complete stranger, albeit a handsome, interesting man, yes; and he had kissed her, but she had drunk too much and she didn't invite the kiss, did she? Nevertheless, she had a deep-seated respect for Grant's perceptive powers. He could read guilt in a face, and guilt was what she felt when she entered the house.

Maggie went right to the medicine cabinet to take a few aspirins, afraid she would wake with a terrific hangover if she didn't. Then she put up some water for tea, changed quickly out of her suit and into a nightgown and robe. She was just calming down and feeling an easy fatigue when she heard the garage door open. A moment later Grant entered, looking somewhat disheveled, disturbed, his tie loosened, his hair messed, his face flushed. He looked like he had been running. He carried a package under his arm. When he saw her sitting there, he paused, and for a moment they just gazed at each other in silence.

'Where have you been, Grant?' she asked quietly. 'You look terrible.'

'Just walking about, thinking, trying to put some sense into the events of the past few weeks. Sorry I didn't get back to you,' he added quickly. 'I just didn't think I would be good company for a cele-bration at the time. I guess you got the partner-ship, huh?'

'Yes,' she said.

'Congratulations.'

'That's it?' She expected a hug, a kiss, the invita-tion to pop open a bottle of champagne.

'For now. I'm tired.' He started away.

'But where did you go? What did you do?' she followed quickly. 'What's that under your arm?'

He paused, took a deep breath, and turned back to her.

'I . . . went to church first,' he said.

'Church? Seriously?'

He smiled.

'I don't know why. I don't know what I expected. It was quiet, meditative, but the only voice I heard was my own. You know, the church was open, but there was no one there, not even a priest.

Just me and all those icons . . . crucified Christs, saints, biblical figures . . . and I suddenly realized that we have become the high priests of the twentieth century, we psychiatrists have replaced Father Understanding and Father Forgiveness, and you know what Maggie?' He drew closer and gazed madly into her eyes. 'It's not because God is dead, it's because the devil is dead, evil is dead. There is no more evil,' he said in a coarse whisper that put a chill in her spine.

'Grant . . .'

'No, listen,' he said, a little more animated. 'I've been thinking this through. That's what took up my time.' He started to pace as he spoke. 'You guys, us guys, the whole infrastructure of so-called morality, legality, ethics . . . we've killed Satan. No one is evil. We're dysfunctional, socially deprived, mentally ill, victims of everything but our own faults. We are no longer responsible, and so how can you blame Satan?' He laughed, a thin, mad laugh.

'Grant, are you all right?'

'Me? Sure. I'm fine. I'm finally . . . fine,' he said, and shook his head. 'I think I'm finally getting everything in perspective so I can better understand my patients and my function.' He stared at the floor a moment and then looked up as if he had come back from another time zone. 'Sorry I missed your big day. I'll make it up to you tenfold tomorrow and tomorrow and tomorrow. Right now, I'm exhausted,' he said. 'And it's not my fault,' he

190

added with a smile. 'I'm just going to put this in the office and go to bed.'

'What is that?'

'A manuscript I received in the mail today. Something very . . . interesting,' he said, and headed for the den.

'Grant!'

He didn't turn back.

Her heart was pounding. When she lifted the cup, her hand trembled so much she couldn't bring the fragile china to her lips. She put it down and took a deep breath. Something terrible, something even more terrible than she had imagined, was happening.

She thought about Landry and went to the telephone. As quietly as she could, she tapped out his number and waited. It rang and rang until his answering machine picked up. She decided not to leave a message.

Grant was already in bed and asleep by the time she put away the dishes and turned off the lights. She stared at him, watched him breathing regularly, his face almost childlike in repose, and then she lowered her head to her own pillow and said a small prayer for the both of them.

Grant was up before she was the next morning. She had been so dead away, she hadn't heard him rise, shower, and dress, which amazed her.

'Wake up, sleepyhead,' he sang.

Her eyelids fluttered. He had come to the doorway of the bedroom carrying a silver tray, on which was a glass of freshly squeezed orange juice and a silver pot of fresh coffee. There was a long-stemmed red rose as well.

'Morning,' he declared, looking bright and revived. 'Thought I'd begin paying homage to the partner.'

'Oh.' She ground the sleep from her eyes. 'Thank you,' she said as he put the tray gingerly on her lap and stepped back. 'I never heard you get up.'

'I was very considerate, moved like a ghost, but you were dead to the world.'

It was as if everything from the night before had been a bad dream. Gone was the wild glint in his eyes. He looked neat and as put together as ever. Mr Perfect.

'Where did you get the rose?'

'I picked it up last night at a street corner and forgot I had left it in the car. So, how did you celebrate without me?' he asked, folding his arms across his chest and leaning against the doorjamb.

'I . . .' She was tempted to tell him the truth, but she wasn't sure how he would take it and she didn't want to spoil the rejuvenation of happiness. 'I went to O'Healies and let the jealous mob buy me drinks and dinner and bow respectfully, even though they dripped with envy and blamed it all on the women's movement.'

Grant laughed.

'I'm sorry I missed that. What about Phil? Was he dripping green?'

'I got the feeling he was already thinking about a new firm, one where he would be a bigger fish,' she said, downing the juice. 'You squeezed the oranges yourself? I'm very impressed.'

'Nothing's too much for the partner,' he kidded.

'I can see where I won't be hearing the end of this for a while.'

Grant laughed and then turned serious as she sipped her coffee.

'Didn't your firm employ a private detective named Landry from time to time?' he asked.

'Landry? Yes. Jack Landry.' Her heart skipped a beat. Had Jack called the house after she had told him specifically not to? 'Why do you ask?'

'There's a story on the morning news about a private detective named Landry.'

'What?' she asked quickly.

'He was killed last night, victim of a mugging in South-Central L.A.'

'What?' Her fingers lost their grip on the handle and the cup hit the saucer, cracking and spilling the coffee over the tray. 'Oh, no.'

Grant rushed forward and lifted the tray carefully from her lap.

'Sorry, I should have waited with bad news,' he said, balancing the tray to keep the liquid contained on it.

'What happened to him?' she asked after catching her breath. She pressed her palm against her heart to keep the beating from drumming the blood right up through her head.

'Just heard bits and pieces. He was found in

his car, gunshot wound to the head, wallet, rings, watch . . . everything of any value missing.'

'South-Central L.A.?'

'That's what I heard,' Grant said. 'Sorry I brought bad news to you so early.' He smiled. 'I made you your favorite omelette. Be waiting in the breakfast nook,' he said, and left her.

She grappled for the remote and turned on the television set, flipping quickly to the local news station. Sports and weather was on. She would have to wait until the top of the hour again, another fifteen minutes. There was nothing to do but shower and dress.

Jack was dead? Murdered? What was he doing in South-Central? Surely it could have had nothing to do with her case, she thought; rather, she hoped. By the time she came out of the shower, the news was starting again and Jack's story was one of the headline events.

It was just as Grant described . . . an apparent robbery, but no sign of a struggle. Wouldn't Jack have put up some resistance? Heartsick, she dressed and went to join Grant for breakfast. He was more animated than ever, as if a good night's rest had washed away all of his mental turmoil.

'I skipped racquetball this morning just so I could whip up this special breakfast.'

'Thank you.'

'Actually, I didn't want those guys kidding me to death about your promotion. I know they're just jealous. Most of them are married to zeros, especially Carl Thornton. They all wish they had a wife as beautiful and as accomplished as mine,' he continued, and served her the omelette. She forced a smile and took a forkful. He stood back. 'Well?'

'It's delicious, Grant. Thanks.'

'Did you call your folks with the good news?'

'Yes. Oh, but I didn't call your mother yet.'

'Oh, no. I'd better do that right away. You know how she gets if she hears news about us from someone else first,' he said, and hurried out to the kitchen.

Her stomach was so tight, she didn't think she could eat half the omelette, much less finish it. Every bite seemed bigger than the one before as Jack's face and voice returned to memory. He was on her case. He was looking into Bois. Somehow it must have taken him to South-Central. Bois was responsible. He had to be. It's my fault, she thought. I put him in harm's way. What does this mean? Who is this patient?

Grant came back, fixing his tie as he entered.

'Be prepared for some sort of celebration you won't be able to stand,' he said. 'She's beaming and planning.' He gazed at her plate. 'I thought you said it was delicious.'

'It is, I just . . .'

'Feel bad about Landry?'

'Yes.'

'Well, they do take risks and they know the danger, not that that justifies it,' he said, and paused, scrutinizing her closer. 'Was he on something for your firm?'

'No,' she said, but dropped her gaze too quickly.

'You saw him recently?'

She took a deep breath. She had to tell him now. What if a police investigation somehow revealed her involvement with Jack and they came around to ask questions? Grant would be even more angry at her for keeping such a thing secret. Besides, what if Bois really was somehow responsible for Jack's death? Would he now direct his attention to her? To Grant?

'Grant,' she said after a deep breath, 'I asked him to do something for me personally.'

Grant's hands froze at the tie knot and then he reached slowly for his jacket.

'Oh? And what might that have been, Mag?'

'You know how worried I've been about you, Grant,' she began. He stared. 'You don't realize how different you've been these past weeks, how you've changed.'

'What did you do, Maggie?'

'I was worried about this new patient and the effect he was having on you. I'm positive I saw someone looking in our window the other night. I mean . . .'

'Maggie, what did you do?' His eyes were like marbles, his lips stretched thin, a whiteness in each corner of his mouth. She swallowed hard before responding.

'I asked Jack to look into the things he was telling you, about Mosley and –'

'You told Jack Landry what a patient of mine told me during a session?'

'I had to see if there was any possibility of truth to it, Grant. You were too involved and you couldn't do it for professional reasons.'

'That's right, and what I couldn't do, you couldn't do. I thought you would respect that confidence.'

'But Jack came back with information that led me to believe there was a good chance of it being true, Grant. This patient wasn't making things up, especially this new situation involving Mrs Mosley.'

'I think I would have discovered that myself, Maggie. I have some ability to discern illusion from reality. That's why they pay me the big bucks.'

'I know. I wasn't worried about your ability; I was worried about you, what might happen next. So I . . .'

'What? What else?'

'Had Jack investigate Jules Bois,' she said quickly, and waited for the ceiling to fall.

'You told him my patient's name and all I told you?' His face reddened and his lips twisted into an even more grotesque grimace of disbelief and anger.

'All in strict confidence, Grant. Jack was a professional. He understood. He might have been killed while on this case, Grant. Don't you see? It's even more serious now.'

'You're not kidding it's even more serious. Never, never in a million years would I have believed that you would betray my trust, Maggie.'

'I didn't.'

'What do you call this investigation behind my back, and one involving a patient of mine? Huh? Do you know what would happen to my career if my patients found out my wife had them investigated? Are you mad? Where do you get the right? You think you're a partner in my practice, too?'

'Grant!'

'You think you can bulldoze everyone, charge through every door, take control of my life, my professional career . . . a professional detective! Christ, was he following me, too?'

'No.'

'I can't believe you did this, Maggie. I only hope my patient never knew. For your sake, more than my own,' he said, and turned.

'Grant!'

He didn't stop. He walked out, slamming his fist against the wall in the kitchen before going into the garage. That door slammed so hard, the house shook.

Maggie sat there, the little she had eaten now up in her throat. The day after the most exciting and significant moment in her professional career, she felt sick and depressed. This patient from hell, as Jack had suggested, somehow, insidiously, had worked his way into their lives and pried her and Grant apart. Now Grant was so angry at her, he wouldn't listen to anything she had to say unless she could bring him something concrete, something so substantial his pride and his ego would take second

198

place and enable him to see clearly. Was it too arrogant of her to take charge or was she just being a good wife, trying to protect the man she loved? And in a real sense, trying to protect herself.

Grant was in a rage all the way to his office. He was so blinded by his anger, he nearly got into two accidents. Horns chastised him, fists waved, and drivers of other cars glared with murderous intent through windshields. Los Angeles was overcast with a thick marine layer and, to Grant, it added to the burden of fury that weighed heavily on his brow. The morning had started well. He had awoken filled with energy and eagerness to get at his work, meet his patients, and work miracles. In minutes, seconds, Maggie had turned it around. Her success had made her arrogant, he thought. Never before would she dare to do anything remotely like this without his knowledge and approval.

As he drew closer to his office building, he tried to calm down. After all, it was important, essential, that he separate his personal life from his work. He couldn't be distracted. He was like a fighter pilot once a patient entered that office. He had to do battle with the demons in their minds and he couldn't afford to make a mistake or he would crash and burn. It was a big responsibility. People put their mental well-being in his hands, and therefore their lives, their happiness, and the happiness of those they loved and who loved them. I'm too important for this nonsense, he thought, and sucked in his breath as he pulled into the garage and became . . . Doctor Grant Blaine.

When he reached his office door, he was surprised to find it still locked. Where was Fay? She was usually a good half hour at her desk by now and she hadn't called to say she would be late. As soon as he entered, he checked the answering machine and saw there were no messages. He settled into his office and waited a good ten minutes before calling her and getting her answering machine. Perhaps something had delayed her, something with her daughter, he thought.

But by the time his first patient had arrived, she still hadn't come to work. The patient, Jerome Ormand, was a thirty-eight-year-old man who suffered agoraphobia. He had a marked fear of being alone or in places from which escape might be difficult or help not available in case he suddenly became incapacitated. Consequently, he would drive a hundred miles to avoid going through a tunnel or over a bridge. He would never get on a crowded train or bus and was even unable to go to a movie theater. He had never been in an elevator. His condition had become so serious, his sister, with whom he lived, was afraid he would soon not leave the house.

The moment Jerome entered the office and noticed Fay was not there, he hesitated. He was a tall, thin man with bushy eyebrows and a head of curly, coarse light brown hair. His brown eyes shifted nervously as he panned the room. He even gazed suspiciously at the ceiling, his nostrils moving in and out like a curious rabbit's. As he stood there perusing, his Adam's apple bobbed and he rubbed the palms of his hands over his thighs.

This was only their second session, but during the first, Grant had analyzed one of Jerome Ormand's habitual nightmares, a dream of being locked in a coffin alive, and discovered that during his youth, his mother often locked him in a closet as punishment, once forgetting he was in there for so many hours, he messed his pants.

'What happened to your secretary?' he asked from the doorway, the door still open behind him.

'She's late. I don't know why. It's no problem, Jerome. Come on in. Make yourself comfortable.'

Remaining where he was, Jerome looked at Fay's empty chair and then at Grant.

'It's unusually hot in here,' he said.

'No. I don't think so, but if you like, we'll open a window in my office. Come on in.'

'You fire her?'

'Oh, no. She'll be here.' Grant stepped toward him. He saw Jerome was beginning to break out in a sweat. 'We can leave the door open until she comes, if you like. Whatever you like, Jerome.'

'You know this office is the farthest from the stairway? Did you know that?'

'Yes. But we're close enough to the emergency exit in case of fire, if that's what you mean.'

'Those sprinkler systems never work. How many fires started and later the firemen found they didn't work, huh?'

'You want to just sit out here until she comes?' Grant asked. He moved to the settee and sat, smiling to demonstrate how relaxed and confident he was. Jerome stared at him a moment and then nodded.

'He said you fired her and I'd be alone with you today. He told me you were having your own problems and might not be able to help me. I would be . . . alone.'

'What?'

'He told me,' he said, nodding.

'Who told you?'

'He said these doors shut automatically in case of fire to keep it from spreading.'

'Who said these things, Jerome?'

Jerome Ormand rose to his feet.

'I gotta go.'

'Wait a minute.'

'I'll come back another time,' he said, and started to turn away.

Grant reached out and seized his arm.

'Wait, Jerome.'

The man spun around, his eyes blazing. As he turned, he dipped into his jacket pocket and brought out a dinner fork, the ends of which had been sharpened. Without warning, he swung around and jabbed it into Grant's neck. The force of the blow sent Grant back against the settee. Blood immediately gushed from the small holes when Grant pulled the fork from his neck. The sight of so much blood so quickly put him in a panic. He stumbled forward.

Jerome Ormand stepped out quickly, closing the door behind him.

'Jesus,' Grant said, gazing down at his blooded hand. He could feel the warm trickle building along his collarbone as the blood flowed.

Has to be the carotid artery, he thought.

He stepped back quickly and seized the phone, while he kept pressure on the artery with his hand and a handkerchief.

Despite the slowing down of the flow of blood, he felt faint. He sat back hard on Fay's desk chair and waited for the operator to pick up while he stared at the picture of the quiet country scene with a cool-looking brook snaking around a bend, over rocks, toward the line of trees. It started to go out of focus.

'What the hell . . . happened?' he muttered, pressing as hard as he could to keep the blood flow diminished.

'Got to stay conscious . . . got to,' he muttered, and resisted the urge to close his eyes, but the lids felt heavier and heavier with every jerk of the second hand on his office wall clock.

'Nine-one-one,' the operator said.

He tried to speak, but it was as if he had slipped and fallen head over heels down a dark well.

14

Work was nearly impossible for Maggie. Her mind drifted, her eyes left the pages, she half listened to phone conversations and the chatter of office employees before heading out to court for a preliminary hearing. There was still a festive air around her. The office staff had ordered flowers and a box of candy. Phil and the other associates bought some champagne for her to enjoy later. She tried hard to put on a happy face, but Grant's raging exit from the house continually replayed in her memory.

Almost as soon as she had arrived at her office, Grant's mother called and rambled on and on about a party of celebration she was organizing, elaborating on the guest list, the menu, until Maggie as politely as possible got off the phone.

'I've got to go to court, Mom,' she said.

'I understand, dear,' Patricia said. 'You must be

twice as busy now that you are one of the bosses. I'll call you later. My son must be a very proud man today,' she added.

The sick feeling at the pit of Maggie's stomach began a slow climb into her throat again. On the way out, she went to the bathroom, washed her face in cold water, took another two aspirins, then headed for the courthouse.

She had just put her folder down on the table and turned to her client when the bailiff approached to tell her there was an emergency phone call for her from her office. She was to call her secretary immediately.

'Immediately?' Her secretary would never interrupt her in court unless it was something terrible.

It felt like a tiny Ping-Pong ball crusted with ice bounced in her stomach. She requested five minutes from the judge, who granted it, but with a look of annoyance, and then she hurried out to the telephone.

'Marsha, it's Maggie. What's up?'

Her secretary quickly told her the emergency room doctor at Cedars-Sinai was looking for her.

'I had a hard time reaching you,' she said. 'You were already out of the car and they kept connecting me to the wrong courtrooms, wrong people. I'm sorry it's taken so long.'

'What did they say? Is it my mother-in-law?'

'No, Mrs Blaine. It's your husband.'

'Grant?'

'Here's the number and the doctor's name,' her

secretary said, and Maggie called. She was on hold for nearly five minutes. By now the judge must be fuming, she thought, but she held on.

'Mrs Blaine?'

'Yes. What is it? What's happened to my husband? A car accident?' she followed with shotgun speed.

'Mrs Blaine. I'm Doctor Saltzman,' he said calmly. 'Your husband was brought into the emergency room with a neck wound,' the deep, formal voice said. It was almost as unemotional as a synthetic voice on a tape recording. No preparation, no niceties, just right to the point, which hit her in the pit of her stomach like something indigestible.

'What? Neck wound? Grant? He's a psychiatrist,' she said, as if that would protect him from any such madness. 'He went to work this morning. You sure you're talking about my husband?'

He rattled off her home address.

'And one of his patients brought him here,' Doctor Saltzman added. 'He found him nearly unconscious in his office.'

'What patient? What happened?'

'Apparently another patient went berserk and was carrying a sharpened dinner fork in his pocket. He struck your husband in the neck. It happened in the office.'

'Oh, no,' she said. 'How is he? How is my husband? Is he dead?'

'As I was saying,' the doctor continued without cloaking his impatience, 'this one patient of your

206

husband's apparently stabbed him with a dinner fork and unfortunately hit the carotid artery. However, your husband had the good sense to keep a pressure point at the wound and stem the flow of blood. Before he passed out, his next patient arrived. Nevertheless, he lost a lot of blood by the time he arrived here. He's in a coma at present, but we have a transfusion under way and I believe it's a good prognosis. He lucked out with the second patient finding him so quickly.'

'What? What's the patient's name?'

'Bois, Jules Bois.'

'I'll be right there,' she gasped, and cradled the phone. She couldn't help but release a small but sharp cry.

The bailiff was at her side.

'Mrs Blaine?'

'What? Oh. I have to speak to the judge. I have a family emergency,' she said, and followed the bailiff into court.

Minutes later, she was pounding the tile in the lobby of the building and rushing to the garage. The attendant nodded and started to speak, but Maggie was already past him, her high heels clicking over the macadam to her automobile. She punched the alarm on her key chain and released the invisible magnetic field. Then she jabbed the key into the ignition and turned it with a vengeance. Her tires squealed as she spun the vehicle out of the garage and into the street.

Traffic was already bottling up the city streets, but

she was filled with a desperation born not only of what she had heard had happened to Grant, but of her uncertainty about what was happening. It couldn't have just been a coincidence that Bois was there at the right moment. The bizarreness put another layer of terror over the one that the doctor had created with his information.

As she drove, her throat tightened to the point where she was afraid she wouldn't be able to breathe. Her chest ached.

'Why didn't I do something more as soon as I heard about Jack this morning? I should have called the police,' she muttered. 'What has this man done to him now?'

She pounded the inside of her palm against the steering wheel when she came to a halt at a red light. Pedestrians, many of them obviously tourists, casually strolled past. Their lives were uncomplicated, carefree at this moment, while she was sitting in the car and coming to the realization that her life, her marriage was crumbling like one of those buildings in the Northridge earthquake.

It was nearly thirty-five minutes before she reached the hospital. The emergency rooms of all the hospitals in American urban areas looked like they were caught up in chaos; Cedars-Sinai in Los Angeles was no different. Wounded, sick, and injured people overflowed the waiting rooms, kept employees filling out forms. All the gurneys looked like they were in use; nurses, technicians, interns were racing around, their eyes tiny mirrors reflecting the agony and confusion. To Maggie, it resembled a war zone. The nurse at the desk smiled at her, however.

'I'm Maggie Blaine. My husband was brought here . . . Doctor Grant Blaine.'

'Oh, yes. He's in seven. Right down the corridor on your right,' she said. 'When you're finished, please stop by to complete the form,' she added.

'When I'm finished,' Maggie muttered, and charged down the corridor.

The sight of Grant spread on the gurney, his face ashen, took her breath away. A nurse was checking the IV bag of blood, which was nearly empty.

'I'm Mrs Blaine,' she said quickly. The nurse turned to her. 'How is he?'

'His blood count's coming up. We're moving him to ICU,' she replied in a calm, cold businesslike manner.

Why wasn't he moved there already? Maggie wondered, and went to Grant's side. She gazed at the wound in his neck, the bandages, the sight of blood, and held his hand. It felt horrifyingly cold to her touch.

'Grant,' she whispered. There was no movement under his eyelids. She gazed at the monitors beeping and studied the lines of light that jetted across the screen. It was all medical gibberish to her. 'Where is Doctor Saltzman?' she asked the nurse.

'He's with another emergency. Someone will be down to take your husband up in a few minutes,' she said, nodding at Grant.

'Do you know what happened?'

The nurse looked at her as if she had asked the most ridiculous question.

'Someone jabbed a fork into his neck is all I was told,' she said. 'There's a policeman in the lobby. I'll let him know you're here,' she added, and left the room.

Maggie turned back to Grant.

'Oh, Grant,' she muttered. 'I'm sorry.' She brought her lips to his cheek and kissed him while she stroked his hair. She heard a knock on the doorjamb and turned to see a police officer.

'Ma'am,' he said. 'I'm Officer Hodges.'

'Do you know what happened?' she demanded quickly.

'Not completely, ma'am, no. That's what we're trying to find out now.'

'Where's Bois?'

'Bois?' He looked at his clipboard. 'That's the man who brought him in. Yes, I spoke with him earlier. All he said was your husband babbled about being stabbed in the neck with a fork. Another, earlier patient apparently –'

'Where is Mr Bois now?'

'I think he left, ma'am.'

'What about my husband's secretary . . . Fay Moffit?'

'His secretary is right outside, but she wasn't at the office when this occurred,' he said.

'Where is she?' Maggie went to the door and saw Fay standing in the hallway, a handkerchief in hand, dabbing her eyes.

'Fay!'

'Oh, Mrs Blaine,' Fay said, hurrying to her. 'How's he doing?'

'The nurse said his blood count was coming up nicely. They're moving him to ICU.'

'I'm so sorry I was late this morning. Maybe if I had been there, too, it wouldn't have happened,' she moaned.

Maggie turned to the police officer.

'You know who really did this, don't you?'

'Mrs Moffit gave me the name of the patient who had the first appointment.'

'No, Bois must have done it himself.'

'You mean the man who found him and brought him here? Why would he stab him and then save his life, Mrs Blaine?'

'He's been doing many things to harm my husband,' Maggie blurted, 'and I think he might be responsible for the death of Jack Landry, a private investigator, who was murdered last night.' Her voice was at a very high pitch, and she knew she sounded mad herself, rambling, but she wanted to get everything out now, desperately.

'Really?' Fay said with surprise.

'Yes. I'll tell you more about it,' Maggie said to the policeman. 'I should have gone directly to the police station this morning. The man's not mentally ill; he's evil. He's been driving my husband mad for weeks and –'

'Mrs Blaine,' Fay said. 'Mr Ormand's been a patient only a couple of weeks. This was only his second session with Doctor Blaine.'

211

'You're not listening. It wasn't Ormand, I tell you,' Maggie said with a cold smile. She turned to the policeman. 'It had to be Jules Bois.'

'Oh, no,' Fay said. She shook her head. 'Not Mr Bois. He would never do such a thing,' she added, her face changing from sadness to indignation. 'Mr Bois is a very kind, gentle man. And he saved Doctor Blaine's life. Just lucky he's had some medical background.'

Maggie stiffened as she focused her attention on Fay Moffit, noticing for the first time how different she looked, how changed was her appearance, the makeup, her hair, and her clothing.

'How do you know so much about him, Fay?'

'I . . . I just do,' she replied, but blushed.

'How?'

Fay looked guiltily at the policeman, whose face was full of confusion.

'You've been seeing one of Grant's patients?' Maggie asked quickly. 'Did Grant know this?' she followed with cross-examiner's speed.

'Well . . . my private life is my own business,' Fay said sharply.

'Not when it involves Grant's patients.'

'Ma'am –' the policeman said.

'Just a minute,' Maggie snapped. 'How long have you been seeing him, Fay? Have you told him things about Grant?' Fay just stared. 'It's very important that you be honest and forthcoming in front of the policeman. This man is dangerous. The police have got to know.'

212

'He is not dangerous. He's very concerned about other patients and he understands their problems,' Fay insisted.

'What other patients?' Maggie narrowed her eyes when Fay looked away. 'You told him about some of Grant's other patients, didn't you?'

'I just came down to see how the doctor was,' Fay said, stepping back.

'Stay away from this man, Fay. Christ.' She spun on the policeman. 'You've got to go after this man. Somehow, he was responsible for this, I tell you. Look at what he's done to my husband's secretary. She's practically under hypnosis.'

'Huh?' The policeman looked at Fay and shook his head.

'Can't you see?' she demanded.

The policeman looked at Fay and then at his clipboard.

'Okay,' he said, 'we'll look into it. First, we'll send someone to question Mr Ormand.'

Maggie turned back to Fay, who was inching farther away with every passing moment.

'Where are you going?'

'I've got to get back to the office and let the other patients know what's happened,' she said.

'Fay.'

'I'll call you, Mrs Blaine.'

'Fay, stay away from that man,' Maggie cried. Fay hurried away.

'I think I have enough for now,' the policeman said. 'We'll be in touch, Mrs Blaine.'

213

'Who's going to be on this case?' she demanded.

'Probably Detective Hartman,' he replied.

'Tom Hartman?'

'Yes, ma'am.'

She had cross-examined Tom Hartman on two different occasions while defending clients. She wasn't on his *my favorite persons* list. She was as sure of that as she was of the vice versa. Nevertheless, this was her husband and her life now. Her view of the police now was different.

'He's got to go after that man,' she said, but the police officer closed his folder. He nodded. 'Don't you understand? He's got to question him closely.'

'I'll give everything to Detective Hartman, who will be in contact with you, I'm sure. I hope he's all right,' he said, nodding at Grant, and then he started away.

The nurse approached.

'If you could stop by the admittance desk, Mrs Blaine,' she said.

'Right,' Maggie said sharply. 'Our paperwork is more important than anything else.'

The nurse pulled her shoulders back and turned away as two attendants arrived to take Grant to ICU.

Maggie sucked in her breath.

There wasn't much she could do now anyway. Get the bureaucratic crap over with, she told herself, and headed for the desk.

Nearly an hour later she was sitting at Grant's bedside in ICU. They permitted her to remain there, talking to him, because the doctor thought it might help bring him back to consciousness faster. She held his hand and rattled on and on, apologizing again for the way she had gone about investigating behind his back, but emphasizing how she was more convinced than ever now that she had done the right thing. She talked about his mother, her current case, plans for a vacation. After a while, she realized she was just babbling. She hadn't even been aware of the activity around her: nurses parading past, other patients being wheeled in with other loved ones standing by, doctors examining, conferring.

She took a deep breath. Perhaps I should give it a rest, she thought, and considered leaving for a while. But before she released Grant's hand and stood, she felt his fingers twitch, and then she saw his eyelids flutter.

'Grant!'

They continued to flutter until they opened.

'He's awake!' she cried. She turned toward the nurse's station. 'My husband . . .'

One of the nurses hurried around the counter.

'Doctor Blaine,' she said. She patted his other hand and checked his monitor. Then she smiled at Maggie. Grant's eyes widened at all the activity going on around him.

'Grant,' Maggie said, leaning over. 'How do you feel?'

His eyelids fluttered and he looked from the monitor and back to her.

'What happened? How did I get here?'

'You were stabbed in the neck and bled profusely,' she said. 'Don't you remember any of it? They said a patient of yours did it with a fork. It happened this morning at your office. Remember?'

Grant shook his head.

'Where am I?'

'You're in ICU, Cedars-Sinai Hospital.' Maggie looked up helplessly at the nurse.

'I'll send for the doctor,' the nurse said, and left them.

'You must remember,' she insisted, turning back to Grant. 'That man, that horrid man Bois, supposedly found you in your office bleeding and brought you to the hospital. The amazing Mr Bois. I told the policeman about him, Grant, and I'm going to follow up now with it. I've got to.'

'Bois?'

'Your patient, Grant . . . the patient from Hell. Surely you couldn't forget him,' she said, and started to laugh, but stopped.

Grant stared at her without expression.

'Don't you remember, Grant?' she asked with more desperation.

He shook his head. An icy sensation flowed down her neck, over her breasts, and across her stomach because of the way he was gazing at her, his eyes void of feeling. She took his hand into hers again and leaned closer.

'Grant . . .' His face remained expressionless, his eyes unchanging, glassy. Then he grimaced as if he had a sharp pain. 'What's wrong, honey?'

'Who are you?' he asked.

'What?'

'Who are you?' he repeated.

The blood drained from her face. It was as if someone had come along and punched her in the stomach. She tried to swallow and felt her throat closed tight. She turned desperately toward the nurse.

'The doctor!' she cried, 'when is he coming?'

15

Maggie stood in the ICU waiting room and gazed numbly out the window. The sky had become totally overcast and there was a light drizzle just dampening the streets enough to make them slick and dangerous. She was so tired, so overwhelmingly tired. She closed her eyes and felt her body sway for a moment and then she heard her name and turned to see Carl Thornton standing in the doorway. She had asked him to come.

'Well?'

'Let's sit here,' Carl said in response, and moved to the settee across from the window. Maggie took a deep breath and joined him.

'When a doctor says please have a seat, it's usually bad news,' Maggie remarked.

Carl smiled.

'It's not good, but I don't think it's as bad as you

believe it is, Mag. Amnesia can follow on the heels of a traumatic event. It's not something permanent. Just be patient.'

'Be patient? He thinks I'm a total stranger.'

'Just keep talking to him and suddenly he'll snap out of it.'

'You're sure?'

'Confident,' he replied.

'But not sure?'

'I think I'm sure. Yes. Leave it to a lawyer to pin me down,' he added with a smile.

'It frightened me,' she admitted.

'I can imagine.'

'You can't. My mind's just going wild with fantastic possibilities. Carl, I'm sure it has something to do with this patient of his, this man Bois. Grant's been disturbed over him ever since he started. He was one of Henry's patients. I feel sure Bois had more to do with the attack on Grant than anyone thinks.'

'I understood it to be a patient named Ormand. He was a referral and it makes sense, Mag. I know about him. He's agoraphobic. Fears – rather, I should say he is terrified – of being alone or in places where escape might be difficult or help not available if he needed it. I had an agoraphobic patient who actually killed his father when his father tried to force him to stay in his room.'

'I don't think it was that man,' Maggie insisted. 'I think it was this other patient, Jules Bois.'

'Wasn't he the one who found Grant and brought him to the hospital?' Carl asked.

'Yes.'

'Doesn't sound like someone out to do him harm, then, does it?'

'Maybe it's part of his madness. If he didn't do it, he got Mr Ormand to do it,' she insisted.

Carl stared at her a moment and then shook his head gently.

'Don't let your imagination take over, Mag, and make you paranoid,' Carl warned. 'We already have one psychiatrist's wife in a mental clinic.'

Maggie looked away and took a deep breath before turning back to him.

'How is Lydia?' she asked.

'More convinced than ever that she did the right thing. That's a hard case,' Carl replied.

Maggie thought a moment.

'I want to see her,' she said.

'What?'

'I want to see her again. Please, arrange it for me, Carl.'

'Sure,' he said, and shrugged. 'But I don't think you'll get anything sensible from her.'

'Nevertheless . . .'

'Fine,' Carl said. He stood. 'From what the doctor says, I don't think Grant will be in ICU much longer.'

'What if he still doesn't remember me?'

'Pretend you're having an affair,' Carl said, smiling. 'I think he might like that.'

Maggie started to smile just as Phil Martin appeared. He looked out of breath.

'I had to park about a mile away. I'm sorry I couldn't get here earlier, Mag. I was down in San Diego on the Langer matter. How's Grant? Jesus,' he added before she could respond. He looked at Carl and then back at her.

'He's going to be all right,' Carl said.

'I used to kid him about the dangers of being around mentally ill people and he would tell me I was in more danger defending criminals. Unfortunately, I was right, huh?'

Maggie shook her head.

'You were both right,' she said.

'Oh?'

'Because Grant's been treating a mentally ill criminal,' she added.

'Oh? Oh, him,' Phil said, his eyes brightening with memory. He glanced at Carl just long enough for Maggie to catch the conspiracy of thoughts.

'Yes,' she said, rising, 'him. Pardon me while I go do something about it.'

She seized her purse and hurried out of the waiting room.

'Where are you going?' Phil called.

'To see the enemy,' Maggie replied, and stepped into the elevator. The door closed on both him and Carl gazing after her, both twin faces of confusion.

A little more than a half hour later, she pulled into the parking lot for the police station and asked the desk sergeant for Detective Hartman.

Hartman was crunched over his desk, his telephone receiver trapped between his shoulder and his ear. A cigarette burned in the glass ashtray blackened with soot and filled with butts, the tiny trail of smoke curling around Hartman's head. He had his jacket off and over the back of his chair, and his heavy shoulders strained the threads of his thinning white shirt. The strands of hair at the back of his head were long and unruly, pouring over his shirt collar and curling to the sides. Maggie recalled him on the witness stand looking more like the defendant than the defendant did himself.

Hartman was scribbling notes on a pad rapidly as he listened. A good minute passed before he said a word. In the meantime, Maggie stood just to his left, a half a foot back, waiting.

'Anything else? You're kidding! Jesus. His ankle? Is that it? All right, thanks.'

As soon as Maggie saw Hartman cradle the receiver, she pounced.

'Excuse me, Detective Hartman?'

Hartman turned slowly and then smiled as soon as he saw her.

'The patrolman on your husband's case told me you would probably be stopping by. How are you, counselor?'

'I'm not exactly in the Christmas mood, if that's what you mean, Detective.'

He nodded and sat back.

'Okay. What can I do for you?'

'I don't think this is an isolated incident involving one of my husband's patients. I think it ties in to other things. What I'm about to tell you is ordinarily confidential, but –'

'So what happens after you tell me,' he snapped, 'I make an arrest that gets thrown out of court?'

'No, this is different. I'm speaking to you off the record,' Maggie said. 'My husband . . . my husband wouldn't approve, but he's not in any condition to make a sensible decision; he wasn't, even before this attack.'

Hartman's eyes widened. He thought a moment and then nodded at the chair beside his desk.

'Have a seat, counselor.'

'Thank you. To get right to the point, Detective, I believe one of Grant's other patients is responsible not only for the attack on him, but for Jack Landry's death and for some other crimes recently committed in Los Angeles.'

'Really? Jack Landry? The private dick?'

'Yes.'

'Landry was mugged, robbed down in South-Central. You say your guy did that?'

'He made it look like that.'

'Why?'

'Because Landry was working for me, following him.'

Hartman whistled through his teeth, nodded, and took up his pen.

'Go on.'

'I hired him after this man began to have a . . . very negative influence on my husband. Grant was very disturbed about him.'

'That's your husband's work, isn't it? Dealing with disturbing people and making them whole again?' Hartman asked, half in jest.

'Yes, but this man is different. He's . . .'

'What?'

'Different,' she said.

Hartman raised his eyebrows.

'You've met him?'

'No, but my husband talked about him enough for me to understand the problem.'

Hartman smirked.

'You have to give me something more to go on, Mrs Blaine. You, of all people, should know that.'

'My husband diagnosed him as a compulsive-obsessive.'

'So?'

'He is driven by the compulsion to instigate evil.'

'Come again?' Hartman said.

'He has an obsessive need to get other people to do evil or illegal things. It pleases him in a sick way. For example, Grant told me the man claimed to have talked Clarence Dunbar into bashing in his wife's head. You know that case?'

'Yeah.' He paused, his eyes narrowing with suspicion. 'Isn't your firm defending him?'

'Yes, but it has nothing to do with this. I am not on that case.'

'Okay,' Hartman said with some obvious skepticism. 'Go on.'

'And then there's a Mrs Mosley, an elderly woman who supposedly overdosed on medication. Grant's patient claimed he talked the woman's daughter-in-law into killing her. The coroner told me that an overdose of nitroglycerin was the cause of death, only he assumed it was because the woman had memory problems and made an error.'

'So?' Hartman said with impatience. 'That sounds logical.'

'There are other examples of his psychotic work I'm sure you'll discover.'

'And just because he has this obsessive need, as you call it, he's able to get anyone he wants to do something terrible, like killing his wife or her mother-in-law?'

'He doesn't just get anyone. He works on just those who are most vulnerable,' Maggie replied. 'I met Clarence Dunbar, questioned him. He's the sort who is emotionally weak, psychologically disturbed, easily influenced. Grant's patient preys on people who have these evil ideas anyway, greedy people, ambitious people. You understand?'

'No. How does he know who these people are?'

'I don't know all of it,' Maggie said with some frustration. 'It's his . . . work, his obsession. Maybe he does research. He hunts them like a . . .'

'Like a what?' Hartman asked.

'Like an obsessive-compulsive personality would,' Maggie replied. 'I believe he gets information from psychiatric files, as well.'

'You have some concrete evidence of this? Something in writing? On tape?' Hartman asked.

'No, I don't. That would be in Grant's files. You

can subpoena them after you investigate and find probable cause.'

'That's a tough one, Mrs Blaine. You know what it's like getting privileged information. It's like asking a priest to testify. You guys would tear us up.'

'Not in this case.'

'Because it involves your husband?' he followed quickly.

'Yes,' she confessed.

'Yeah, fine, but what do you have for us? I mean, what do I do, go up to him and ask him point-blank if he had an obsessive need to get a woman to kill her mother-in-law?'

'Just start an investigation. You'll see.'

The detective gazed at her a moment.

'According to the patrolman, this is the guy' – he fished through some paperwork – 'who found your husband bleeding to death, rushed him to the hospital?'

'Yes.'

'Bois, Jules Bois,' Hartman read.

'That's him. He's very clever. He did all that to cover up his involvement in the attack.'

'But you think he'll just up and confess to us like he confessed to your husband?'

'He could. It's part of his sickness.'

'What if he doesn't confess?'

'He must have had something to do with Landry's death,' Maggie insisted, struggling to impress him. 'He surely had something to do with Doctor Flemming's death.'

226

'Doctor Flemming?' Hartman sat back. 'Wasn't he that psychiatrist in Brentwood whose wife shot him?'

'Yes,' she said.

'So, what, is this guy all over the city talking people into killing their wives, their husbands, their mothers-in-law . . . I mean, how's he come to this psychiatrist in Brentwood?'

'He was seeing him before he came to see my husband,' Maggie said.

'And you think he talked the psychiatrist's wife into shooting him?'

'Drove her to it, maybe. I don't know all the answers, but you've got to start a serious investigation of him,' Maggie insisted. 'Look into his background. See who he really is and what he really does. That's what Jack Landry was trying to find out for me when he was murdered. Maybe Bois saw Jack follow him that day and realized I had hired him. Don't you see the possibilities?' Maggie asked.

'Okay,' Hartman said, standing. 'Don't bust a blood vessel. We'll go question the guy, see where he was the night of Landry's death and what he knows about today's exciting events.'

'My husband's secretary . . .' Maggie said, and paused to look away a moment. She couldn't help feeling like an informer, ratting on people who once trusted her.

'What about her?'

'I think she's been seeing this patient, this Jules Bois, socially. I think she might have given him some information about some of Grant's other patients, one of them being the man accused of stabbing Grant.'

'Ormand?'

'Yes. Have you spoken to him? I'm sure he'll be able to tie Jules Bois to this, now that you know what to ask.'

'You don't know?' Hartman responded.

Maggie held her breath.

'Know what?'

'I thought that was part of why you came here to blame this other guy. When they went to pick up Ormand, they found him in his closet, wearing a necktie, only the necktie was tied to a hook just high enough above him to keep his feet from reaching the floor. Suicide.'

Maggie shook her head.

'That can't be. It was definitely a murder,' she said.

'Oh. And why is that, Sherlock?'

'Because I just learned Jerome Ormand was an agoraphobic. He was terrified of being closed in, trapped. That's why he was seeing Grant, Don't you understand? The man would never put himself into a closet.'

Hartman shrugged.

'Or maybe it was his way of getting the courage or the inclination to commit suicide. I'm sure there's a psychiatrist out there who would testify for another defendant at the drop of a retainer – aren't you, Mrs Blaine?' he asked sharply.

Maybe Grant wasn't just babbling last night, Maggie thought sadly. Maybe he was right. Maybe lawyers, psychiatrists, even policemen had killed Satan. There was no guilt anymore. Even Bois, even Bois would go unpunished.

'I've told you a great deal more than I should have,' she said slowly, her voice tired and depressed enough to impress Hartman, 'in the hope that you would initiate an investigation.'

'I'll check on this,' Hartman promised.

'Thank you.'

'How's your husband?'

'He's . . . getting better,' she said.

'At least someone is,' Hartman quipped.

When they brought Lydia Flemming into the visitors' lounge, Maggie was surprised to see how well put together she was. She looked as though she had been brought directly from her home and not from some room on a mental ward. Her hair was brushed and neat. She wore makeup and a pretty light blue dress with sapphire earrings. The moment she saw Maggie, she smiled, but then, just as suddenly, the smile evaporated.

'It's Grant, isn't it?' she said just before she sat in the wide-armed, heavy-cushioned chair across from Maggie. Spiders with legs of ice ran down her spine.

'How did you know that?'

'I can see it in your face. You look like I looked when I gazed at myself in the mirror just before . . .

just before I lost Henry,' she said, and took a deep breath. She gazed around the lounge. 'It's really very comfortable here. Everyone's been quite considerate and I have a nice room with a window that looks out on the gardens and the fountain. I feel . . . safe.

'The children,' she continued, 'haven't been here. They make their duty calls, but I hear the strain in the voices. They think of me now as the woman who killed their father.'

'Aren't you?'

'No,' Lydia said, shaking her head. 'Someone else killed him long before I did, but' – she sighed – 'no one's ever going to believe that, I'm afraid. No one but you, perhaps,' she added, glancing up at Maggie.

'We didn't talk very much at the police station, Lydia. I was too upset. I'm sorry. I had to turn you over to Phil Martin.'

'I understand. I don't mind. I feel safe,' she reemphasized. 'What's happened?' she asked, her face turning serious.

She seems so sane, Maggie thought, so much the Lydia Flemming I remember.

'One of Grant's patients attacked him this morning and nearly killed him, stabbed him in the neck with a sharp fork.'

'Oh, dear. Henry grappled with a patient once. The man struck him on the temple with one of Henry's trophies, but Henry was a strong man, a football player, college wrestler. He took him

230

down quickly and restrained him, and then blamed himself for it.'

'Yes,' Maggie said, nodding. 'Grant will, too.'

Lydia smiled and nodded.

'Lydia, tell me about Henry. Why did you think he was no longer Henry?'

Tears came to her eyes. She sat quietly a long moment and then took a deep breath.

'I don't mean to upset you,' Maggie said.

'It's all right. It's not easy for me to tell anyone these things. The doctors here try to get me to talk about it, but I can't talk to them.' She leaned forward and whispered. 'I don't trust them.'

'Why not?'

'I'm not sure who they're working for,' she said. Maggie nodded. This was the paranoia, she thought, and wondered now if Carl Thornton was right: she had put herself into the madness and would get nothing substantial from Lydia Flemming.

Lydia looked at the attendant in the doorway and then at Maggie. She smiled.

'But somehow . . . maybe because of our friendship . . . I feel I can tell you. I feel I should tell you. You have Grant to worry about or you wouldn't have come.'

'I appreciate that, Lydia. Whatever it is, I know it's difficult for you.'

'You don't know how difficult.' She took another deep breath, looked away and then back at Maggie. 'Henry began taking on some of the characteristics of some of his patients,' she began.

'How do you mean?'

'I'm not even an amateur psychiatrist, Maggie, even though I spent a good deal of my adult life living with a psychiatrist, but I could recognize symptoms of paranoia, for one. It got so he locked the doors and closed curtains as soon as he arrived home. I would find him staring out the windows sometimes, watching the street. When I asked him what he was looking for, he would snap at me, "Nothing!" Often at night I would wake and find him missing from the bed. When I looked for him, I usually found him downstairs peering out the window or in his office just pacing.'

'He never told you why?'

'No. In fact, he got more and more belligerent about my inquiring. It was as if he wanted to drive me away from him, as if he thought . . .'

'What?'

'That whatever or whoever was after him would harm me if I was too close to him.' She sat back. 'It went that way for a while and then he began to undergo an even more dramatic personality change. It was never like Henry to forget to call me if he wasn't coming home or if he would be home very late. Henry was never selfish, never self-centered. He always thought about me first. Suddenly he stopped being interested in anything but himself. He never even asked about the children or cared to see our grandchildren.

'When he returned home from work, he would go right to that den and light up his computer. He told me he was working on some new book, some new theory about guilt.'

'Guilt?'

'Guilt being the cause of all our psychological problems and it being the fault of religion. Henry usually kept his current works on the long table in the den, the pages spread out for his editing. Often he would ask me to proofread for him, but not this time. This time he didn't want me anywhere near what he was doing.'

'So he was writing a book about it, too,' Maggie mused, her thoughts returning to Grant at the hospital.

'That's not the worst of it,' Lydia said quickly, as if she were afraid Maggie would lose interest or miss the point. She swallowed. 'He began . . .'

'What?'

She shook her head and began to cry. Maggie rose from the chair and went to her, putting her arm around Lydia's shoulders and holding her. She felt her shaking. The attendant at the door widened his eyes. After a moment Lydia took a deep breath and nodded.

'I'm all right.'

'If this is too difficult for you, I'll come back another time, Lydia.'

'No, no, I'll be all right. I want you to hear it,' she said. Maggie returned to the chair. The attendant relaxed and leaned against the jamb again.

Lydia closed her eyes, took a deep breath, and continued. 'I did become an amateur psychiatrist.

I went to Henry's reference material and I looked it up.'

'What?'

'What psychiatrists call paraphilias, disorders in which unusual or bizarre imagery or acts are necessary for sexual excitement.'

Maggie stared. She tightened her face with determination.

'That's why I say Henry took on the characteristics of some of his patients. It was as if the madness were infectious, especially the bizarre.'

'What do you mean, exactly?' Maggie asked.

'It got so he wouldn't go to bed with me unless he wore some article of women's clothing. I didn't know where he got these things or whose they might be. Of course, it was a turnoff for me, but he didn't seem to care. After a while it was more like a rape anyway,' she said with shame.

'More like rape?'

'I want you to see something,' she said, and began to unbutton her blouse. Maggie sat transfixed as Lydia pulled her right arm out of the sleeve and then lowered the brassiere cup over her right breast until Maggie saw the ugly abrasion that had become a scar.

'My God . . . what?'

'He bit me while we were having sex and wouldn't release or ease up. It got so he enjoyed inflicting a little pain on me whenever we were together like that. Finally I shut him out of my bedroom and he slept in the den.'

She started to cry. The attendant came forward.

'I'm all right. Please,' Lydia said.

'I'd better get her back to her room, ma'am,' he told Maggie.

'She's okay. Doctor Thornton said this would be okay,' Maggie insisted. The attendant retreated, reluctantly.

Lydia reduced her voice to a whisper.

'I couldn't tell anyone these things. My husband . . . one of the most respected psychiatrists in Los Angeles; in the country, for that matter . . . of course, I never told the children.'

'I wish you had told me sooner.'

'So do I, but he was erratic. Sometimes,' she said, wiping away the tears, 'he would come home and seem so normal and apologetic. I would think whatever this was . . . experiment, whatever, it was over, but it never ended. It was as if someone or something had gotten into his brain and poisoned him.'

Maggie nodded, her eyes brightening with the possibilities.

'Lydia, Grant has a former patient of Henry's. He told him his name is Jules Bois.'

'Does he claim to suffer from a compulsion, an obsession to instigate evil in others?'

'Yes,' Maggie said, her eyes widening with excitement.

'When he was seeing Henry, he called himself Thomas Forcas. Have you met him?'

'No. Did you ever meet Forcas?'

'No.'

'Grant described him as a tall, distinguished-looking man,' Maggie said.

'It's what I was afraid of,' Lydia replied. 'You don't have much more time.'

'Why not?'

'By the time he had tracked him to Henry, it was too late for me.'

'By the time who tracked him to Henry?'

'Father Dimmesdale,' she said. She leaned closer. 'I called him just before . . . before I killed that creature in Henry's body,' she whispered. 'He told me what to do. I never forgot his phone number. It is etched in my brain. 555–6666.'

She reached out and took Maggie's hand into hers.

'Call him, call Father Dimmesdale, and maybe, just maybe you won't have to kill Grant,' Lydia said.

16

Maggie found herself trembling when she returned to her vehicle and got behind the steering wheel. Lydia Flemming was swimming in a pool of madness, just as Carl Thornton had described; but what had put her there? Were they real events or imagined? That scar on her breast was real enough, but the descriptions of Henry were so astounding, how could there be any truth to them? If Henry was so weird, why hadn't any of his associates seen it? Was he only bizarre around Lydia? And who exactly was this Father Dimmesdale? Why would a priest be calling her and advising her to kill her own husband? Was he real or also something manufactured by madness?

Lydia's eyes had become electric at the end of their conversation and filled with wild static, the colors like neon, jetting through Maggie's own and into her brain, burning down to the vault of her deepest fears, rattling her very bones. Just maybe she wouldn't have to kill Grant? How did someone so gentle and pacific become so trigger-happy? Who in his or her wildest imaginings could have envisioned that little woman holding a .38 on her husband and actually pulling the trigger?

There are things about ourselves we die not knowing, Maggie thought. The biggest mystery is our own identity. We don't live long enough to make all the discoveries or perhaps the most important ones, she thought.

She sighed.

What was left to do? Maybe Grant would become stronger because of all this. He would become wiser and more in control of himself. People wake up when they hear distant bells tolling for them. They had almost tolled for him.

She really was very tired now and not very hungry. She drove home, made herself a slice of toast and some tea, and settled down to return the phone calls that had mounted up on the answering machine. Grant's mother took his recuperation for granted, barely pausing between descriptions of charity and social events to ask a question. If people were reincarnated out of the animal world or vice versa, Patricia Blaine was surely a descendant of or headed for life as an ostrich, Maggie thought.

Her own mother was sympathetic and very concerned. She volunteered to come right to Los Angeles, but Maggie assured her it wasn't necessary. The phone calls to friends went quickly when she explained how tired she was. It was true. She couldn't wait to soak in a warm bath and then crawl into bed. The bubbly water soothed her, helped her to calm down and meditate. For a few minutes at least, it felt as if she had slipped back into the safety and security of the womb itself.

Afterward, she fell asleep quickly, but she woke once during the night and heard what sounded like fingernails on the windowpane. She sat up and listened and then she went to the window that looked out on the street. Was that a deep shadow or was it a man silhouetted in the soft streetlight? she wondered. She stared and waited, but the shape took no form, nor did it move. Satisfied, she went to the bathroom. However, as she returned to her bed, she gazed out again and saw the shadow was gone.

It put a chill into her. She checked the house alarm to be sure it was armed before returning to bed. It took quite a while to fall back to sleep despite her fatigue and after she did, her dreams were fantastic, colorful and troubling. She rose early, deciding to go to her office first and check her messages before going to the hospital. She called the nurses' station first and was told Grant had had a very comfortable night and was going to be put on a regular diet immediately. The doctor hadn't been in yet, but they were expecting him shortly.

'Has his memory improved any?' she followed, holding her breath.

'Not much, Mrs Grant, but as he grows stronger, that's sure to happen,' the nurse predicted.

Buoyed by that, Maggie regained some of her characteristic energy and went to the office, churning through her messages, dictating letters, and rearranging her schedule. The partners stopped by and were happy to hear about Grant's physical progress. Everyone had the same faith in time healing his amnesia.

Just before she prepared to leave for the hospital, Maggie received a call from Carl Thornton.

'How did your visit with Lydia go?' he asked.

'You were right, I guess. She said so many disturbing things about Henry it was like visiting someone in the *Twilight Zone*.'

'Yes, I know. It's part of her illness,' he said.

'There was one thing, Carl, a scar on her breast. Did she ever tell you about it and explain how it got there?' Maggie asked, curious as to how Carl handled that aspect.

'No,' he said. 'That's a new one. How did it get there?'

'I don't even want to repeat it,' Maggie said.

'I understand.'

'Did you get a chance to see Grant this morning?'

'First thing.'

'And?'

'Give it time, Maggie. He'll get back to his old self before you know it,' Carl promised.

'Once he recuperates, could any of that amnesia return?'

240

'No, I doubt that. Call me if you need me. Anytime,' he added.

Thinking about it all reminded her of Bois and she decided to call Detective Hartman.

'I was going to call you after lunch, counselor. I interviewed your notorious Mr Bois last night.'

'And?'

'For one thing, he has a solid alibi for the night of Landry's death. He was having dinner with his next-door neighbor, an elderly lady right out of a Norman Rockwell painting entitled *Everyone's Grandmother*. They've sort of adopted each other since he moved into the building. I don't think I would have felt more out of place and off the mark if I had gone to interview the Pope.'

'What did you find out about him?' Maggie pursued.

'He was quite candid, actually. He's independently wealthy now and had once been a financial manager, among other things. He freely admitted he had been seeing your husband for a problem with depression. I didn't think it was right for me to question him any further about it.'

'Depression. He's lying.'

'Yeah, well, the only way to confirm that is to question your husband, who he highly respects, by the way. Will your husband answer questions about him when he's up to it?'

She hesitated.

'I didn't think he would, especially since the man is the reason your husband's still alive. Look, counselor, I don't know what your purpose is here, but I have my suspicions, and I can tell you that you're not going to manipulate this law enforcement agency. We don't have the manpower for these sort of games. Clarence Dunbar should go to the gas chamber.'

'This isn't about Dunbar,' Maggie protested.

'Well, it's not about Jules Bois, either.'

'I'm telling you I think the man's dangerous,' she insisted.

'Then maybe you ought to be the next patient your husband has . . . It sounds like rampant paranoia. Got to go. I have some real criminals to pursue,' Hartman quipped, and hung up.

Maggie sat fuming with the receiver in her hand for a moment and then quietly placed it in the cradle.

Maybe Jack Landry was working on another case and was actually the victim of a mugging. Maybe she had seen nothing more than a shadow outside the house, but that didn't explain away the dramatic changes in Grant, and it certainly didn't explain what had happened to Henry Flemming and why Lydia had done what she had done.

Maggie looked at the phone, recalled Lydia Flemming's warning, and went to tap out the number that had been etched in her memory.

The priest seemed to answer before the phone even rang.

'Hello.'

'Father Dimmesdale?' Maggie asked.

'Yes?'

'My name is Maggie Blaine. My husband is Doctor Grant Blaine, a psychiatrist in Los Angeles.'

'Who gave you my name and number?' the priest demanded.

'Pardon?'

'Who told you to call me?'

'Do you remember a Doctor Henry Flemming?'

'Of course. His wife shot him.'

'She told me to call you,' Maggie said.

The priest was silent a moment.

'I understand. In that case, Mrs Blaine, when do you want to come to see me?'

'Pardon?'

'I understand why you've called.' He had a deep, resonant voice, commanding and authoritative.

Maggie hesitated, a bit apprehensive. What was she getting herself into? She should just forget all this and go over to the hospital to help revive Grant's memory, but then the priest added something.

'I'd advise you to come to see me as soon as possible. In fact, it might already be too late for you, too.'

Maggie pulled into the driveway of the small house off Melrose Avenue in West Hollywood. With the late afternoon sun now sinking below the top of the Hollywood Hills, shadows crawled over the roofs, streets, and lawns.

Like many of the homes on this block, Father

Dimmesdale's Spanish-style two-bedroom was weathered and worn with age, its pale white finish marred with spidery cracks. Some of the tiles on the roof looked loose and broken. The patch of lawn wasn't maintained, but there were a half dozen healthy-looking orange, lemon, and grapefruit trees and rows of philodendron lining the walkway and bordering the front of the arched entrance.

Maggie turned off her engine and sat a moment. Her insides were still trembling. She took a deep breath to calm herself. What was she doing here? She told herself that just possibly this priest knew something about Henry Flemming's situation, something that might help explain all that had happened and was happening.

She got out of her car and walked to the front door, on which hung an enormous wooden cross. She looked for the door buzzer and saw the button was missing, only wires exposed, so she knocked and waited. Moments later, a short, plump man with bushy gray hair and thick, untrimmed gray eyebrows peered out at her through the opened door. He wore a clerical white collar and a dark blue jacket and trousers. Dangling over his chest on a thick silver chain was a jeweled silver cross, the stem covered with chips of sapphire.

Dimmesdale's hands were small enough to appear stunted. On his left pinkie, he wore a yellowish green polished stone in a silver setting. The priest stood barely five feet one or two. Although he wore a suit, he had his feet in a pair of fur-lined, worn black leather slippers and no socks. Dimmesdale's small, dark eyes looked lost in his swollen face. Bloated cheeks, thick ruby lips, and a bulbous nose seemed to be exploding on his relatively small skull.

'Mrs Blaine?'

'Yes,' Maggie said. Dimmesdale didn't invite her in immediately. He stood there, scrutinizing her for a moment, before stepping back.

'Come in,' he said.

Maggie stepped into the small alcove and Father Dimmesdale, after gazing outside a moment to see if there was anyone else with her, closed the door. There was a light fixture above them, but it was missing a bulb. The illumination from the room on the left and the corridor threw a soft light over the beige walls, which were literally inundated with religious paintings, scenes of the Nativity, the Sermon on the Mount, the Rising of Lazarus, all of the realistic school. It was like walking into a gallery of spiritual art.

'This way, please,' Father Dimmesdale said, indicating the room to the left. They crossed over the worn rug and entered what resembled a private prayer room in a sanctuary. Dozens of candles burned in silver holders on the mantel, above which was a replica of Jesus on the Cross. To the right were portraits of the Virgin Mary. Covering the small coffee table were chunks of agate, in the center of which was another print of Jesus at Golgotha. The air was heavy with the scent of garlic and Maggie saw it in dishes and even in vases where there would normally be flowers.

'Sit, please,' Father Dimmesdale said. Maggie took the worn, overstuffed chair and Dimmesdale sat on the settee across from her.

'How do you know Lydia Flemming?' he asked.

'My husband trained under Doctor Flemming and we all became very good friends. We all sort of drifted apart this past year. I'm a trial attorney, too busy for my own good, and Grant, my husband, became very busy with his practice, too.'

Dimmesdale nodded and smiled as if this were the same old story.

'After Doctor Flemming's tragic death, one of his patients contacted your husband to continue his therapy with him?'

'Yes,' Maggie said with surprise.

'And it's because of this patient that you called me?'

'Yes.'

'It's not just accidental that he chose your husband,' he said. 'We'll have to talk about the reasons.'

'Reasons?'

'Go on with your story first. I need to know the details.'

Maggie quickly explained what had happened to Grant and how Bois had come to the rescue.

'Brilliant new move. He astounds me all the time,' Dimmesdale said. 'Getting back to why this all might not be coincidental . . . your husband's not a religious man, is he?'

'No.' Maggie started to smile. 'Although he recently went to church, but for whatever reason he went, he was unsatisfied, even angry.'

'Religion, as we know it, is a failure in his eyes. He was always, shall we say, skeptical.'

'Yes.'

'I understand. There are other vulnerabilities, I'm sure, but that would take hours and hours of discovery. It's sufficient that he has an atheistic frame of mind to work on,' Dimmesdale said.

'I would not go so far as to say Grant's an atheist.'

'It doesn't matter. He was unprotected.'

'Unprotected?'

'In a universe divided between the forces of good and the forces of evil, religion provides us with the only weapons, the only salvation,' Father Dimmesdale said. 'Forgive me if I sound like a preacher,' he said, but he didn't relax his intense gaze. 'Our fortress is our faith and virtue. Once those are weakened, once the fiend knows where we are vulnerable, he attacks.'

'Fiend?'

'Satan,' Father Dimmesdale said.

Maggie relaxed with disappointment. She had been hoping to confront one of the more open-minded, well-educated members of the church, someone schooled in psychology and therefore perhaps someone Henry Flemming would have confided in for advice. The priest appeared to sense it and smiled.

'You think I'm bonkers, a candidate for your husband?'

'Well, no, I . . .'

'Lydia Flemming came to me because she learned I was an expert on such matters.'

'What matters?'

'Demons, evil.'

'Oh?'

'You're disappointed?'

'Well, I called you because I was hoping this patient of Grant's, who was also a patient of Henry's, might have been someone you knew, perhaps someone who had gone to confession. I was hoping to get some more background on the man,' Maggie added. 'Something concrete I could give to the police. He has everyone fooled, even them.'

'I'll give you background,' Dimmesdale said. 'But it's not the sort of thing you expected, hoped for, not that I blame you for that. I wish what I have to say wasn't true, but, alas,' he said with a sigh, 'it is, and painfully so. You're not a religious woman, either?'

'No,' Maggie replied quickly. Dimmesdale nodded and leaned forward.

'This patient of Doctor Flemming's was a man who called himself Forcas.'

'Yes. Then she did reveal his patient's name to you,' Maggie said, impressed.

'I told you. She came in a state of desperation. Revealing her husband's patient's name was the least of her concerns at the time.' Dimmesdale smiled. 'You know he has a sense of humor when he dabbles with our souls.'

Maggie raised her eyebrows in question.

'Who?'

'Lucifer.'

'Lucifer?'

'Satan, Beelzebub, Old Scratch. In the New Testament, the name *Satan* appears thirty-four times, while the expression *Devil* occurs thirty-six times. In the New Testament Satan is also termed the Dragon. The Prince of Air,' Father Dimmesdale continued.

'You said sense of humor?' Maggie repeated.

'Yes. The names he chooses, for example. Forras, or Forcas, is a renowned president in hell. Here,' Dimmesdale said, rising and going to his bookcase. He pulled a volume from the bottom shelf and brought it to Maggie, opening it to an illustration of Forcas on a pony. Maggie saw that it was a book on demonology.

'What's the name he's using as your husband's patient?'

Maggie hesitated.

'He didn't call himself Forcas, did he?'

'No.' If the things she had done in the past had enraged Grant, this would drive him over a cliff, she thought. But she felt the desperation Father Dimmesdale had painted Lydia with. After a moment Maggie said, 'Jules Bois.'

Again Dimmesdale smiled.

'The name also has some meaning for him. Let me show you.'

Dimmesdale flipped through the pages of the book until he found the chapter 'Demons in Literature' and ran his finger down to a reference to a play entitled *The Nuptials of Satan*, published in 1890.

'Note the author's name,' he said.

Maggie read.

'Jules Bois!'

'Who,' Dimmesdale said, raising the book to read, 'depicts Satan as a beautiful athletic youth, whose crackling hair reflects the heavenly stars like a glistening sea. The fiend loves flattery.'

He snapped the book closed and returned to his settee.

'According to what Lydia Flemming told me, Doctor Flemming was losing control of himself, first in small ways and then in bigger and more dramatic ones. It began with him becoming forgetful, neglectful, terribly distracted. All of his other patients fell to the wayside.

'He was plagued by dreams, visions, and haunted by the memories of his past indiscretions, sins, all of the memories of which had been stirred and resurrected by our unusual patient. Is this beginning to sound familiar?'

Maggie nodded, barely permitting herself to breathe.

'Which brings us back to why he chose your husband. Something led him to believe he would be vulnerable. You see,' Father Dimmesdale continued, 'the Devil knows only our evil thoughts. If he knew everything, he would not only be the

Ape of God, he would be what he intended to be.'

Dimmesdale sat back, pressing the tips of his fingers together to form a cathedral with his hands.

'You say you're not religious now, but do you have very much in the way of religious training . . . background?'

'Not really. But let me understand you, Father. You think my husband's patient believes he is Satan?' Maggie asked.

'No, Mrs Blaine. I think he *is* Satan.'

Maggie started to smile.

'Did he show your husband in some way that he knew of something immoral or illegal he might have done, something he wouldn't have expected anyone else to know?'

Maggie's smile quickly faded as she felt a warmth crawl up her chest, over her neck, and settle in her cheeks. She recalled the first time Grant had come home disturbed about Jules Bois because Bois knew about some of his past indiscretions.

'Yes,' she said. Dimmesdale nodded.

'There's more, isn't there? He told your husband about his most current victims and either you or your husband confirmed his stories?'

'Yes, but from a purely legal viewpoint, I can't be sure as to how much of a role he really did play. I wouldn't know how to prosecute him.'

'He is the archenemy of every pious act, the deceiver of men, but he must first be given the opportunity. Since he can read the evil thoughts in our minds, he chooses those who express them and are most vulnerable to his attack. Then he leads us to wickedness. The Devil can't get into a human soul, but he can get into our bodies. When he is completely victorious, he possesses us. We would need to be exorcised. This is what eventually happened to Doctor Flemming, I'm afraid. And what could very likely happen to your husband, if it hasn't already.

'I understand your skepticism,' Father Dimmesdale continued quickly. 'Ironically, it's that very skepticism that the fiend relies upon because it keeps us from being vigilant. You want to be skeptical; you don't want a universe in which there is an active, conscious evil at work. You would rather believe that evil is the by-product of social and psychological problems, something that can be corrected and eventually destroyed.'

Maggie nodded.

'Grant thinks we've destroyed Satan, destroyed the concept of evil. He's talking about redefining guilt, blaming religion for psychological problems in society today.'

'Is he . . . writing a book?'

'I don't know. I think so. He had a manuscript the other night.'

Dimmesdale nodded.

'He's nearly his, if not already so.'

Maggie winced.

'I thought, even for the church, belief in the Devil was a symbolic thing, that we had left the Middle

Ages,' Maggie said, a little more sharply than she had intended.

'Yes, we have left the Middle Ages, and so has Satan. Satan moves with the times; evil metamorphoses as well as good.' He leaned forward. 'Satan has chosen your husband and your husband's profession lately. He has found a way to turn the sword of psychoanalytic thought against itself and use it as his new weapon. In a sense he always did. He appealed to our paranoia, our illusions or delusions, he built upon our . . . what psychiatrists call . . . id, the animal in us, to get us to succumb to temptation and evil.

'Now, with our emphasis on the psychological to explain human behavior, our tendency at times is to forgive or mitigate our evil acts by claiming they are the result of psychological disorders, mental aberrations, temporary insanities . . . John W. Hinckley, Jr., for example. Remember him? He tried to assassinate President Ronald Reagan and succeeded in wounding him, remember? Our jury found him not guilty of criminal conduct by reason of insanity. Hinckley was a troubled young man, his family had nearly committed him to a mental hospital . . . on and on. It's what forensic psychiatrists call the cognitive standard or the M'Naughten rule, the incapability of knowing right from wrong at the time of the act, correct?' Dimmesdale smiled. 'Children who kill their parents, no matter how viciously or determinedly, must be forgiven because their parents abused them; policemen who beat their fugitives nearly to death must be understood because of the pressure under which they work; on and on it goes.'

'That's what Grant's been saying.'

'Of course. It fits. Imagine if there had been one other person in the Garden of Eden. Imagine if this one other person was a psychiatrist who was then asked by Adam to testify for Eve.

'"Lord," he would say, "Eve was under great strain. She felt unappreciated and was very insecure. She was paranoid. Everything was so perfect, she kept expecting something terrible to happen, especially after the dire warning.

'"And Lord, she was innocent. How would she recognize the face of evil? It wasn't even in her subconscious. No, Lord, Eve did not know what she was doing. Please, Lord, apply the cognitive rule."

'We should certainly apply it to Cain,' he continued. 'Look at what mental turmoil he lived under because of his brother Abel. If he had only been able to go into analysis, he might not have committed the first murder.'

Maggie started to smile.

'Don't look down on my ideas, Mrs Blaine,' Dimmesdale said sternly. 'Lydia Flemming realized too late that her husband had been invaded. His own patients, because of his weakness, were falling victim; and the same will happen to your husband's patients,' Dimmesdale prophesied.

Maggie shook her head.

'You'll have to come to these conclusions yourself.

But if you wait too long . . . somewhere some other psychiatrist will be getting a call from a former patient of Doctor Blaine, who will either have committed suicide or perhaps even murdered someone himself,' Dimmesdale predicted with cold certainty.

'Well,' Maggie said. She was trying to think of a graceful way to flee this house and this strange priest. 'Thank you for sharing your thoughts.'

Dimmesdale laughed.

'My thoughts won't help you if you don't believe in what I say.'

'Even if I did, what could I do against . . .' She had trouble saying it, but did. 'The Devil?'

'You must destroy the vessel in which Lucifer has poured his molten hate-filled self. As you see from my home, I have surrounded myself with those weapons that have proven effective against the fiend since time began. Once he gets past your wall of faith and virtue, you are vulnerable and must battle him with whatever has proven effective since Eden. Certain gems, such as the chrysolite and the agate, have been known to put the Devil to flight, as well as herbs and plants like garlic and rue. Salt is one of the things that puts real fear into the Devil.'

'Why salt?'

'It's the symbol of immortality and eternity. A dish of salt was often placed on the body of the deceased,' Dimmesdale explained. 'But alas, my dear, I believe it is too late for these remedies, for he has entered your husband's fortress. No, you can do only what I said . . . destroy his vessel.'

Dimmesdale went to the cabinet and opened the top drawer slowly. He reached in and brought out something wrapped in an embroidered piece of a shroud. He placed it on the table and carefully, reverently, peeled the material back to reveal a silver cross, the bottom of the stem of which was sharpened into a pointed blade. It glittered in the candlelight.

'The cross has always been blinding to the Devil. It is our most sacred symbol and the one that reminds him of Christ's sacrifice to drive evil from this world. It reiterates Satan's ultimate defeat and he cannot face it.

'But to be sure we will not fail . . .' Dimmesdale returned to the cabinet and brought out a small pewter bottle. He opened it. 'In here I have holy water, which in itself would singe and burn the fiend.' He tipped the bottle over the stem of the cross and poured a tiny stream of the water over it.

Maggie watched, wide-eyed, and then looked up at the small man.

'What . . . what am I supposed to do with that?'

'Drive it into his heart,' Dimmesdale said without hesitation. 'Before he drives himself into your husband completely.'

He wrapped the cross in the shroud again and then handed it to her.

'Take it and go. It's all I can do for you now.'

Maggie took it but shook her head.

'I can't kill a man.'

'No one is telling you to kill a man. Would I, a

priest, tell you to kill another man? You won't be killing a man, but you must kill the body in which the Devil currently resides.'

'If you're so certain of all this and you are sure this man is the Devil, why don't you destroy him yourself, Father?' Maggie challenged.

The priest looked away.

'I've told you how he can seize upon the evil in our hearts, Mrs Blaine. In my case . . . let's just say, I know I am vulnerable. I have sinned.'

The sincerity of his confession made her feel less aggressive. She started away.

'One final test to satisfy your doubt,' he said, walking beside her. 'As I have told you, the Devil is the Ape of God, copying that with which the Creator has endowed man. But being an imitator, he is never capable of completely assimilating the original. Something's always missing. If he is perfect in the sense that he is exactly like you and me, then he is merely a man with extraordinary powers; but if he is not . . .' He opened the door and she stepped out.

'God be with you, Mrs Blaine,' Dimmesdale said, and closed the door behind her.

17

Maggie took a deep breath and looked at the well-lit lobby of the building. An elderly gentleman came out and walked up the street, but other than that, there was very little activity. After her disappointing visit with this Father Dimmesdale, she decided she had to confront this man once and for all. It was almost out of curiosity as much as anything else. Who was this man who could influence, control, and fool so many people? Perhaps if she confronted him, she could get him to leave them alone, to stay away from Grant.

She opened the car door and stepped out slowly. At the front of the building, she took another deep breath and then pressed the button next to the name Jules Bois. A moment later, he spoke.

'Yes?'

'Mr Bois, my name is Maggie Blaine. I'm Doctor Blaine's wife and I'd like to see you.'

'Well . . . of course. I hope he's all right,' the nearly muffled voice replied.

'Yes, he's all right,' she said.

'Good. Please. Come right up,' he said, and she heard the buzzer unlock the front door. She took another deep breath for courage and entered. She pushed the button for the elevator. The doors opened immediately and she stepped in.

A few moments later, she stepped out and up to the apartment door. Shortly after she pushed the buzzer, the door was opened, but instead of Bois, an elderly lady gazed out at her.

'Oh, I'm looking for Mr Bois,' Maggie said.

'This is his apartment. I was just leaving. He asked me to answer the door. Please, come in,' she said. Maggie entered the apartment and the elderly lady closed the door.

'I'm Amanda Lucy, his next-door neighbor,' the elderly lady said.

'How do you do?' Maggie said, and thought this must be the nice old lady Hartman had referred to.

'Mr Bois will be out in a moment. Nice to have met you, dear,' she said, and left the apartment.

Maggie gazed around. Everything looked so neat, clean, and new. He was no slob, that was for sure. She stepped gingerly into the living room and a moment later, appearing almost out of thin air, Jules Bois came up behind her.

'So you've found me,' he said, and she spun around.

What she saw almost caused her to drop not only

the wrapped cross, but her purse as well. Her heart pounded, and a cold sweat broke out on the back of her neck. Her cheeks were immediately flushed. She actually felt faint and feared she would go unconscious.

'You? You're Mr Bois? But I thought . . . you were an attorney.'

'I am, and when I'm an attorney,' he said, 'I'm Thomas Becket.'

The man who had nearly seduced her, the man who had taken her to dinner in that cozy Italian restaurant, stood before her in his robe, his hair neatly brushed, his face cleanly shaven, and reeking of a sweet cologne.

'It's sort of an original idea, I think,' he said, smiling warmly. 'If you can be more than one person, why not have more than one name?' he said. 'I have a whole set of friends, acquaintances, who know me as Thomas Becket, and a whole set who know me as Jules Bois, when I'm Jules Bois.'

Maggie shook her head, her mouth agape. He laughed.

'We did have an enjoyable evening, didn't we? I don't mean to pry, but did you ever find out why your husband was unreachable on such an auspicious occasion?'

'Yes,' she said, her voice raspy, 'I have the feeling it was because of you.'

'Me?'

'Who are you? I mean, really?' she asked.

'I'm one of those fortunate people who are many

things,' he replied calmly. 'Please, have a seat. I'd love to hear why you have come to see me.' He stepped forward, gesturing toward the beige settee.

Maggie retreated quickly, thinking now she would just run out, but when her gaze went to Bois' bare feet, she paused. All the toes on the left foot were gone. It turned her into a statue of ice. What was it Father Dimmesdale had said about the final test? 'The devil is the Ape of God, but being an imitator, he is never capable of completely assimilating the original. Something's always missing. If he's the same as you and me, then he's merely a man, but if he's not . . .'

'I see you're looking at my foot. Lawn mower accident years and years ago. My father had me cutting the grass before I was really old enough to handle a power mower. I must say, it presents a problem for me whenever I go to buy shoes. So' – he put his hands on his hips – 'if you didn't know I was Thomas Becket, why did you come to see me?'

'I . . . want you to stop seeing my husband. I want you to leave him alone. I don't know what you're up to or who you really are, but I know you've done evil things,' she said, her throat so dry now, she was afraid she wouldn't be able to speak.

'Really?'

He stepped toward her. Maggie instinctively retreated and at the same time pulled the cloth from the cross.

'What is that? A cross?'

'It's been bathed in holy water,' she said, 'by a priest.'

Bois smiled. Then he shook his head.

'Who do you think I am?' He stepped toward her and she backed away. 'Dracula?' he said, and laughed. 'I must say, this is the most original come-on I've ever experienced. Bravo, Mrs Blaine. This could be a very exciting night . . . for both of us,' he continued, and undid the strap on his robe.

Maggie shook her head as if to deny the reality of this confrontation. This was insane. How did she let herself get into this? What made her think she could frighten or reason with such a man?

'We'll make love like you've never made love before,' he said. 'A woman with your drive and energy should have a lover who can give her what she deserves.'

'Stay back,' Maggie warned. 'I know you were seeing Henry Flemming and I know what you did to him. I've told the police.'

'Henry Flemming did everything to himself, and to his wife, I might add. He was already more troubled than I was when we first met. I tried to help him, just as I've been trying to help Grant.'

'You won't anymore,' Maggie predicted. 'I won't let you.'

'Oh, you don't have to worry, Mrs Blaine. I'm finished with your husband,' Bois said, 'but I'm not finished with you.'

Bois came forward again. She turned toward the

doorway. Bois saw where she was looking and laughed.

'Are you expecting someone else? The cavalry, perhaps?' Bois laughed again and came at her.

She started to turn away, intending to rush past him and out the door, but he scooped her at the waist and pulled her toward him.

'Why did you really come up here, Maggie? Admit it to yourself and enjoy the bountiful pleasures of self-indulgence. Relax. It's always better that way,' he said, and brought his lips to her face. She tried to turn away, but he seized her head with his left hand and forced her to turn his way. She felt his erection building, prodding.

'Give it up, Mrs Blaine,' he whispered into her ear. 'As an attorney, you can see the difficulty of accusing me of rape. You came up here, and after we had a tryst, a romantic dinner, too. Who will the world believe – you, Mag Pie? Just lay back and enjoy,' he added, pushing her to the settee.

'Let me go, damn you!'

She seized his shoulder and dug in her nails.

He grasped her at the throat and held her back as he dropped the robe from his body. Then he moved over her. Without hesitation, desperate and in a frenzy, she brought her right hand around, the cross now grasped in her fingers tightly, and drove it hard and fast, with all her strength, into Bois' left side, just under his armpit.

He gasped, released his hold on her, gazed into her

eyes, smiled, and stepped back. Then his expression changed, the joviality leaving his face.

'You weren't kidding,' he said. 'There is holy water on this.'

He folded before her, falling on his right side, the sharpened cross embedded so that the Christ icon faced her. Blood streamed down and over his chest. He shuddered and then went still.

Maggie's first thought was to flee. She stepped past him and went to the apartment door. When she opened it, she found the corridor empty. She rushed out to the elevator, hit the button, and lunged in when the doors opened. As she caught her breath and the elevator descended, the realization of what she had done settled in.

'My God!' she cried. 'I must have killed him!'

The doors opened on an empty lobby. She stood there a moment and then went out slowly, deliberately, to her car. She got in, picked up the car phone, and dialed 911.

'This is Maggie Blaine,' she said. She rattled off the address. 'I've just stabbed a man in self-defense. I think he's dead or dying. Send an ambulance.'

The bubble light on the police car behind her resembled a toy top, mesmerizing with its spinning. Maggie sat quietly in her automobile. Outside, on the sidewalk, two uniformed policemen spoke softly. Another black and white pulled up in front of her and two more uniformed officers got out and began a conversation with the two who had already arrived.

Everyone was waiting for Detective Hartman to come down from the apartment. When he finally appeared, all eyes were on him. He paused in the doorway and looked at Maggie. She was staring down and didn't see him approach the car from the passenger's side until he reached for the door handle.

She looked up sharply as he got in. For a moment he just sat there staring out the front window of the automobile. Then he took a deep breath and turned to her.

'I think most people, even defense lawyers, would say I've been very patient with you, Mrs Blaine. Some might even call me a horse's ass.'

'What are you talking about?'

He stared and then smirked.

'There's no body up there; dead body, that is. And what's more, there's no blood. When someone is stabbed and falls to the floor, he or she usually bleeds and some of that blood stains the carpet.'

'What?' She shook her head. 'I did it. He grabbed me, tried to rape me, and I . . . I did it.'

Hartman stared at her, gazed out the side window a moment, and then turned back.

'All right. How did you get up there?'

'How did I get up there? I went to the front, pushed the buzzer by his name, and when he buzzed me in, I went up.'

'You spoke to him through the intercom?'

'Yes. Look, when I got to the apartment, there was a neighbor there. I forgot her name. Mrs . . . Lucy?'

'Yes, that's his neighbor. I spoke with her before and I spoke with her now. She told me Mr Bois left earlier today.'

'Left? Left for where?'

'He didn't tell her. He asked her to look after his things until he sends for them.'

Maggie shook her head.

'That's not true. That can't be true. She's lying.'

'You insist you killed him?'

'I know I killed him!' Maggie cried.

'Okay.' Hartman opened the door. 'Let's go upstairs together.'

Maggie got out of the car. Her legs were shaking, but she held together and followed Hartman into the building.

'Why did you come here, Mrs Blaine?' Hartman asked as they rode up the elevator.

'To put an end to all this, to confront this man, a man Father Dimmesdale believes is the Devil himself,' she blurted.

Hartman's eyebrows rose.

'Father Dimmesdale? And who might he be?'

'Someone Mrs Flemming told me to see,' Maggie said as the doors opened.

'Mrs Flemming? The one who shot her husband?'

'Yes.'

'Isn't she in the loony bin?'

Maggie looked toward the apartment door. It was open and Hartman's associate, a younger detective, was talking to Amanda Lucy. The elderly lady

266

paused to look as Maggie and Detective Hartman approached.

'Where did the body fall?' Hartman asked.

Maggie looked at the floor. It was clean, spotless, not a drop of blood and no Bois.

'Right there,' she said, pointing. 'You remember me, don't you?' she asked Mrs Lucy.

The old lady looked at the young detective first and then at Maggie before shaking her head.

'I'm sorry, I don't.'

'I was just up here! You let me in,' Maggie cried. 'What is this?'

'Oh, dear,' Mrs Lucy said. She brought her hand to her mouth and her eyes went wide and frantic.

'Take it easy, Mrs Blaine,' Hartman said, stepping forward. 'You're frightening her.'

'Frightening her? What do you think she's doing to me?'

Hartman seized her at the elbow and pulled her back before turning to the elderly woman.

'You can go, ma'am,' he told the elderly lady. She looked very grateful and hurried past Maggie and out the door.

'She's lying. She must be part of this.'

'Part of what? Is she hiding his body? Did she clean up the blood? Why?' Hartman asked. 'What's going on, Mrs Blaine? Are you a one-woman team out to wear down the Los Angeles Police Department?'

Hartman's young partner smiled.

'I . . . don't understand,' Maggie said.

'Imagine how I feel,' Hartman replied.

She glanced at him and then at the floor.

'You checked the other rooms, the bathroom, closets?'

'You want me to find the body of someone you killed that bad? Yes, of course we checked around. If you go look in the closets, you'll find most everything's gone. From the dresser drawers as well.'

'I did stab him in self-defense,' she insisted. She shook her head. 'I did. He attacked me right here.'

'Okay. On the way out we'll check the garbage chute. Maybe he had a good cleaning lady, right, Carnesi?'

'Right,' the young detective said.

Maggie straightened up, regaining her composure. She blinked back the tears at her eyelids.

'Is it all right if I leave, then?' she said.

'Frankly, Mrs Blaine, I don't give a damn,' Hartman said in his best Clark Gable voice, and Carnesi roared.

Maggie hurried out to the elevator. Her heart was pounding as she hit the button and traveled down. All the uniformed policemen, aware of the situation, stared at her as she walked to her car. She took a deep breath, started the engine, and drove away, her hands shaking every time she lifted them from the wheel.

The car phone rang. She fumbled it and then took a firmer grip.

'Hello.'

'Maggie, it's Phil. The hospital has been looking for you.'

'Grant?'

'Yes, he's apparently been asking for you.'

'What?'

'The amnesia, it's over,' Phil said.

'Oh, God,' Maggie said. She started to cry, sucked in her breath, and headed for the hospital.

Grant was actually sitting up in bed and eating a soft-diet early dinner when she arrived at his room. He looked ravenously hungry and practically ignored her arrival.

'Hi,' he said quickly, and put another spoonful of oatmeal into his mouth. She kissed him on the cheek and he reached for his coffee.

'How are you, Grant?'

'I feel like Rip van Winkle, and from what they tell me, it hasn't been that long.'

'No. No one expected this fast a recovery.'

'Beat Christ, huh?'

'Pardon?'

'My resurrection. His took three days,' Grant said, and laughed.

'Oh. Yes. I guess it must feel sort of like a resurrection to you.' She pulled a chair up to the bed and sat. Grant paused and considered her.

'You look worse than me,' he said. 'I guess you've been overwrought with worry. I'm sorry, honey.'

'Do you remember all of it now, Grant? What happened to you at the office?'

'Sure,' he said. 'Mr Ormand did not appreciate

my efforts to have him stay, so he forked me.' Grant laughed. 'Go fork yourself,' he said.

Maggie smiled with confusion.

'How can you laugh about it, Grant? You nearly died.'

'It wasn't personal,' he said. 'I just happened to be at the other end of the fork at the wrong time. A little carelessness, that's all. Mr Ormand needs more tender loving care. He has to be eased out of his psychosis, not tugged. I should have known better.'

'He won't be eased out of anything,' Maggie said.

'What do you mean?'

'I guess I'll be the one to tell you first.'

'Tell me what?'

'He's dead, Grant. The police found him hanging in the closet.'

Grant paused and then nodded.

'Gosh, that's too bad. I suppose he couldn't live with the guilt. See what guilt can do to you, Maggie?' He shook his head and looked despondent.

'It wasn't your fault, Grant. If it was anyone's fault, I'm sure it was that man's.'

'That man's? Who?'

'Jules Bois or whoever he is. Grant . . .' She bit down on her lower lip, tears streaming down her cheeks.

'What is it, sweetheart? I'm going to be all right.'

'It's not that.'

'You haven't done anything else, have you, Maggie? It was enough you put that detective on Mr Bois,' he said in a soft tone.

270

She sat back and pressed her lips together as if to keep herself from talking.

'What have you done now, my love?'

'Grant, a man attacked you, nearly killed you. Bois just happens to come upon the scene in time? What do you say about that?'

'I'd say I was a lucky man.'

'Don't you think this is all too convenient, Grant?'

'Criminal attorney's paranoia again? Come on, Maggie. Bois was just early for his appointment. We should be grateful.'

'Grateful?' She started to laugh. 'Did you know that Fay has been seeing this man socially?'

'Fay's been a very lonely woman, neglected, very insecure. I can't blame her for reaching out and finally pleasing herself. Mr Bois can be very charming.'

'But . . .'

'Stop worrying. No one got Jerome Ormand to do this to me. He had a logical reaction to what I had done to him.'

'Grant, I went to his apartment. I confronted him and he tried to rape me, so I stabbed him,' she said.

'What?'

'But when the police came, there wasn't any body, and there wasn't any blood. What's more, the neighbor, an elderly lady, who was there when I first arrived, claimed she had never seen me before. And she was the one who let me into the apartment.'

'You stabbed him but there wasn't any body or any blood.'

'Yes.'

Grant stared at her a moment.

'Maggie, you're the one who sounds like she should be in this bed.'

'I know. I'm going mad.' She took a deep breath and sat up. 'But I won't let this happen. I won't let him do this to us,' she said firmly.

'Who? Do what?'

'Never mind. We've got to get you up and around first. That's the priority,' she said.

Grant shook his head.

'Stabbings, no bodies, no blood? Lying elderly neighbors? I think maybe both of us are due for a vacation, Mag.' He closed his eyes and leaned back against his pillow. 'You'll tell me all of this later and I'll figure out what happened. Maybe . . . you've been hallucinating? You're not the only one. Right now, I'm suddenly tired, very tired.'

'Okay. We'll talk about it later, Grant. For now, you just rest.'

'Right,' he said, nodding, still with his eyes closed.

She watched him awhile. His breathing grew regular, and in moments he was asleep.

Carl Thornton was just coming down the hallway when she emerged from the room.

'I hear he's back.'

'Yes,' she said. 'You were right.' She leaned against the wall to steady herself and Carl grabbed her arm.

272

'Whoa. What's wrong, Maggie?'

'I need a strong cup of coffee, maybe something stronger.'

'Let's go down to the hospital cafeteria. The coffee here is usually pretty stale by this time of day. It should take the hair off your chest,' he said, and held her arm as they went toward the elevator.

On the way down, she began to tell him what she had done and what had occurred.

'Maybe you just wounded him, Mag, or nicked him and he fainted. Then he woke up and left.'

'I felt that sharpened cross go into his body, Carl,' Maggie said. They were at the table, sipping coffee.

'No evidence of blood and the old lady doesn't remember you?'

'Yes. As you can imagine, the police, especially Detective Hartman, are somewhat upset with me.'

'I can imagine,' Carl said, laughing. 'So the old woman next door claims he's gone?'

'That's what she told the police.'

'Good riddance.'

'But that doesn't explain it, does it? It's all so . . . strange – Lydia Flemming, the priest, my stabbing no one, Grant's miraculous recovery . . .'

'Not so miraculous. I predicted his recovery, remember?'

'Yes. Yes, you did. Thank you, Carl.'

'It's all right. He'll be home in a few days and you'll get your lives back on track.'

She smiled.

'I hope so.'

'I know so,' Carl said.

'But what if that man didn't leave, Carl? What if he starts all this again?'

Carl considered.

'Let me do some digging around. It's not ethical for one psychotherapist to investigate another's patients, but in this case . . .'

'Yes, please Carl. Do what you can or I'll . . . I'll go mad myself!'

He stared at her a moment. Her hair was disheveled, her face flushed. He had never seen Maggie Blaine this way.

'Okay, Maggie. I'll do it.'

'Thank you, Carl. Thank you,' she said, squeezing his hand. Then she closed her eyes, the exhaustion hitting her like a punch in the stomach.

'You'd better go home and get some rest, Maggie.'

'Okay.'

'Can you make it on your own?'

'Yes, I'm fine, Carl. Thank you,' she said, rising.

'I'll call you tomorrow, and I'll look in on Grant before I leave the hospital.'

She smiled and then went home.

When she arrived, she decided to make herself a cup of warm milk. She got undressed and into her nightgown first and then warmed the milk. As she sipped it, she reviewed the events of the past few hours, feeling now it had all been a dream, a horrible nightmare. Maybe Grant was right: maybe she had hallucinated everything.

As she wandered back toward the bedroom, cup

steaming in her hands, she paused at Grant's den and turned on the lights. She had the strange sensation that someone had been there, even though the alarm pad on the garage door had indicated no one had entered this house. Still, she moved about the office, checking the windows to be sure they were locked and not opened, and then she stopped at the desk and looked down at the manuscript Grant had been working on. It looked like three, four hundred printed pages.

She gazed at the title page.

THE SEVENTH WAVE by Grant Blaine, *A Study of the Negative Effects of Guilt on the Human Psyche.*

She wasn't going to read any of it now, even though she had always wondered what it was about and why Grant was so secretive about it. Before she turned away, however, she spotted a folded page with just enough of a signature visible to demand her interest. She unfolded it and read.

The manuscript I promised you. Henry would have wanted you to finish it and get it published.

Best,
Jules Bois

It was as if the paper were on fire. She dropped it and stepped away. Her heart pounded so hard, she thought she would faint. Then she stepped forward again, now her curiosity piqued, and gazed at the front page, the preface.

The idea that guilt is the root cause of most of our psychological difficulties has more merit than we would first believe. We've got to stop worrying about being selfish. First, we must please ourselves and when we are happy, we will best be able to help others. Guilt is the great incapacitator and unfortunately, most of our so-called organized religions weigh us down with it. Confession, asking forgiveness, ten Hail Marys, fast for Yom Kippur . . . atone, atone, atone, it's maddening, it's what makes us mad.

We no longer measure things in the traditional Judeo-Christian way. The mind is its own place and, as John Milton wrote, 'makes a heaven of hell or a hell of heaven.' In other words, we've got to come to a realistic understanding of guilt and how it can incapacitate us. Once we do that, we realize being selfish isn't as bad as the corporate religious groups tell us it is.

Once we understand that evil as we were taught it no longer exists in our sophisticated world, we can throw off the burden of remorse and become happier, well-adjusted, and more productive people.

Maggie stepped away from the desk, her eyes glued to the pages as if they might jump up after her. These weren't Grant's words; these couldn't be Grant's thoughts. She felt an inherent evil in them, an evil that reached the bottom of her stomach and made her cringe.

Suddenly she was filled with rage and determination. She put the cup of warm milk down and went to the fireplace. She turned on the gas, lit the fake logs, and went back to the desk. In a swift, impulsive, but decisive move, she brought the packet of pages to the fire and cast them in. They exploded in sparks, flying up the chimney, and then . . .

It was as if she heard someone scream. She actually put her hands over her ears. It only lasted a few seconds and it was gone. The pages folded into the flames and were quickly reduced to ashes.

A great sense of relief came over her. She smiled, watched the flames consume the last piece of paper, and then turned down the fire. She stared at the ashes a moment before turning and leaving the den, putting the lights out behind her.

After she crawled under the blanket and started to close her eyes, the phone rang. It was the hospital.

'I'm sorry to bother you, Mrs Blaine, but your husband won't go to sleep until he speaks to you.'

'Oh? Okay. Thank you.'

'Maggie.'

'Grant? Are you all right?'

'Are you all right? I woke up, realized you had been here and left, and remembered some of the things you babbled. Are you all right?'

'Yes, Grant. I'm okay now, darling.'

'Great. I'll be home before you know it, Maggie,

and things will be different. We've got to get serious about becoming parents, honey. That's the first thing that came to my mind when I realized what had happened to me.'

'I think you're right Grant.'

'What about partnerships, law cases, careers . . .'

'We'll find a way to do it all. We'll make the compromises that matter.'

'Good. Okay. Have a good night's sleep.'

'You, too, honey.'

'Good night.'

'Good night,' she said, and hung up.

There were shadows in this house; there were shadows outside. But suddenly she no longer was afraid of them.

18

Carl Thornton reached her at the office toward the end of the day. She had gone to the hospital to have lunch with Grant and had met with his doctors, who told her he would be going home after another day. Buoyed by the good news, she attacked her work with familiar vigor. It really did feel like a cloud had been lifted.

Before Carl called, however, she received a call from Father Dimmesdale.

'You've done well,' he told her.

She explained what had happened, but he didn't seem a bit fazed.

'It's what happens. You met the fiend and drove him away,' he insisted.

When she hung up, she wondered if he wasn't right. The mere thought of it put ice in her spine. How could an intelligent, well-educated,

279

and successful professional woman in the nineties believe in such fantasy, the fodder for horror movies? Carl Thornton, fortunately, she thought, came to her rescue. He told her to meet him for a drink at O'Healies. He was there waiting for her at a booth when she arrived.

'Why did you choose this place?' she asked as she slid in across from him.

'I know it's a favorite lawyer's hangout. Why?'

'Nothing. Just that . . . I met that man here. He pretended to be an attorney.'

'That figures.'

'Why?'

He ordered them drinks and then sat forward. His face was taut, serious, his eyes a bit narrow.

'Using one of those timeworn expressions, we have what we might call a loose cannon,' he said. 'Every profession – lawyers, doctors, teachers, police – has a built-in good ole boys' club, Maggie. We all cover for our own, even if it means lying, distorting evidence, ignoring, literally burying the truth sometimes. I guess it's a form of professional paranoia. No one wants to be tainted by someone else in his field, and everyone fears the wrath of the public or the tendency of the public to treat everyone as if he or she were the same as the bad apple.'

Maggie shook her head.

'I'm not following.'

'Cops cover up for bad cops because they don't want people to think all cops are bad. It's the same for lawyers, doctors . . . we all need a certain amount

280

of blind faith in order to function, keep our clientele, as it were.'

'What does this have to do with this man who calls himself Jules Bois, Carl?'

'I spoke first with Michael Sacks, one of Henry Flemming's associates, who told me about this patient who went by the name of Thomas Forcas.'

'Yes?' Maggie said.

'According to Michael, in the beginning, Henry was skeptical about him and tracked him back to a Doctor Theodore Denning in San Francisco, a psychiatrist of some note. He's published a number of articles in prestigious journals and lately has written a book on psychogenic fugue, a book I believe came out of his experiences with a patient named Colin Barret.'

'Who is he?'

'Are you hungry? This might take a while, and –'

'The thought of eating makes my stomach do somersaults.'

Carl nodded and continued.

'Colin Barret is Thomas Forcas, a.k.a. Jules Bois,' he said. Maggie sat back.

'So, he's a patient who's been to a few psychiatrists and each time he gives them a different name?'

'He's more than that,' Carl said, 'which brings me back to professional paranoia.'

Maggie held her breath. Was Carl going to confirm Father Dimmesdale's theory?

'What do you mean, he's more?'

'He's a psychiatrist himself, Maggie,' Carl said.

She sat back, not stunned and shocked by the revelation as much as she was frightened by it. From her own experiences with clients who had been treated by psychologists and psychiatrists, from counselors of all ilk, and from Grant's stories and professional activities, she had, as well as most people she knew, developed the belief that people who were trained to get into our deepest thoughts, unwrap our most secret subconscious images, and somehow get us to face the truths about ourselves were modern-day wizards, professionals with power, talented, blessed, educated, whatever . . . they had mental weapons as deadly as guns and knives. They could cause people to doubt their loves, their hates, the wisdom of their own lives. They could influence great changes, and of course forensic psychologists and psychiatrists could literally determine an individual's fate and freedom.

It was as if Carl had told her about a psychotic policeman or a psychotic brain surgeon.

She smiled and Carl's eyebrows lifted.

'What's so funny?'

'In a sense I'm relieved,' she said.

'Oh?'

'He's not Satan, even though I'll swear to the day I die that I stabbed him in that apartment.'

Carl laughed.

'No, he's not Satan, but I would venture to guess that he thinks he is.'

'Really? What else do you know?'

282

'I spoke with Doctor Denning. At first he was reluctant to say anything, of course, but once I explained and described it all, he relented and agreed to join me in this . . . pursuit, I guess you could say.'

'Why don't you just go to the police? They would believe you before they would believe me, and now they will believe most of what I've said,' she declared excitedly.

'We've got a problem with that.'

'What?'

'First, as you know, what went on between Colin Barret and his psychiatrist is privileged information, and second, what am I going to tell them? You've already had that experience with Detective Hartman. There's nothing concrete, no smoking gun. A man who is brilliant when he is a psychiatrist manipulates people to do bad things? None of the people really understand what's happening to them. You interviewed Dunbar and saw that for yourself. You don't have to be a psychiatrist to understand the problem, but even if these victims understood what had happened to them, what's their defense? The Devil made me do it?'

Maggie nodded, disappointed.

'What is psychogenic fugue?' she asked. 'I don't recall Grant ever mentioning it to me.'

'It's a dissociative disorder. Unexpected travel away from home or customary work locale with assumption of a new identity and an inability to recall one's previous identity.'

'A form of amnesia?'

'Precisely. Barret was an atypical self-made man. He was orphaned at five and placed in four different foster homes before remaining in one permanently and eventually being adopted by his foster parents, William and Katrina Barret.

'Contrary to what is more commonly the case with children passed from one familial setting to another, Colin appeared to be stable and was an excellent student. He won an academic scholarship to college and then was awarded a grant to continue in medical school. He never married.

'A little more than three years after he had set up his practice, he demonstrated the first signs of psychosocial stress. Both his foster parents were killed in a gruesome traffic accident involving a tractor-trailer truck whose driver was drunk. Once again, he was an orphan. Although his psychogenic fugue was relatively brief then, it was, nevertheless, quite dramatic.

'Barret left home, proceeded to get on the highway and hitchhike almost across country, claiming to be a freelance writer doing a book on Americana.'

'A book? He gave Grant a manuscript he claimed Henry had been working on with him and he asked Grant to finish the work. Grant was actually working on it,' Maggie revealed.

'Really. Where is it?'

'I burned it in the fireplace last night, Carl. It was horrible . . . a justification for evil acts.'

Carl's eyes grew small for a moment and then he shook his head.

'Grant might be upset about that.'

'I don't care. I don't want anything to do with that man around us anymore,' she said firmly. 'Tell me what else you've learned, though.'

Carl sipped his drink and continued.

'Two weeks after his disappearance, he returned to his true identity while he was languishing in a motel. He flew back home to return to his practice. He had the presence of mind, however, to seek psychiatric help himself and began therapy with Doctor Denning, who was a little over a hundred miles from his home. Distance gave him a sense of security. He was naturally afraid that his own patients would discover he was in analysis and it would hurt his own practice.

'The bouts of psychogenic fugue continued periodically, the longest seizure being a few days less than two months. Incredibly, because of his brilliance, perhaps, Barret's patients continued to hold him in high regard whenever he did function normally, none knowing, of course, that he did have his own psychological problems.

'However, Doctor Denning revealed that about this time Barret's disorder was taking on a strange new twist. Although Barret still began sudden and unexpected travel and was unable during the period to recall his past, the new identities he assumed always had some similar characteristics: advising people, influencing them, always to do evil.'

'The very thing we ascribe to the Devil,' Maggie said.

'Yes. Troubled by what he was doing, the schizo-phrenia had a deep effect on him. A part of him wanted to be cured, and a part of him enjoyed the sense of power, this godlike identity. Denning began to find himself in a new relationship with his patient, one of combativeness. In the end he determined Barret needed even more treatment and recommended he see someone who specialized in his problem and perhaps go into a clinical setting.'

'In other words,' Maggie concluded, 'Doctor Denning had grown afraid of his patient and wanted to end the relationship?'

'Yes.'

'And that was when he first saw Henry, but as Forcas?' Maggie concluded.

'Yes.'

'My God. Does Grant know any of this?'

'A little. I started to lay the groundwork with him today. I want to take it a bit slower with him, under the circumstances,' he added.

Maggie took a long sip on her drink and then sat back.

'What about this Father Dimmesdale? How does he fit in?'

'Lydia did tell me about him. I called the monsig-nor, who is a personal friend, and he told me about Father Dimmesdale. Seems he was encouraged to retire after the disclosure of an episode with some young priest.'

'His sin,' Maggie muttered, 'why he couldn't con-front the Devil?'

'What?'

'Nothing.'

'Anyway, according to the monsignor, who sees himself as more than an amateur psychiatrist, Dimmesdale's reaction to all this was to develop acute paranoia, seeing Satan everywhere, even in the higher echelon of the church itself.'

'How did Lydia come to him?'

'It was the other way around. One of Dimmesdale's parishioners was tempted to do evil by the then Thomas Forcas, which put Dimmesdale on the case, trailing him to Henry, who apparently just about threw him out of his office. You remember Henry's attitude about religion.'

'Yes.'

'That only served to convince Dimmesdale Henry was in the hands of the Devil. That, combined with what was happening to Lydia . . . well, anyway, the rest you know,' Carl said.

'But Carl, I swear to you, I drove that sharpened cross into him.'

'My guess now is you did wound him. Did he say anything right after you struck him?'

She thought a moment and then widened her eyes.

'Yes. He said something like "You did dip that in holy water," and then he collapsed.'

Carl smiled and shook his head.

'What?' Maggie asked.

'He survived the wound, and you might have cured him.'

'What?'

'You killed **the Devil** in him. He probably believed that, especially in light of his survival,' Carl said.

'But the old lady. Why did she lie?'

'I don't know. He was a charmer. He might have convinced her you were the bad guy and not him. It doesn't matter now. He's not dead and maybe, just maybe, his evil nature has been exorcised.

'Funny,' Carl continued, 'a loony priest and a desperate wife drove the Devil out of our Mr Bois. Well, that's it. That's what I learned and now you know it all.'

'Do you think it really is over, Carl?'

'Yes. You'll take Grant home and he won't remember much of it. Believe me.'

She felt her body finally relax.

'Where do you think this madman is?'

'Wandering about, looking for a new identity. He's to be pitied now.'

'I have trouble with that,' she said.

Carl laughed.

'Understood.'

'Thanks, Carl.'

'Hey, it's all in a day's work.'

Maggie laughed.

It was the first time in quite a while and it felt real good.

Two days later Grant was released and Maggie brought him home. He was weak but in very good spirits. After his mother visited, Grant rose from bed and insisted on having dinner in the dining room. Maggie protested.

'I'm tired of being treated as an invalid,' he said. 'The faster I see myself as recuperating, the faster I'll recuperate. Hospital, doctors, nurses reinforce the image of sickness, weakness, and patients accept that view and don't get well as fast as they should.'

'That's quite a sweeping generalization, Grant. Not everyone is a hypochondriac because of the way their doctors and nurses treat them.'

'Nevertheless, it's a big problem,' he insisted. 'The power of suggestion can be used positively or negatively.'

He wanted some wine with their meal and some music. Everything did indeed look wonderful and she was beginning to relax and become reassured herself. After dinner, he said he would return to bed, but he stopped at his den-office and entered. She watched him and waited, anticipating his discovery that his manuscript was missing. Her heart pounded.

When she heard nothing after a good ten minutes, she went to the den door and peered in. He was sitting behind his desk, just staring ahead.

'Grant?'

'Oh. Funny,' he said. 'I came in here as if I had something to do, something to read, and for the life of me, I can't remember what it was.'

She let out a hot breath.

'I'm sure it's not important, Grant. You'll recuperate, return to work, and the important things will return to your memory.'

'Yes,' he said. 'You're right.'

He rose.

'I guess I'm not as strong as I thought. I'd better get to bed.'

'That's very wise, Doctor,' she said, smiling.

He paused at the doorway.

'I haven't told you how much I loved you lately, have I?'

'No, not lately,' she teased.

'Well, I'll make up for it tenfold.'

'I'll hold you to that promise, Doctor Blaine.'

He laughed and rolled his eyes. She watched him return to the bedroom and then she returned to the kitchen to clean up. By the time she looked in on him, he was dead asleep. She fixed his blanket, kissed his cheek, and went out to watch some television. She didn't realize how tired she was herself until her eyes snapped open and she saw the *Letterman* show was coming to an end.

She rose, turned off the set, rubbed her cheeks, and started for the bedroom when she heard the strangest sound. It resembled a clock being wound. Confused, she listened harder and then realized it was coming from the den. She went to it slowly and peered in. The room was dark, but the computer monitor was lit, the glow threw a pool of light over the chair for a moment giving her the illusion that someone was sitting there.

Had Grant turned on the computer and forgotten to turn it off when he left? She also remembered it could be triggered on by an incoming E-mail.

Cautiously, her heart thumping, she walked to the desk and came around to gaze at the screen. Words were flying across it as they were being sent. She leaned in to read them, and then she recoiled as if a snake had popped out at her.

The book . . . *The Seventh Wave* . . . it was coming in page by page.

She uttered a cry and then she got on her hands and knees and located the computer power cord. With a firm tug, she jerked the plug out of the wall and the computer went dark. Then she stood up and gazed at it. The silence was reassuring, but she was full of trepidation.

It took her hours to fall asleep. She said nothing to Grant about the phenomenon, but after she had made him breakfast, she called Carl Thornton.

'That's too bad,' he said. 'I was hoping you actually had rid the man of some of his schizophrenia. But I wouldn't worry. He won't be back.'

'How can you be so sure, Carl?'

'He moves on to greener pastures. It's the Devil's way, so it will be his. The computer was just his way of letting you know you can't kill him. Fits the profile of Satan . . . arrogant, defiant.'

'How do you know so much about it, Carl?'

'It's my work, Maggie. I have to understand the evil mind. We're doing an awful lot of forensic psychology these days.'

'You'd even testify for Satan?' she asked, half facetiously.

'Hey, everyone's entitled to a defense,' he said,

laughing. 'Don't worry. It'll be all right.'

'I wish there was a way to get the police involved in this, Carl.'

'Somehow, but somewhere else, they probably will be,' he predicted.

A week later, Grant returned to work. He kept Fay on and the events that had interrupted their lives so dramatically began to fade. Grant never asked Maggie about the manuscript and he never mentioned Bois' name, except to tell her Bois didn't pay for his last session. She laughed. It was a healthy complaint.

One night nearly five months later, she put her fork down at dinner, folded her hands, and sat back. Grant paused, lifted his eyebrows curiously, and looked at her.

'What?'

'I have something to tell you,' she began, 'a confession to make.'

'Okay. I'm good at hearing those. What is it?'

'It involves us and our future.'

'You have my attention, counselor.'

She smiled.

'I'm pregnant,' she said.

Epilogue

Doctor Froman sat back in his chair and pressed his fingers together in cathedral fashion. His thick, dark brown eyebrows dipped toward each other as his forehead wrinkled. He had full, very feminine lips and a narrow face with a sharp turn at the jawbone. Not particularly a handsome man, Jules thought, but a man with expressive eyes, the doorways to the soul, wide open, exposing that soul.

He smiled at him.

'Why so amazed, Doctor Froman?'

'Just the way you said it . . . you died and were reborn?'

'Well,' Bois said with a sigh, 'she stabbed me and just missed my heart, but the wound was deep enough to be as near to fatal as could be. Fortunately, I got medical attention from a close friend quickly and I was able to recuperate. But when someone you love and trust tries to kill you . . . well, that's a form of dying, wouldn't you agree?'

'Yes, I suppose so.'

'And when you return to life, renewed with even stronger vision, that's a resurrection of sorts, too.'

Froman nodded.

Bois smiled.

'It sort of makes you feel . . .'

'Yes, how does it make you feel?' Doctor Froman asked, and, like a good psychiatrist, leaned forward to show real interest in the answer.

Bois smiled.

'Immortal,' he said.

And then he laughed.

And then it all began again.